ADVENTURES
OF
JOE HARPER

A NOVEL

PHONG NGUYEN

Outpost19 | San Francisco
outpost19.com

Nguyen, Phong
        The Adventures of Joe Harper/ Phong Nguyen
        ISBN: 9781944853044 (pbk)

Library of Congress Control Number: 2016912998

Cover art by Sarah Nguyen.

OUTPOST19

ORIGINAL
PROVOCATIVE
READING

THE ADVENTURES OF JOE HARPER

(MISSOURI, 1871)

This book is dedicated to

Mark Twain

who, though I stand knee-high to his genius,
would not, I believe, try to shake me off his leg,

and Emily Saunders

grandmother, & the first person I ever
heard say the words, "I'm from Missouri."

"As the two boys walked sorrowing along, they made a new compact to stand by each other and be brothers and never separate till death relieved them of their troubles. Then they began to lay their plans. Joe was for being a hermit, and living on crusts in a remote cave, and dying, some time, of cold and want and grief; but after listening to Tom, he conceded that there were some conspicuous advantages about a life of crime, and so he consented to be a pirate."

—Mark Twain, *The Adventures of Tom Sawyer*

Chapter I

The day had come to die proper. You mightn't think life had nothing more to offer a 35-year-old Joe Harper, but then again you mightn't have abandoned all your kin and returned home ten years on to find a St. Petersburg full of strangers; or you mightn't have reached a body's threshold for sinning, when each day is a new excuse to poke an old wound; or you just mightn't have been born with a bitter taste on your tongue and a holler in your heart.

I'd been p'inted in the direction of hell a long time; now I'd set my feet a goin'.

My compass read South, though I scarcely needed it to read me the right way. For all my folly and failures as a man, ten years at sea had learned me to navigate by open sky. My aim was the Ozarks, a region rumored to have more oxbow lakes and karst springs than people in it, and I reckoned it would take me only another week as long as I kept the sun on my left cheek in the morning, and on my right after noon. Half a-way to the prize now, I had just won the keystone that day and was ready to celebrate alone with a sour drink and a crust of bread.

I'd started out at Cave Hollow up where Injun Joe been buried alive, but since I didn't aim to remember my wayward boyhood every day 'til I growed old, I struck out for the Ozarks where caves was plentiful and folks warn't known for asking questions. All I knowed for sure was that ruther than listen to the current of the Mississippi below the cliff face all day pulling at me to drift on, soon I'd be hearing the soft slurp of waves on a rocky shore somewhere closed off from any other body of water.

On the way down thar I ran acrost a one-road town with a saloon that once'd been used to waylay travelers turning south from the east-west road. The burg itself was barely there, just the bones of buildings, with the houses spaced at such a distance from one another you wondered if the owners warn't being extra mindful of the range of buckshot.

Their saloon was a former country home where ruther than putting up bird-feeders it offered up its walls to woodpeckers. A porch had been hastily built to take in sudden business moving in the other direction—from south to north, in the aftermath of Lincoln's war. It hadn't rained for days, yet the roof looked badly rained-on. As for the old saloon itself, 't was well occupied with rum-dums, though most was asleep or mighty close to 't.

Seeing my ragged shoulder bag and my generally hungry appearance, the proprietor cleared all the cash from the bar top and didn't mind that I seen him do it. His yaller hair flared out from his brow and temples like a lion's mane and his beard, of a slightly darker hue, was trimmed to a p'int. Behind him were his wife and another feller, sleek as a leopard, who served drinks. "Where you running from?" his wife says before I even take the stool. I hadn't made it far enough into the hills yet that I was rid of the hen mothers whose occupation was to nose into others' business.

"St. Petersburg. But I ain't a-running." She could see plainly I hadn't a pack to lay down, much less a horse to haul it on. The counter had used to be white, with tan streaks made up to look like ivory—the one lavish detail in an otherwise run-down saloon—which had faded and soiled to a cracked brown. Even so, they judged me a vagabond, unworthy of sharing patronage with the drunken wastrels and assorted scoundrels who commanded the share of the room. My misfortune was that I'd have to wait 'til they were done a-pestering me before I could get on my way and properly call myself a hermit on his way to a lonely death.

"What are your plans?" she says, and I had sudden visions of Susie and Faith and Mama Sereny and Aunt Lily and Tom's Aunt Polly and the one thousand women I growed up under and had at long last broken away from.

"To live until I'm dead," I says. "Preferably someplace southern and lonesome."

The barman nodded like he heard it all before, and I s'pose he must have. "Think that you'll find the right life there?" he says. His tolerance for brooding strangers was lower than the missus'.

The second feller kep' checking over his shoulder, showing his whiskers, his face pockmarked like a leopard's skin. His arms were bare, to show the work he put into 'em, I reckon, and the muscle moved beneath the skin like rats burrowing through a sack of feed. They was powerful suspicious of this stranger in their midst, I reckoned, and it was this other feller's job to sort out suspicious strangers. I'd just walked in the door, hardly, and it already brung back to me the reason I designed never to see hide or hair of another human being for the duration of my mortal life. "Just the ordinary sort. I've taken up too many high-minded dreams already."

To this news he only nodded, for he couldn't have knowed how many years I'd spent following that rascal Tom Sawyer, drunk with the borrowed vision of a man worthy of the title "Joe Harper the Terror of the High Seas," and how much harm I'd done in the world trying to live up to that name.

"You ain't unique," he says. The barman dasn't lie.

"Leastways you'll be warm," he says, "down South." His wife spat on the counter and scrubbed it fiercely, though the froth of her mouth did naught to erase the filth that was caught between the cracks.

I sat ca'm and pacific 'til I glimpsed they was both staring at me like a deer tick.

"D'you got any three-day loaves in back?" I ask.

"D'you got any nickels?" he says.

"I was goin' to ask for the crusts, if you had left-overs."

3

"I don't store old food," he says.

As a St. Petersburg boy, I reckoned this was the height of human folly. "None of your patrons is poor?"

"The wise ones carry coins when they walk into a saloon," he says.

"No," the wife says, as if to her husband, just loud enough to absorb from where I sat, "The wise ones move on, 'stead of taking up precious air in Lone Jack."

Her hint was blunt as a butter knife. "I guess I ain't wise," I says.

"It's the foolish you oughter worry about," the woman says, slowly and full of hidden intention. "They git lost sometimes and you never hear from 'em agin."

The only thing that kep' my mouth from pronouncing "This *is* lost, ma'am," was my manners from having been raised under those one-thousand women I tole you about.

"D'you got a spare room to let?" I ask.

"D'you got any nickels?" the man says.

I reached in my poke and fingered the two di'monds I kep' from my pirating days. I weighed the risk of revealing them with the risk of starving, and judging that there wouldn't be another saloon on this road until the great saloon in the sky, I chanced it. Pulling them out of the poke and placing them on the bartop, I says, "Sorry, no. I only got di'monds, and I don't aim to buy the building."

She hid it well, but the wife she flashed a wolfish smile. The barman he kep' a face of a stone lion. "I'll entertain your ruse, and let on those are real di'monds," he says, "I s'pose I'd give you a month's room and board for the big'un."

"I s'pose you won't," I says. "You never seen a di'mond like this 'less you been to El Dorado."

He looked at his wife but she warn't taking her eyes off the di'monds. Though she was old enough to be sunken cheeked and worry-lined, and half the weight of her husband, you could see by the rim of her one wide eye that she was the one to be a-feared. "All right. You can have the swill ale and crumbs, but I ain't cooking for you. One night is all you are welcome to."

I judged the free food and drink would suit me, but I dasn't take a free bed. It could 'a been an act of Christian charity, I s'pose, but I reckoned these good country folks just wanted to rob this vagabond of his di'monds while he slep'.

Chapter II

By the time I staggered out through the swinging door of the saloon, muddle-headed from sour ale, the ripe darkness was at its fullness, before the rotting. It is at this tar-black hour that I am most ambitious to find a cave to disappear into and grieve 'til my death. For more'n ten years I kept my conscience clean by s'posing one day I'd come home and find forgiveness, never imagining there warn't a home to return to, nor any forgiveness to be found. With Mama Sereny in the ground, there was no one to ask or offer approval for this plan. I thunk maybe I'd better to hunt up Tom Sawyer and ask him why he abandoned me to go and work for the law. But with the endless Osage plains laid out before me, half of 'em felled by tornaders and ready to be turned into so many board feet of timber, even I—known in St. Petersburg for being learn'd indoors and immune to whims of superstition—was turned to thoughts of haunting, or at least occurrences of the bizarre.

I had just enough sense left to reckon I was being followed into the darkness by the barman's goon. When I heard the crackle of leather behind me, I turned about, and for a minute I thought I seen his leopard-face in the darkness, among a thousand imagined terrors, but 't was just the inviting lights of the saloon where a free bed was a-tempting me.

That's the last time I flash a di'mond amongst strangers, I resolved, no matter how hungry I get. For I had sworn, after I'd quit piracy—which, it took me too long to figure out, was plain murder and savagery, with nothing Romantic in it at all—that nothing in the world would ever bring me again to a state of dependence on another human soul. For relying on Tom Sawyer, I was sentenced to wander, carrying with me more guilt and grief than a moral man can stand. And if I ever expected redemption at the hands of my Mama, it warn't a coming now. It was therefore my burden, as I seen it, to be alone forever. So I stalked on, Southward, into the incarnations of my own fear.

As the darkness deepened to nothing I start to worry, by and by, that I might come upon a deep place where the sun had gone silent forever. The wind assisted in this dark vision as it went to work shaking the highest, most cumbrous branches, riffling their leaves like bible pages and dropping their hedgeapples along the gutters of the path, where they thumped and rolled just outside my sight.

From the journeying he described to me at great length on his homecoming those twenty-odd years ago, I reckon Huck was a bolder traveler than I. A baker's dozen of negroes couldn't aright the unsettled, one-legged feeling I get in the thrum of night in an unfamiliar woods.

The stories I remember best from reading lessons always tole about a hero *finding* a home: 'Dysseus pining for the shores of his Itchica; or Dainty chasing a lady called Beet-Rice, a lady who they say was the only home he'd ever know. Why is it then, that all the travelers I personally know—Huck Finn and Tom Sawyer and Nat Parsons—just have the one ambition to get as much distance as possible between them and St. Petersburg?

After ten years away, it warn't my home: Mama Sereny gone; sissies all married; the gang gone to war and come back different, or ain't come back at-all. Now, as the darkness became complete, I thunk more and more about what it meant to die. Is it just walking blind into a dark woods? Or shrinking away piece by piece until nothing was left? I was always curious, but somehow I could never strike a place where it happened all a-sudden. My imagination wouldn't let it. But when I set my mind upon it, death's egg cracking and opening and letting out the life inside so that nothing was left but a body's shell—blamed if it didn't sound like a welcome break from the rotten-egged feeling I carried around at the pit of me.

Pretty soon I judged I'd be worn down and weary by the time I arrived anywhere worth arriving. But by and by in the distance I seen a rectangular light like from a window lamp, then another—bright orange eyes in the face of night. As a future hermit, I reckoned this must be a hermit's hideaway, but the homeful kind, so I had a mind to knock on this cottage door in the middle of the night, and I 'most done it too, but then stumbled all a sudden into what felt like a fish net, and git all tangled up in it.

Since the fearful dark had rendered me of unsound mind, at first I judged it was a giant spider-web—the kind that's weaved, I *s'pose*, by a giant spider. But after thrashing around and untangling my arm, I seen that my spider-web was but a hemp rope hammock tied between two trees. I 'most cut it. I can get that-a-way at times when I've a mind to, and the old pirate in me come out of his ship-in-a-bottle. But Mama Sereny's voice come out in me instead and says, "Joe Harper, don't you do it."

"I warn't goin' to," I says. "Reminds me of a spider-web, and you knows how I feel about critters."

She kep' quiet, though I could hear in my head her lips pinch together.

"Cutting a rope is bad luck," I says, "to seafaring folks."

"Scratch luck," she says. "I taught you better than to cow to superstition. And how's a body supposed to dwell in a cave the rest of his life without cottoning to critters?"

"I'll get used to 'em," I says. "But blamed if I'll ever get used to womenfolk."

"It must be hard to get used to folks taking such good care of you," she says, and I flushed the way she always make me.

"One way or t' other," I says. "I'm making my own way in the world."

8

"I'm mortal proud," she says.

As if joining in on the palaver, a rough voice come up in the dark and says, "Who're you talking to out there, you muggins?" By that time in our chat I'd settled on the hammock and was mumbling my way to sleep, but this one rousted me.

"Why'd you creep up like that and who're you?" I says.

"I'm Lee and this is my home, so I judge I can walk or run or creep anyways I like. Who're you?" But for the light in the house yonder, it was unwelcome dark, so I heard him but I ain't seen him.

"I'm Joe Harper, but I don't s'pose that means shucks to you."

"You don't s'pose, do you? That's right. You just shut your mouth and I'll s'pose for the both of us." I couldn't see nothing, but I get a niggling sense that he was a-holding a gun p'inted in my general direction. "Now tell me what you're after, sleeping in a man's hammock who never offered you his hammock to sleep in."

As I was trying to follow these instructions, I thought to myself how it would be a considerable long time before I ever find any peace. "So which is it? Should I shut my mouth, or tell how's I got here?"

"How about you just confess what you are running from, or running towards?" he says, more ca'm now that he judged me a harmless tramp.

I paused before I spoke, since it seemed a bigger question than he meant it. "There's an inn up in Lone Jack, and they followed me halfway here. They's probably still prowling around in the dark, a-waiting for me to double back."

"Why didn't you say so straight off?" he says. "You've got good reason to be a-feared. Them's wicked beasts, and that she-wolf is the worst of the bunch."

"Well," I says, "I didn't say straight-off because your first question was 'Who're you?' It would a' been queer to say, 'I'm being chased by the barman and his wife'." Lee allowed it was so, and we could a' gone on that way until the dawn come, but Lee finally located my arm with his'n and dragged me into his two-room cabin in the lonely woods.

It was the sparsest, Lincolniest cabin-in-the-woods you could picture, and I allowed he must live alone because I knowed what a house looks like when womenfolk lives in it. There was a wood table for eating, and one chair that wobbled so bad it would answer for a rocking chair. I could make out the outline of a four-poster bed in the connected room on the southern end of the cabin, the only sizable thing in an otherwise empty home. When we stepped into the light, I noticed he ain't the hulking, wild woodsman I'd imagined, but a sallow-faced Chinese feller in fine clothes such as I only seen on Sundays in St. Petersburg. It was hard to read his age because there was only the slightest delta on the outside of each eye, and when he took off his hat I seen there was flecks of gray where the hair parted at his left temple.

"Explain yourself," he says.

"Well, the truth is," I says, "I'm on a mission to find a cave to dwell inside and be a hermit." The man Lee looked like he never considered any other way. "Hey, maybe *you* can learn me to be a hermit," I says, and I meant it too. He looked like he'd drank from the cup of solitude to the last drop.

I wanted to ask how he come to be so far from the railroad, but then I noticed he didn't talk like t' other Chinee, neither. As an old pirate, I seen my share of foreign sorts, but only knowed two other of his kind, and after I met them Tom and I gone into fits talking gibberish and scurrying round the deck to ape their shuffling walk. In years since, Tom had seen plenty and swears they ain't worthy of one tenth of a man's trust. So I asks him anyways, "How'd you come to be so far from the railroad?"

"You pudd'nhead," he says, "don't you know they finished building the railroad after the big one?" I grimaced, since I only knowed old soldiers to call it the big one. It was just Lincoln's war to the rest of us.

"You mean after you done finished laying the railroad, you just… stuck around?"

He turn his face to me like he means me to guess, like the answer was right there in front of me, which I s'pose 't was.

"Why, who give you permission?" I says.

"What d'you mean, *who give me permission*?" he says. "I was born here, warn't I? My parents was Christian, warn't they?"

That one did stump me. "If you's born here, how come you's Chinee?"

Lee set up a bedroll and some linens in the middle of his kitchen floor, and pushed the chairs to the wall. "I allow I'd have to learn you much more than a day's worth if I'm gonna settle that one to your satisfaction."

I seen he aimed to drop the subject, but after I took a think, I got it up again. "Is lots of folks of Christian parents born Chinee?"

He smiled like he thought I was giving him a-ribbing. "I've had a few transgressions with otherwise faithful Christian ladies, but I ain't goin' to say *lots* of folks is born that way." Lee snuffed the light, and left me to find the bedroll. "Sorry I hain't got a trundle, but it's a sight better than a hammock." He opened the door to escape into his bedroom for the night, letting in an edge of orange light.

Chapter III

The morning chill rousted me and I didn't right away figure out where I was, but remembered the sound of howling all night, and immediately I heard it again and discovered 't was just the wind. It blew so steady it pasted a brown leaf against the middle of the East-facing window and riffled it for a while then drifted it down to the sill. As I rose, I had a Rip Van Winkle feeling that I'd missed all of September and 't was already full-blown autumn. With the wind a-ripping outside, I was mighty glad not to be out in a hammock.

It was enough to convince me to double-up the blanket and press my face deeper into the pillow, allowing the wind to lull me back into the shadder-world. Back in my head somers deep, I heard Mama say, "D'you see, Joe? You don't need to dwell in a cave to be your own man. You're in a warm place, but don't let yourself be taken-care-of." But the forces of comfort was too strong for it, and I slep'.

—

Dreams is memories and memories is dreams. My strange tentacular history convinced me that there was as much truth in one as t' other. So when I closed my eyes I had the sense of leaving the world and coming home to it at once. That partic'lar night the vision I had was as bright and thick with color as a circus poster, and I had the notion I was a witness to it, ruther than its principle actor.

The two-horse wagon took the uphill road to St. Petersburg ploddingly. I'd seen abler animals give up on the Northern Missouri terrain and turn t' other way, content to nibble at the grass on the mid-range of the hills. But I was crossing now over the threshold of the town that once knew me as a boy, and I would not turn back for any enticement.

Every rock and tree and bend in the road glowed with the light of the familiar.

When I arrove at the edge of town, the squat house I growed up in looked sunken and sadder than I ever recalled. It had been painted a violet that purposed to be cheerful but came out a shade too dark to accomplish it. Otherwise 't was just as I'd left it when at 22 years old I boarded passage on a steamship headed down the Mississippi to the Gulf and to my destiny.

I lifted the latch and stepped through the doorway. Though it hadn't been my proper home in more'n ten years, I couldn't bring myself to knock on Mama Sereny's door like an uninvited guest. The space inside felt smaller, sure, than I remembered it, but I felt smaller too somehow. I scarcely recognized any of the furnishings. The stairs had a new wood railing of a darker hue than the steps themselves, and each stairstep showed depressions worn by more'n ten years of feet that warn't my own.

My sissies' bedroom was now the suite, and Mama Sereny's room was an adjunct to it—a guest room. Did Mama Sereny take a second husband in her dotage? It seemed most unlike her to do so, since she scarcely wanted a first one. Then I seen the row of family pictures on the mantle, and just as this old pirate was about to become tender about himself and his boyhood, he looked closer and seen that they was full of nothing but strangers.

It would have come quicker to a less mulish sort than me that the house I stood in was inhabited by a family other than that which had borne me. I tried to picture Mama Sereny up and leaving her lifelong home and I couldn't reckon how or why. If she warn't home, where in the blamed world was she?

Stepping out onto the street, I stood there tipping a bit on my heels, but otherwise stock-still as foot traffic moved to and fro before me. One face after another brought the promise of the familiar, but each one appeared stranger and stranger until I reckoned I could stand there forever and never meet my kin.

After an eternity of shifting from one sole to the other, my feet took me on the south-going road, but not before a detour at the St. Petersburg cemetery, where I saw Mama for the last time.

—

When I woke by and by, I seen Lee sitting at the table, scratching out a letter with a quill that was ruther fine for this cabin or this county. I dasn't disturb the man who give me such a good turn, but I'd recently struck that age where just laying in bed makes a body ache. I had to roust myself just to distract from the body's habit of decrepitude.

Once we'd said our g'mornings, Lee dropt his pen and offered me a stool to sit on. I took it, and he shuffled away his papers before I could ask what they was for. The autumn wind hit the cabin on the broad side, and shook the door on its hinges.

"D'you ever hear voices inside?" I says, just from the habit of always saying what was on my mind.

"You mean the wind?" says Lee.

"No, Lee," I says. "I mean like in your own head. It would make a hermit's life a mite easier if a body could just make its own company."

"Oh, I see," he says. "No, not voices. *Visions*, yes. Either way, a hermit does need his imagination."

"Visions?" I says.

"Yep. I had a vision last night," he says, and I think fondly of what it might be like to see Mama again some day, ruther than just listening to her prattle. How long would it be before I could summon up a full-on vision that a-way? "Matter of fact, it was what brought me outside, where I found you a-babbling on and wrapped up in a hammock."

"What about the vision?" I says.

"It was a lady," he says. "Young and pretty, out of place."

"Well, I reckon it *was* a vision," I says, with a hint of mischief in it.

Lee tsks at me. "It warn't *that* sort of vision," he says. He looked like he was a-goin' to say more, but he declined.

He sat like a statue long enough for the wind to rattle the door again, and this time I shook too, as I had been turning over an image in my head: the barman and his wife with her one eye wide. Right then I wondered if I should offer Lee one of my di'monds, to repay him for his hospitality. But then I just start to pity him because nobody ever heard of a rich chinaman, and reckoned there might be a good reason for it. Maybe if I could turn him normal first, he could get rich and buy himself some proper furniture for his cabin?

"All right," Lee says. "I'll learn you to be a hermit. I'm fixing to leave soon, and I could use a squire. But as my study, you're obliged to do as I say. That clear?"

"Yes'sir," I says. I'd been a first-mate all my life, in one way or t' other, so I knowed exactly what to do. I only worried there was even more, now, to be indebted to him for.

"First off, a hermit only says as much as he needs to get by, and sometimes less." Lee was adamant on this p'int. We sat acrost the table coffin-quiet, and if this was my first test, I reckon I was within the margin of success.

Then Lee stood up to answer a boiling kettle, but before he could snuff the flame, I struck an idea like I was striking a vein of ore. "I know how you can git normal!" I says, and he looked over at me like I'd growed a second head. "But you mightn't like it, because you have to use a partic'lar kinder knife to trade blood with a normal Christian." I stopped there because I didn't mean to let on I'd offer *my* blood, and I warn't even sure that it mightn't turn *me* half-Chinee.

All a sudden he give me a look full of brimstone, but it turned out to be a spark that never catched. "Okay, Doctor," he says, a-standing up from his chair. "What sorter knife?"

"A ce-re-mo-ni-al knife," I says. "I seem to recall."

"D'you mean a serrated knife?" he says.

"I reckon they's similar enough," I says with a shrug.

"Would a sawblade answer?" he says, walking over and drawing out a jagged-edged wood saw from a luggage box that was plopped down in the dusty corner.

"I reckon," I says, because there warn't any other place in the cabin to store knives. "Wait, d'you mean to trade blood with *me*, Lee?"

"Warn't it your idea?" he says.

"Yessir," I says, "but…."

"Nevermind, Joe," he says, sitting back down and looking up from his breakfast platter. "Why don't you take this saw, go outside, and cut some logs out of the trees that was felled by the wind? We'll talk about trading blood and turning into proper Christians afterwards."

It was a relief to hear we would work before we bled, so I went out in the woods and done it. And after I spent most the whole day sawing enough logs to set us up for four winters, I walked inside, et a few pinches of oats and salted meat, then collapsed on my bedroll. Thank goodness, I thought. He'll have to wait for the morning to cut me.

Next day, when Lee shook me awake, he looked a bit wild, though Sunday-dressed just as he'd been the day before. "I gotta light out," he says, hushed. "They're out front, ready to hunt me up. You can stand your ground and make a home here, or come be my squire. Makes no difference to me."

Though I hain't let on, I was expecting breakfast 'stead of a quandary. My palms start to sweat and my heart galloped, for I hadn't faced a juncture like this since I called myself Joe Harper Terror of the High Seas. "Leastways grab me my coat," I says.

"No, Joe," he says, a-whispering. "Here's your boots. Let's git!" He pushed me out the back door what he used to get rid of kitchen waste, but then I see he come along with me. I struggle to shod my bare feet while we was a-running.

Among scores of thoughts I aimed to ask him when I finally stirred up was this one: "When you live all on your lonesome, how does you keep from going deranged?" But now I see he *had* gone deranged from his hermitage, and I despaired of my chances of ever dying a reasonable recluse.

"Where're you leading me, Lee?" I asked, but like a proper hermit he answered me with silence. I turned back towards the cabin, and through the layers of trees growing thicker with distance, I seen the barman with his goon charging inside Lee's home. Then I spied that wolf-wife, standing off a ways, staring back at me, but at that distance, with her one bad eye, I prayed she took me for a bounding deer.

In the deep woods we'd come to, the whole morning was dappled with strange movement, with light falling on the branches of trees in imperfect circles, like a spray of buckshot. The shadders of sunrise colored the forest floor orange, so that for a moment I felt the sky were below me, not above.

"I knowed it was a-coming, but I guess folks got wind of my sinful ways," Lee says.

"They just figured out you warn't Christian? Couldn't they see plain as day you was Chinee?" This was too many for me. "See now, *that's* why I says you should'a just asked a body's permission to stay."

"They knowed I was Chinese, Joe Harper, but they just learned this morning... that I failed to respect the Lord's commandment about coveting." He reflected. "Or, that I respected too well His commandment about loving thy neighbor."

"Well, which is the greater?" I asks.

"That's the trouble," he says. "Nobody owns it's one or

t' other."

"Well which come first in scripture? If it's a principle, He'd probably let you know about it first, wouldn't He?"

"That's so, 'cept what if He say it one way first, then change His mind and say it another," Lee reasoned.

"You do talk like a heathen, Lee. Everybody knows how the Lord fixes his mind on a thing and don't change it for man or the devil," I says.

"He changed His mind about Ham, ain't he?" Lee says.

I allowed He did. "But just because them Canaanites couldn't eat ham and now *we* can doesn't mean that He changed His mind about big things like coveting and such."

"You just quit your gabbing about pig's meat, Joe, I'm talking about *Ham*, Noah's son, who the Lord made a slave. Now he done freed the slaves, so *there's* a Lord who changed His mind."

"Changing His mind had nothin' to do with it!" I says. This one I learned well on Sundays, because after Lincoln's war I paid close attention to the preachers who had been telling us our whole lives long that slavery was a holy thing and that abolitionists was the devil's messengers. "It's 'God's plan,' that is. History keeps happening the way it does because it's *His plan*, not because he keep changing His mind. Shows how much a heathen Chinee knows about the holy scripture!"

We were in the unmarked woods now, headed south by way of a deer path, where I'd been headed all along. The oaks and elms hadn't learned it was autumn yet, but the poplars and birches was ablaze with orange and yaller leaves.

"Really now, Lee, are you goin' to make me guess where we's headed? Because I got an education as a boy, so I know *every* state and its capital," I says.

"West," he says, and I didn't have the spirit to tell him 't was otherwise. His kind once'd come from the land where the sun a-rises, and now Lee forgot which direction home was.

Chapter IV

Next day we come upon a shallow cave—not the sort I'd aim to settle in, yet found myself standing before it humbler than any sinner who ever stood at the gates of his church. The wind brought a chill, too, that give us both gooseflesh. "You'll get there, someday, darling," Mama Sereny's voice come up in me again. "You'll find a cave to call your home, sure as you're born."

Virginia creeper run up all the old trees—having turned the young ones to kindling long ago—and formed a canopy of vines that draped in front of its mossy cave entrance, but still deeper in, all the color went away and, though you could see plumb to the end of the shallow cave, turned into a different kind of darkness from outdoor darkness, all womby and inviting.

"It wouldn't answer for a home," Lee says. "A rainstorm'd soak through your linens, and a possum'd snatch your food. Never mind snakes." Lee was taking up the burden of teaching me the hermit ways. We moved further south, steering well off the deer path, into the thick and viney woods.

"I knows how to handle a snake," I says. "But I was kinder hoping a dry cave won't have bugs."

I was expecting a scornful laugh and to be called a numbskull, but 'stead Lee chewed on it a moment and says, "In a dry cave you don't worry about a tick or a louse, long as you don't keep animals. But if you're near still water then you've got gnats in the evening and mosquitoes at night, and if it's a large lake you may get horseflies, which live on dead things that washes up on the beach." Now why should I have felt just then a twinge of envy at the thought of a dead thing washing up on the sand? I learned long ago not to make apologies for the strange paths my mind a-wanders on. It's just how I was made.

Lee took out a Jim Bowie knife and made quick work of the vines, and we clumb up a whole passel of trees that fell and died but warn't yet joined with the earth. So I acted the part of Spanish explorer taming the great wilderness, and remembered how I'd partnered with Tom Sawyer in the year or so between the time when we learned to play pirates and the time *we* become pirates—and before Tom give up piracy and become the law, working to capture or kill rascal pirates like us.

Mama Sereny always did say Tom Sawyer was a bad egg, and wrong in the head.

Though it was warmer now, and not so buggy or windy, and I had slept two nights in a cabin, I still felt lost in a dark woods, bushwhacking and clambering until my arms growed tired and my calves took sore. I started to wonder whether following Lee through the woods was wise, or whether I oughter listen to Mama Sereny and find a cave nearby to hermit on my own and die.

Just then the wood opened up and we seen in the clearing a couple 'a railway lines stretching out to the horizon yonder, and I was thinking, "*Now* we got to civilization at last, and things'll be all smooth sailing from here."

"Now don't you go thinking, 'this is civilization at last, and things'll be all smooth sailing from here'," Lee says.

"There ain't nothing wrong with a hopeful thought," I says, but what I was thinking was How'd a body read a man's mind like that? Is it natural or unnatural? In the end I judged Lee was a foreign man with foreign powers, and there warn't any cause to question it.

Then Lee started walking 'longside the tracks West, and I seen why he was so keen on walking South and *letting on* it's West. I followed just a pace behind him. "No rest or nothin', Lee? Here's a man who don't waste time."

He looked at me and looked back at the place where the tracks meet on the horizon, where we was headed. "A hermit don't *waste* time or *kill* time, nor *spend* it neither, 'cause the Lord's hours ain't pesky coons or pennies in a market. He passes time, just the way God intended," he says.

"What's the diff'rence?" I asks.

"Joe Harper, what you don't know could fill a subscription library," he says, and I 'most wondered if in Lee I hadn't just found the Chinese Tom Sawyer. "*Passing* the time is con*temp*lative. A hermit's line is to watch time go by, observant-like, and notice things like the feel of the air and the sounds of all the creturs in the nighttime."

I allowed it was so, but it sound to me like the dullest way to spend a body's time.

When it was noon and our shadders warn't no bigger than a circle round our feet, I reckoned we warn't ever goin' to stop, so I says, "How far does the train track go on? We've been walking all morning and it seems we ain't made no progress getting there."

"Why, Joe, it goes all the way to the coast, to the Pacific ocean!"

That one shook me sure as clouds make rain. I imagined what kind of endless cave I'd find on the shores of the Pacific. I reckoned a cold, hungry death would be an even grander fate out there. "That's a fine thing!" I says. "Piracy only ever took me back and forth on the Atlantic."

Lee squinted his narrow eyes at me. "You, a pirate? Must 'a been the chuckle-headiest bunch of pirates that ever wore long johns," he says.

"The mischief they were!" I says. "Tom and his gang was the blood-thirstiest pirates this side of the British Empire. Although they started out slow, kind of shallow-water pirates hogging catches from fishermen, and it ended up in a bad way since Tom and me wound up on either side of the pirating line."

Lee didn't slow down at all as he walked. If anything, he quickened his pace. "I can't seem to cipher it out, Joe. What's on t' other side of the pirating line?"

"Oh, well Tom's become a *Privateer*," I says, mournful.

Lee looked at me skeptical, though his regular look was skeptical enough already to doubt ten thousand Joe Harper stories. "I been acrost the continent and I hain't ever heard talk of a Privateer."

"That's because a Privateer is known mostly to pirates and other seafaring folks, not landlocked continentals." I confess I was happy to know a thing or two Lee don't.

"All right, what's a Privateer?" he says.

"A Privateer gets permission from the govment to set up a corpsoration that boards strange ships or stops folks in the street or wherever and bully them till they gets a holt of people's money."

"Why, Joe, that's a whopper if I ever heard one. That ain't no diff'rent from being a pirate."

"It ain't so. A pirate ain't got the govment's permission to take folks' money, do he?" I says, but Lee growed tired of all the pirate talk, and his only answer was to kick the dirt in his path.

As we fell back on our hermity silence, I felt a powerful urge to hear Mama Sereny's voice, but I dasn't speak to her in front of Lee. So I took quiet and repeated the Jesus prayer under my breath instead, since it was the only prayer I knowed other than the bedtime prayer: "Lord, Jesus Christ, have mercy on me, the sinner." And as I walked, and as I went over the words again and again, I ached with the wish that Mama Sereny could hear 'em, and I reckoned in my heart I was speaking to her ruther than to Him. "Lord, Jesus Christ, have mercy on me, the sinner. Lord, Jesus Christ, have mercy on me, the sinner. Lord, Jesus Christ, have mercy on me, the sinner."

Chapter V

By and by we come upon a goods station where an engine idled with forty freight cars full of nothing. I wondered how come there was a train at a goods station with no goods on it, but I dasn't say anything and run the risk of sounding like a muggins in front of old Lee. Meanwhile he scoped out the cleanest and sparest car to set up in. I didn't know why we was hopping a freight train, but I was mighty glad to quit walking.

The freight cars was all lined up empty like they was expecting the corn yonder to climb into the boxcars and shuck themselves. Lee clumb into one that looked new and looked around, though there warn't nothing to look at but the inside of a freight car.

"Fetch some straw from the stables, would you, Joe?" says Lee.

I looked and don't see any stables, but a tiny shed somers off on t' other side of the goods station. Then I judged my walking days warn't over by a long sight. After arguing the p'int of whether we really ought to soil the freight car with straw after we took such an effort to find the cleanest and emptiest of the bunch, I headed out for the horse shed that must a' been 'most a half mile away from the tracks.

When I near the horse shed, I seen it warn't part of the goods station at all, but belong to a farm that shaped its border. I clumb over a wood fence and sallied over to the shutters to look over 'em. Then blamed if there warn't already a body in the horse shed!—a woman in a black dress with a black bonnet with black shoes sat in the hay like a brooding hen. The only bit of color on her was a brown apron, and that just barely brown like a hen's egg. Her nose and cheeks formed three gentle peaks and her eyes were green pools—pools!—flecked with gray like I never seen before on a lady, and shaped with a tail on each end that followed the path of her yellow lashes. Her blink was like speech, and her gaze was like a sermon.

"Sorry, ma'am," I says. "I didn't mean to disturb you."

She jump up like a snake uncoiling in the sun and grab my arm, whispering as loud as a whisper could get and still be rightly called a whisper, "Keep mum, vould you?"

I've sailed the Atlantic north, south, east, and west, but I hain't ever learned to listen when told. "Why? What're you afeard of?"

She blushed when she seen I ain't somebody she knowed, but sat me down where I couldn't be seen by folks passing by the horse shed. "De boy Abram has been after me vor marrying. And don't mistake me, sir—marriage is a holy thing ordained by God—but I'm not ready!" Her talk was clipped and full of patter, strange to my ear.

"Marry? But I thought you was a widow," I says, not meaning to stare at her stark black clothes from top to bottom.

"How could I be a *vidow*?" she says. "I'm twenty-two years dis month!"

"Excuse me, ma'am," I says. "I reckoned from the dress that you was in mourning, and I figured you was in such a state of grief you plumb forgot how to talk."

Then she judged it was safe, and she quit loud-whispering and flick the remnants of hay from her black dress. "Vhy didn't you just come out and ask?" she says, more patient now that she had me estimated. "I'm Pennsylvania Dutch, that's vhy."

I supposed all Pennsylvanians talk Pennsylvanian that a-way. "Now since I know how old you are, and I know where you're from, and I know who you're about to marry, s'pose you tell me your name?"

She come back to herself when she hear me put it straight that a-way. "My name is Ruth, and though I know

24

I'll be married under God someday, I'll never marry Abram Hershberger!"

I raise my hands up like she was accusing me of being Abram Hershberger in disguise, and says, "All right, so bide your time and find another boy to marry."

She looked aggrieved. "Dat's de problem, sir. Der ain't but de one."

"So you'll just be running away from the same boy all the rest of your days?" I says.

"Dat's de vay of it," she says, looking down at her feet.

I looked down too, and I noticed I dropped my poke. Ruth and I crouched down at just the same time to pick it up. We both went for the strings, and our hands touched by an accident. 'T was a simple touch, but it felt more like my skin was playing at lightning. She pulled her slender hand away, but we both kep' crouching down thar between the swinging door and the bales.

"Why ain't you marry some stranger?" I says, a-whispering for some reason.

"I vould be shunned," she says, standing at the last, "by my people vorever."

"Why don't you marry *nobody*?" I says.

When she seen how close our bodies become, she dasn't answer, but lift up her cupped hands between us and showed me a di'mond what fell out of my poke. I plucked it out of her hands more quickly than respectfully, and thanked her ten times.

It was a rare soul—man or woman—who would 'a done the same, and the more I thunk on't, the more it charmed me that that sweet Pennsylvania Dutch girl could hand over a d'imond she found nestled in the hay of her own horse shed.

"Well," I says, and though I knowed I'd find cause to regret it soon enough, I blurt out, "I s'pose you can come our way." It come back to me then, what Lee did say about my habit of carelessly s'posing.

25

"Honor bright?"

"Honor bright," I says, too quick to take it back. "I'm speaking true."

Here I aimed to double my quota of companions on the road. If I warn't the sorriest hermit there ever was, I don't know who is.

"Are you out on your own?" she says.

"Just me and a Chinaman," I says. "Heading West." Her face contorts like she's curious but disapproving of this fact.

All a sudden I hear the engine clatter off in the distance, and I 'most forgot to grab an armful of the hay before I blew open the shutters and spaded up the ground, galloping mightily like I was one of that shed's intended dwellers. It was the longest quarter mile I ever run, but the shortest work I ever made of it. I passed the caboose and reached the hindmost freight car before I remembered my erstwhile invitation to the twenty-two-year-old Pennsylvania Dutch girl I left behind, Ruth, who swore never to marry the only eligible man her town had produced, Abram Hershberger.

I had to check each car as I passed for some sign of Lee, until the engine pick up speed and the cars begin to pass *me*, so I sped up though my legs was burning miserable and my eyes was stinging from the dust and wind. Finally I catched the right one, and Lee reached his arm out, and I clumb up to the mount, and flung myself into the dank metal box. I turn around right away and look back for any sign of Ruth, but there warn't any. I felt a twinge that could just as easily have been a cramp.

Lee gave me a smile and a slap on the back, then he looked at the load I brought. "I asked you to get *straw*," says Lee. "This'n here is hay."

"What's the diff'rence?" I says. There's plenty of boys in St. Petersburg who knowed the answer to that question, but I was the only one raised indoors by a thousand worried women.

"Well, one's grain stalks, and t' other is dried long-grass," he says. "But more importantly, one's for laying on, and t' other's for eating."

I throw down the hay and lay on it, yet the Lord didn't see fit to strike me down. "I reckon it'll answer for a bed," I says.

He 'most argued the p'int, but the train whistle blew as we breezed through a town called Lotawana on the way to Kansas. "Joe Harper, I never asked your opinion," he says.

The sky was 'most dark. The last blue of it stuck to the wall of the car, and Lee's perfect white shirt, which started to look faded and day-worn. Outside, the corn was running and running and running, making a blur of the fields and homes, so that only an unimpressionable moon seemed to hang in one place while the earth whirled beneath it.

"Those corpsorations you was talking about," says Lee as the darkness come in. "Are they in the mercenarying business?"

"Sure they are," I says. "Why're you wanting to know?"

"I just wonder. Ever since the big one ended, there's been a lot of wickedness out West." This'n here was a sorrowful Lee I ain't never seen before. "Not just thievery or mischief neither. But killings and round-ups. It make sense now, I s'pose, that it's corpsorations, because in most places killing folks is 'gainst the law, just as piracy is 'gainst the law."

"Not if it's got the govment's permission," I says.

"I guess it's so," he says with a bit of strain to his lip, like it was trying to pull his mouth into a frown. "I've always wondered why the law don't ever stop folks from 'saulting and murdering my kinfolk. And sometimes it's the law that's doing the 'saulting! Now I know, it's Privateers working for corpsorations with permission from the govment." Lee looked like the low-downest Chinee that ever drove a railroad spike. "I've lived in the forsaken wilds of Missouri too long, and now I been chased out of my home. So it's high time I returned West."

"If they's 'saulting and murdering Chinee out West," I says, "why're you so eager to go back?"

"Oh, that's just the way home is, I suppose," he says, "ain't it?"

Now I wondered if Lee really was a hermit at all, or just *letting on* he was, so I'd stay on as his squire for the ride home, but in the end I kep' his company, for pity ruther than for education.

Chapter VI

Life ain't so easy on a train, I judged, as I wake up again and again from the knocks and rattles on each bend in the track, and the train whistle call out every time we come upon a cow town, which was all of Missouri. I 'most wondered whether Lee spoke true when he said that hay won't answer for a bed, though straw will. My neck was powerful sore from keeping my head from jostling round on every bump on the rail, and I was eager to blame my pillow.

When Mama Sereny's voice come up in me now, she strikes a disapp'inted tone. "I saw how you was looking at that Dutch girl, Joe Harper," she says, her voice a cold rag on my forehead. "She ain't right for you."

"I warn't looking any partic'lar way," I says.

"Now if you don't want to go through with this business of becoming a hermit and dying alone in a cave, it's one thing; but if you do, and you lose sight of your plan and settle down with a young lady just because you lack the will to say no, that's another thing entirely."

"Nobody needs to say no to nobody, because nobody never made no kinder invitation to nobody," I says, before I realize that it's my Mama I'm talkin' to, and she never abided back-talk from anyone. "But I'm awful sorry, Mama, for making you ashamed of your only son."

"Don't ask forgiveness of *me*, Joe Harper," she says. "Ask forgiveness of the Lord for every one of your sins."

"They's too many, Mama," I says. But under my breath I whispered the only prayer I knowed: "Lord, Jesus Christ, have mercy on me, the sinner. Lord, Jesus Christ, have mercy on me, the sinner."

Her voice went the way of the wind, but I made a vow to learn some new prayers and get so busy with prayers I wouldn't ever be distracted by womenfolk, and become my own man and my Mama's soul would be happy by and by.

Then I notice that the train warn't in any partic'lar rush, that the clacking of wheels was becoming irregular. I look outside and all was darkness, but the darkness moved more slowly now than before. By and by the darkness was interrupted by a lamplight yonder, then a handful, then a score. In the orange-y light I spied a water tank on which some wandering vagabond had wrote, "Don't Expect Much." For some reason those words was awful precious to me, and I made it my talisman, to hold close and repeat over and over again on my journey like another prayer.

"Lee, git up," I says. You could hear the steam hiss now that the whistle had quit. "I think she's making another stop."

Turned out Lee was just as awake as I'd been. But he stirred up now righteous quick. "We're on the high line," he says. "We held down too long."

"Where're we goin' to turn up?" I says.

"In the train yard, I'd reckon."

"About where's?"

"Independence," he says, grim as a schoolmaster.

"Inde*pen*dents?" I says. "Well ain't that sorter where we been meaning to end up? As independents?"

"No, Joe, this'n here is nobody's destination. Tramps call her the queen city of the trails, 'cause she's easy to hop, but ain't nobody end up here on purpose," Lee says.

By and by the engine come to a complete stop, and from the lamps I seen it *is* a train yard, and an endless flat one. To a seafarer such as I'd been, the vastness of the yard brung up only one unshakeable association: the ocean-wide. 'Cept these rail lines—that flow out, and cross, and never jink nor double-back—are unnatural straight and seem to tie together like strings being pulled together on the horizon. But in the night, it was just as colorless dark as the sea, and just as good a cause for fear.

So when I heard bodies a-bustling outside of the car,

I took still, like there was sharks that swum underneath the gravel of the roadbed. Lee and I sat quiet, and moved to the back of the box where the shadders was deepest. It was a powerful long time before any thing or any body appeared in the rectangle of light in the wall from where the door hanged open. When it did, 't was a man's hand that pulled the door shut and latched us in, our view of the outside world shrinking until 't was no more than a sliver.

When enough time was passed, and I reckoned it was safe to say, "D'you think he knows we's stuck in the box?" I says it, but Lee covered up my mouth with his hand.

"Maybe it's the bulls," he whispers, meaning the railroad workers assigned to keep out the stowaways—or tramps, I s'pose they's called on land.

"Or maybe it's Ruth come to fetch us out!" I says in a louder kind of whisper.

"Ruth?" he says, looking at me askance, sidelong, and quizzical. I s'pose she made such an impression on me that I reckoned he'd know her, even though 't was I who'd laid eyes on her.

"She's a girl twenty-two years old who don't ever aim to marry," I says. "But she thought she'd try tramping for a while."

"The trail's no place for a lady," Lee says with a weary breath out the side of his mouth. "*Nobody's* comin' to rescue us, Joe."

"Then how're we goin' to get out of this fix?" I says. The silence Lee answered with was more troubling than anything he could 'a spoken.

There's naught to do in the dark but sniff, so we done it. I even slep' and woke up with my head resting on Lee's bony shoulder, which served better'n hay for a pillow.

Chapter VII

By and by we hear bodies a-shuffling outside again, whereupon Lee and I tighten up into ourselves and will the silence and the darkness deeper still. The latch is pulled, and the door drawed open; the light falls on us and we can't see a mite through the squinting of our eyes. From all the balloon juice I'd heard about the tramp's trail, I was expecting to see a swarm of broad-backed bulls, armed with hammers, grinning with the anticipation of their evil deed, descending upon us and extorting the price of a hobo ticket from our hides.

Instead when my eyes come back to me all I seen was city tramps, two of 'em, one tall and t' other short, got up in scarfs and gloves though it warn't yet the first frost. "Hey, boes," the tall one says. "This your call?" I never fancied myself a tramp, but my experience at the Lone Jack saloon learned me that I can handily pass for one, and even Lee was starting to look the part, with his glad rags worn down from three days on the road.

Lee and I hopped out of the box like we was born to 't. The taller tramp had a mop of black hair and a mustache that'd never been trimmed. The short one had the coldest, clearest blue eyes you ever seen, so you practically never noticed the rest of him.

"Thanks, and I owe you," I says, but Lee shot me a look meaning it was probably true but wrong of me to say so.

The tall one nodded and walked forward like we was meant to follow, and he had the sort of air to him that that's just what we done. The short one looked at me and Lee suspicious, and says, "How come yous riding in on the fifteen? Don't yous know that's a bad road?"

"We made it here, didn't we?" Lee says. I noticed the four of us ranged in height (with me and Lee in the middle) so from behind we must 'a looked like stair-steps or a church organ. But Lee, walking next to the short feller, towered over him and evil-eyed him, mean as a frothing dog.

The tall one stopped us in our tracks and put on a smile. "Let's not start a row, boys. We all got to get along in the jungle. This'n here is Jersey Joe," he p'ints to his companion, "and I'm Trombo."

We shook hands like gentlemen, and I was about to introduce myself too when Lee stepped in and says, "I'm Frisco Dan, and this'n here is Mutton-chop," referring, I can only guess, to my burnsides.

"Mutton-chop?" says Jersey Joe. "What kind of monicker is that?"

"In the West he's known as Missouri Joe, but down here everybody knows him, so he's just Mutton-chop to you, boy." Lee says to Jersey Joe, though instead of mad-dogging him this time, he just put on his old camel-face.

"If I'm Missouri Joe, and this'n here is Jersey Joe, and this'n here is Frisco Dan, how come you's just Trombo?" I says.

Lee cut in again, "You keep kidding us, Mutton-chop. You know too well Trombo's a tramp-royal, and a Chicago bo, which is why his monicker stands alone like yours do." I nodded and walked on, aiming to still my restless curiosity.

By and by we got to the hobo jungle where dozens of tramps in snapper rags was set up with tents and makeshift tables right next to the train yard, engaged in the various occupations of the bo—trading stories of the Wander Path, snoozing, boozing, playing rummy, and eating mulligan. The life of the pirate as I recalled was full of stories and games too, all manner of idleness, but 't was the full pot of food that drew my eye that day. When I got close I seen the mess of bubbling brown stew that these boes called by the name of mulligan, and my yawning appetite snapped shut like an oyster.

Try as we might to fit in, at first Lee and I turned up our

noses at the stew, which looked like burnt bits of corn roiling in a vat of waste. But by and by our stomachs got the better of us, and we et the mulligan. As luck would have it, the hobo "food" was more bland than foul-tasting. It warn't a bit like eating an old shoe as I'd reckoned. 'T was a sight better than that. 'T was more like eating a *new* shoe.

In my part of Missouri, growing up we always et quietly. Dinner was sober and prayerful, with me and Mama, my five sisters, our Aunties, and the presence of the Lord. But that warn't how these tramps was raised. After sitting down to just one cup of mulligan, I learned these partic'lar tramps' names was Texas Jim, Arkansas Jack, Ohio Eddie, and Canada Pete. And a couple 'a Chicago boes went by the monickers of Star-line Sam and Red-eye Munson. Lee proceeded to introduce himself as Frisco Dan and me as Mutton-chop.

Once we got comfortable amongst our new friends, I turned to one side and says to Trombo: "Why d'you wear scarves and gloves and such in the autumn? The cold hain't even come in yet."

"We ride the rods, bo," Trombo says. "Now the two of you is riding blind baggage, up in the boxcars, but when it comes to the bad roads around Hobohemia"—that was Chicago, he learned me later—"or the queen city, when the shacks catch you riding blind, they don't ever let you out."

"So you barnacle underneath the train where the rods is?" I says with new appreciation at the sheer gumption of this rabble.

Trombo nods. "Or you ride up on deck, like Star-line Sam," Trombo says. "Either way, you needs gloves and scarves so your fingers and ears don't get bit by the wind. Just learn yourself to tie up a scarf real good, because if you're riding the rods, and let out too much slack, with the rest of it wrapped around your neck, that'd be the end of Mutton-chop's tramping life."

Trombo says this with a half-smile, like he's on to me—

like he knows we're just hobby hoboes, but doesn't seem to mind much. "If there's any bo whose a real tramp-royal, it's Star-line Sam."

"He's the best there is, eh?" I says.

"No sir," says Trombo. "The best freight hopper you won't never see in the jungle. He sticks to hisself, and don't ever let him be seen by nobody." Just when it seemed as though he warn't goin' to say shucks more, Trombo puts in, "He's called the Airedale, and he's free as the wind."

I looked into the distance above the trees to the West as the sun crawled over the Independence water tower, and I imagined the wild and wily grit of the Airedale—who traveled so much amongst the crowds but remained unseen—lonely and suffering and anonymous. Then my eyes refocused, and I saw only the swarm of gnats in front of me, and was returned to the smallness of one man in a hobo jungle.

Listening to the boes' stories, I gathered this much: that Texas Jim was a remittance man—his wife un-married him and found herself a rich feller to raise their kids, then paid Jim fifty dollars every six months just to stay away from home, so he was a pitiable fool in the eyes of his kin, and a celebrated character and a rich man in the eyes of these brethren of the road. Ohio Eddie was a scissor bill—a grown man with no property to his name who still believed in spite of all evidence to the contrary in the goodness of fate; he couldn't find work hauling bricks but still thought he'd be President someday. Jersey Joe I figured right away—I knew his sort too well from my years a-pirating. I *was* his sort, once.

As for Trombo, nobody knew what to make of him. He struck 'em all first off as a superior feller, high-minded like a mission stiff. When they learned he was Bohunk, and furthermore a Bohunk of the chosen tribe, they figured him for an easy mark, which he warn't. It was the jack-rollers that tried to rob him blind who first learned that Trombo was a first-class pugilist who could no longer fight in the circuit once the promoters learned he was a son of Shem, so took to the Wander Path since he warn't getting paid for what he done best. Now they all had him figured, though. Trombo was just a big ole, who'd do the hard work for anyone, just so as he could feel useful again.

Each man had come to hoboing on his own circurious route, but all the men shared this in common: a loud contempt for bozoes and scenery bums—samplers of The Life such as I secretly was.

My queasiness come back all a sudden, and I a-feared that the ringing in my ear was the bee's buzz. "How comes there are hornets out when it's near winter?" I says, tugging my shirt closer around my shoulders. Then I notice the flies come to share in our mulligan, and start thinking on the tiny eggs they laid everywhere. "Don't any body ever mind the maggots?"

Just then Lee cuffed me and pull me in next to him and says, "What're you doin', Joe?" I notice now that Lee looks a-feared too, but it ain't the bugs he's bothering about. "Why're you asking so many blamed questions? You want them to think we's geycats?"

It seemed an odd kind of question for him to ask, but I answered it the best I could think how. "I ain't any sort of cat, Lee," I says.

"You muggins," says Lee. "Geycats is tramps who's new to the tramping life, like them road kids." He p'inted to the pair of tramps who brung with 'em a dirtied-up kid with ash smeared on his face and clothes, no more than ten years old, one for each of 'em. It 'most gave me the jim-jams *and* the fantods to see those boys, out in the weather, sipping their Peoria soup from a cup, and no mama in sight.

I nodded at Lee, and I done my best to be unmoved by the sight of the road kids. But being inclined toward hermitage, the only way I knowed to make conversation was to ask questions, so I turned to the feller on t' other side of me, and says, "What's your name?"

"Arkan-saw Jack," he says, and no more, too busy shucking corn for the mulligan. He wore a farmer hat and looked like he shaved his chin with a Jim Bowie knife.

"Where're you from?" I says.

"Arkan-saw," he says, and no more than that either.

"I thought about goin' to Arkansas once," I says, looking at my lap. "But I changed my mind."

He nodded and went back to his shucking.

Fitting in and letting on I was a tramp of the road was a tougher business than I'd reckoned. "Is there a family relation 'tween Kansas and *Ar*-kansas?" I asked. Here again I thunk I was making the harmlessest, ildest talk, but Arkansas Jack put on the meanest, ugliest face I ever seen, and set his jaw.

"There ain't *nothin'* between Arkansaw and that blamed half-a-state," he says, jumping to his feet and raking his fingers through his beard as though his white hair were all the proof he needed. "You know why they call it *Cain's-ass*? 'Cause the only men fool enough to set their backsides on it are sinners and wanderers. It's the last refuge for every undesirable no other state ever wanted. You're asking me about Cain's-ass? You must take me for a cunt-lipped yaller dog, 'cause the only kind of man I ever met from Cain's-ass was a cunt-lipped yaller dog. And I wouldn't deserve the name of Arkansaw Jack if I 'lowed you to sit there and stain the good name of Arkansaw."

Trombo spoke up now, standing to his full height and breadth, and the air of threat introduced by Arkansas Jack just steamed out like a slowing engine. "Who d'you think you're talking to, Arkansas? We're all of us sinners and wanderers, and you're the sinningest of the bunch."

The whole affair turned out to be a ruse for Jersey Joe to lift my poke and Lee's satchel. He held up our things above his head and asked how badly we wanted them back. In this way he meant to learn the value of their contents. It's a good thing I reckon that Jersey Joe was so thick-headed, because if he'd 'a poured out my poke he would have learned too well the value of what it contained, as a score of yeggs would 'a stampeded him just for the boast of saying for the rest of their lives, "yes, I once'd been a rich man."

I looked to Trombo for help again. "Ain't there laws in the jungle?"

He nodded at me, but he dasn't intervene.

"They's rules, for sure, when it comes to boes in the jungle," says Jersey Joe. "But you two ain't boes, and ain't tramps neither. You're just jungle buzzards—bums looking to eat our food and take what ain't yours." I couldn't help but notice that Jersey Joe was the one who took what warn't his. He bent down to unwrap his bindle, to throw our pokes in with his things, but Lee saw his chance and leapt up to swat that yegg on his ear, landing him on the ground by the rocks.

"I'm a bum, you say? A jungle buzzard? Just because I ain't no bindle-stiff, you dingbats can't recognize the bona fide, dyed-in-the-wool Airedale when you see him? Why, I breakfast on tramps like you and leave you curled up in a chamberpot before dinnertime. When you're forced to lay your bedroll in the woods, and skeered to fall asleep, I'm your bogeyman; and when you ride your last train up to the big tunnel in the sky, I'll be your conductor."

Jersey Joe got to his feet and stared back at Lee with his sky-clear eyes, then throwed us our pokes and lit out. That's when I judged Lee warn't a bo, or a hermit, but maybe he was the Airedale too!

Chapter VIII

From then on those boes embraced me like I was one of the tribe, and they looked up to Lee like a true tramp-royal. Lee explained to Trombo and the others that he was soon to retire from The Life and aimed to learn me in the secrets of freight-hopping before he was Westbound, so he had to let on that *I* was a tramp-royal to keep them from sniffing him out as the Airedale. A real crowd had formed now, and every direction Lee went, he met another brother intent on learning the mysteries of the path, and envious of me for being the beneficiary of his teaching.

In partic'lar, a local bo named Toke—hardly more than a road kid—followed us around and asked us questions about The Life. Everyone who knew Toke held him in high esteem for his prowess in the art of borrowing. Though still a boy of nineteen, he took on debts with a prodigious mastery found elsewhere only in the musical arts. Ten dollars, fifteen, one hundred and fifty—it warn't no trouble at-all for that boy to collect loans the way a tide collects algae. Added to this was the fact that Toke had a skill for dodging his creditors, and when he failed at evasion, he took out loans from another unsuspecting soul in order to make a payment to the former. On occasion his sense of honor inclined him to forgo the indignity of cadging for a loan, and he was obliged to take, ruther than borrow, that sum of money from his unsuspecting creditor—which practice the hobos referred to as "jack-rolling." So Toke was a yegg like Jersey Joe, pinching from working folks in the town, but he'd always dreamed of being the Airedale. Problem was that for all his wanderlust, he was just a Wallie—some down-and-out kid from the city—and never once rode him a train beyond Missouri.

Toke asks us, "So what kinds of things is it okay to jack-roll, and what kinds of things ain't?"

I shook my head at this yegg, practically a road kid, worrying only about what things he can take.

Lee, he don't blink. "Gooseberries, spuds, the papers," he listed them on his fingers.

"Tobacker?" Toke asks.

"No, bo," says Lee. "Tobacker is as good as cash up in the stir."

"What about things I find, just layin' around?" he says, and he kep' going on in that way until I learned to stop listening.

We did pick up a few things from Toke: that if you got "saved" at the mission church you'd get bread and a bed, that all the bad roads were coming in to Independence ruther than going out, and that if we moved on West, there was a man who lived on the Kansas side and was named Guy van der Loost who was good to tramps—who Trombo confirmed was one of the best men Missouri ever made. I reckoned we would pay him tribute, as we was ready for a proper meal.

"You was too young for the big one," says Trombo to Toke. "But they say Guy fought for the North *and* the South."

"The mischief he did," says Toke. "And where was *you* during Lincoln's war?"

Trombo looked shameful sad, but he don't make any apologies. "I always fought for pay, so's I could eat," says Trombo. "But I couldn't ever figure out what they was fighting about, so I sat it out."

"Me as well," says Red-Eye Munson. "There was all kinds of confusion in those days. What does the problems between rebels and slaves and such got to do with Missouri?"

There was general agreement on this score, and no body in that jungle could find any reason to fault Guy for fighting on both sides of the war, so we decided to seek him out.

But as we head back to the train yard, I noticed that the critters was swarming up now and getting bolder, then a bunch of 'em blowed against my cheek, uncommon warm.

"Ho!" I says to Lee. "Them ain't critters at-all!" What I thought were a swarm of gnats spiraling through the air of the hobo jungle was really bits of blackened coal dust from the ash cloud, raised up out of the cinders of the trainyard!

On the boxcar thar we come upon a piteous sight—a deafie, a man who couldn't hear or say nothin', just tucked in a corner of the car and covered in rags from sole to crown. He made grunting sounds now and then, when he couldn't help it, and suddenly I was wishing I was like him, born short of two senses, not caring a whit about how the noises I make will sound to the wide world.

It turned dark again, and I was weary of traveling, so we stuck with the occupied car instead of padfooting it. Lee and me was becoming regular midnight cargo. Hopping the car with us was Trombo, Red-Eye Munson, and the boy Toke—who'd stolen a jug of tiger milk from some rum dum in the jungle and was about to make himself scarce by hopping to the city.

Red-Eye had the most peculiar bo story of all, I do believe. He was just a man in Chicago worked at a bank and rode the local rail to work every day. Day by day he found it harder and harder to sleep in his bed at home, and easier and easier to sleep on his morning route to work. Until one day he's pacing around the house at night, unsleeping, when he reckoned to take a walk. On his way home, waiting at a crossing for a freight train to pass him by—and it's taking forever, just dragging on like them fifty-car trains do when they're full of goods—without a thought he hopped it. He didn't even bother to find his way inside, he just clumb up a ladder, found himself on deck, and fell into the best sleep he ever had in his life. Now have you ever heard of another man like Red-Eye who traveled the country in search of only a good night's sleep?

When I seen Toke and Trombo fell asleep—and when the train started up it didn't take Munson but a minute to tramp off to the shadder-world—I asks Lee, "Is you really the Airedale?"

Lee got on a sudden smile, the kind that takes the whole face with it, but he didn't say yes or no. "As much as you're a pirate, I am." I reckoned it was okay that Lee judged my life at sea to be a big fish story. This a-way I had less to answer for.

"If you don't trust me, Lee, why did you 'low me in your home, to sleep on your floor?" I says.

He shrugged. "It's a sight better'n a hammock," he says. "Ain't a body 'lowed to help out another lost soul without being asked what-for?"

"But what did you figure I was there for?" I says.

He chewed on this one before saying, "I figured you was just a man, but I was hoping you were a kinder god."

This was too many for me. "A god?"

"Yeah," he says. "I warn't counting on it, but I reckon it happens. Don't you know the story of Bag-ass and Philly-man?"

Trombo spoke up from the rear end of the boxcar without ever opening his eyes. "Was they the boes who was twins, and kep' making trouble, thinking 't was t' other one who would get the rap?"

"No, bo," says Lee. "Bag-ass and Philly-man warn't boes at-all; they was a loving couple from ancient grease who lived in a town what lost its sense of hospitality. Didn't no one of their neighbors welcome strangers into their homes. So the god Zoos comes to town dressed up like a vagabond—"

"—like a plain ol' tramp?" I says.

"*Just* like a tramp, and his road kid Herpes with him, and they goes from one house to t' other, cadging for grub and bedroll, but ain't nobody offer a set-down, much less a bed."

I shake my head. "That's just the way of it," I says.

"But when they come to Bag-ass and Philly-man's house, they take them in, no question. The god Zoos and Herpes gets their fill of biddles and beans and they even roast 'em up a pig's vest. And after they're done with the meal, Bag-ass and Philly-man offer them *their* bed and a couple 'a goose-down pillows they warmed by setting 'em above the hearth stove."

I 'most cried when I heard this partic'lar bo story, thinking on the generosity and kindness toward strangers shown by that grease-y old couple.

"Don't shed your tears yet, Joe; you ain't even heard the end of the story," he says.

"Why? What happen then?" I says.

"Well, when that old couple come to serve 'em some wine, they see that the pot just keeps filling itself over and over, and they recognize this old tramp and his road kid as the gods they rightly was. They get down on their knees and offer a sacrifice, but these gods never want any. Instead they say, 'this whole town is rotten and we're goin' to wipe it out, but your house can stay as long as you turn it into a temple and always welcome weary strangers, and if you do, we'll grant you both one wish.' Bag-ass and Philly-man don't even need to think, they already knowed what they want. It's what they always wanted, which is, when they come to die, to do so together, ruther than to 'low one of 'em to bury t' other. Sure 'nough, after a lifetime of tending to the temple and welcoming every stranger who come through, they look at each other one day and notice leaves and moss and bark is growing on 'em. So Bag-ass she leans in to her husband, and Philly-man he leans in to his wife, and they have just enough motion in 'em to reach out and embrace t' other before they's turned to trees. And to this day they're still tangled up that a-way, and will continue to be as long as there's a god Zoos."

The sky had turned dark and star-speckled now, and maybe it's 'cause I was bone-tired, but the tears come fast and plenty. I'm one of those, I've learned, who don't ever sob or sniffle, but just lets loose a tap of tears until my collar is wet. "There's good folks out there for certain," I says. Lee nods.

"You missed the p'int of the story entirely," says Trombo, his eyes closed in imitation of sleep.

"What d'you mean?" I says.

"I mean that it seems to me the p'int of the story is that gods is no good at cadging for food. They've got all the knowhow when it comes to making and unmaking the world and such, but when it comes to falling on the hospitality of others, they's got plenty to learn," he says.

I thought to argue, since the bo story had affected me so, but I reckoned he had it square.

I barely got to sleep before I was rousted by Trombo, who wake us up one by one, 'cept for Red-Eye. Even the deafie get up, though he kept his face hidden in the dark corner of the box. "Wake up, boes. It's Kansas City." On the open end of the box, we see the lights of the city up ahead.

"Well, that's swell, ain't it? I slep' more'n I thought if we's already in Kansas!" I says.

Too tired to razz me, Lee just come out and says, "That's Kansas City, *Missouri*, Joe." Then it seems he couldn't help himself any more. "Hain't you lived in Missouri your whole life long? Didn't you tell me you got an education?"

"I did and I had, 'cept I unlearned it when I took up pirating," I says. But the more I puzzle it out, the less sense it do seem to make. Kansas left its own city in Missouri and left it's whole self in the middle of Arkansas. It's the curiosest state, I do believe.

Chapter IX

Here was Trombo, the boy Toke, Lee, and me. We got out at the Union station, and padfoot it to the West Bottoms, but then we have to cross the Kansas River. Trouble is there warn't any bridges, just ferry-boats that only take thin ones for payment, and between the four of us we've got two di'monds and zero nickels. After trailing up and down the banks, we finally come upon a feller in a float house willing to transport us who took hobo money—wooden nickels—which Trombo was strong in.

But the oarsman was so old he looked like he was made of skin-clothes, so I wondered whether he could even lift his own burden, much less row four grown men across the Kansas River. He swore he'd get us to t' other side, but wondered aloud whether we'd ever find our way back. I reckoned the joke was on him, though, since me and Lee at least never planned on coming back this way again.

The air was full of all sorter mists: some low-riding clouds that moved fast near above us, a few wisps rising from the water as the evening frost come in, and smoke from a fire on the far bank, obscuring the skyline and making the wide river look like a harbor. We could see the fire plain from where we stood on the float house, yet the air around us was uncommon cold.

Another fire—that was the setting sun—burned between the water and a bridge still under construction. There was workingmen on it hauling lumber, small as mites in the distance, using the last bit of sunlight to see by. It must 'a been a weekday, though I cain't say which.

We docked on a low place beside a bluff that, despite being only my height, appeared to be the highest p'int in the topography of Kansas. Beyond it, a long field ending in a row of one-story wood buildings ranged before us, suggesting the endless plains awaiting. The spacious green of a park pleased my eyes, after dwelling these days in the city 'mongst urban folk. This here was Kaw Point, which stood apart from the surrounding neighborhood like a village—or like a book illustration of a village.

Since it was close to full dark, folks strolled up and down the walkways 'longside the park, holding hands and looking placid at the unstepped grass. Trombo, Toke, Lee and I walked through it.

When we reached the piece that was cobblestoned, there was benches and tables set up throughout. Some of the ripest folks I ever seen sat at those tables—gray beards long as trousers, faces old as Methuselah—and played chess. I fancied some of them were philosophers.

Finally, when we get to that stretch of road where Toke promised we'd meet the famous Guy van der Loost, who fought for both the union and the rebel armies, I seen there warn't one saloon, but seven, all beside one another, without a church in sight. I had to stand there and count 'em, in p'int of fact. Yes, there were seven. "Go on," I says. "Which one is it, Toke?"

Toke just stood dumbly—even dumber than regular. "I cain't remember. Somehow I only ever showed up at The Summit when I was already a few drinks below sober."

"D'you mean you never once showed up at The Summit in your right mind and in the daytime?" But as soon as I said it, it seemed a profligate question.

"What should we do?" Trombo says. For a hobo, he looked mighty uncomfortable in a crowd. Or p'rhaps just among the quality.

In the ten minutes it took to get from the riverbank to the saloons, somehow our lot hadn't improved any, so we were left with no money *and* no partic'lar destination. Lee come up with the idea that we should round up the empties on the tables we could find and let Toke drink up the swill left at the bottom. In this way, Toke could bluff the feeling of showing up stunk and, Lee guessed, his compass for free drinks would direct him.

This satisfied Toke, who was always fond of yegging. So we stood around like geycats, watching the boy Toke get boozy and boozier, until it seemed like he was about to jack-roll some accoutered gentleman for just a sip of his brandy. Then we stepped in, figuring the boy was well-battered.

By and by we land at Guy's doorstep just as The Summit got busy with the night crowd, and he *still* opened his doors to us tramps and give us each a stool to set ourselves on. I could see he was a man earned his reputation for kindness and charity. But when the last of us walked in the door, which was Lee, he says with a frown, "who's the yeller feller?"

Ruther than bark back, like I seen him do many a time, Lee took a big step back out the door, put his hand on my shoulder—where I felt his hand a-trembling—and says, "I'll catch up with you, Joe." It was too much society for a hermit, I s'posed, but then I wondered, Why was Lee a-feared? I kep' wondering it, until I walked inside and looked around, where four Johnny Laws was playing seven-up, surrounded by empty cups.

Next day at six, the dog's hour, Guy unlocked his doors and let the early morning folks in. The tan counter shone almost bronze in the daylight. A clean mirror behind a shelf clogged with bottles reflected the light from the window and sent out a spectrum that was cruel to the eyes. As I just begin to stir, having fallen asleep at the bar, I seen Guy had already hosted a new batch of Johnny Laws coming in off their beat, 'lowing them one last game of seven-up and one more fistful of whiskey so they'd have something to sleep off. I took a tired minute to appreciate a place that can host every kind of man, from tramps to tramp-catchers, without trouble. There was even a drunk negro in there the night before, as I recall. But still no Lee.

One feller from last night who stuck around was a salesman who set up at the bar, dropped his valise, and laid his head down on the counter. This morning, he was still at it, drinking and grumbling, but he kep' looking at the door after every sip. I reckon he was trying to muster the strength to kick back the stool and get out. "The Irish is named Whelan," Guy says, nodding toward t' other end of the bar. "A man so proud he'll swear President Grant is half-Irish, and if he asked you the time and you said Seven O'clock, he'd tell you that Seven O'clock was an Irishman too."

"He a regular?" I says.

Guy shaked his head. "He's more'n a regular. He's furniture."

I reckon Guy took ample pride in how his saloon welcomed every soul, provided a second home to the lost; and Whelan was in the running for the most-lost sumbitch that ever drank whiskey for breakfast. And in my ten years a pirate and my weeks in the tramping life, I seen the competition.

Toke came in that morning with an antique musket, hefting it in front of him like a prized fish. His short hair was brushed back, making it stick up part of the way like stepped-on grass. The kid looked even skinnier with no coat, and had a way of raising his eyebrows when he talked that made him look surprised by his own words. Guy was t' other way, I s'pose: heavy around the middle, and as excitable as an Indian chief.

"Ain't she a beauty?" Toke says, cradling the musket. He placed it on the wood grain by the cask ale.

Leaning over it so he can smell the gunpowder, Guy shrugged. "It's not from the war, I'll tell you that much," he says.

"Not the war between the states, my friend," Toke says,

running his fingers along the Dutch lock, a hundred-year-old span of iron, admirably worn. "The War of Independence. It belonged to my great-grampa."

"Seeing as you hain't put a musket ball through me, I reckon you brung it in hoping to sell it," Guy says. "Does this look like a pawnshop to you, Toke?"

"Come on, Guy," Toke says. "It's a gift. I figure since my dad's passed it'd be better to get rid of the old things." He fidgeted, looking away from the gun, and scanned the room, lingering on the tap. I'd come around on Toke, had even learned to like him, but I swear no man ever wore his weaknesses so openly as him. "But... I s'pose, if you was interested, I'd take a week of drinks in trade."

Guy stared at him an uncomfortable long time. "Take your treasure and bury it, Toke. In my place, no good man ever goes thirsty."

Toke brushed back his prickly hair, muttered his thanks, and waited a full forty seconds before filling his glass.

Chapter X

As the day passed along in the saloon dark, I started to become familiar with the company at The Summit, and it seemed to me the whole Van der Loost family was employed there. Guy's little brother John worked the bar and his littlest brother Tim swept up. But between John's pious scolding and Tim's hollering, there warn't much time for work. Tim preferred persiflage, and John favored the art of the jeremiad. "You teetotalling sumbitch," Tim says. Then he turned toward Guy like he was tattling and says, "As soon as John showed up last night he started cutting customers off at three drinks. Ain't it true, Joe?" I half-nod, not wanting to come between feuding brothers.

John polished the counter, ignoring the wily runt in front of him. "This way of life—the kind of business you run—isn't long for this world," he says, dropping his Christian wisdom on the saloon floor like rose petals.

"Nothing is, Johnny," Guy says, dropping his saloon wisdom on him like a horse pile.

John had wet-looking hair that fell down on his broad forehead in pointy strands, and manly features that stood in contrast to the bruised expressions he often wore. He could 'a been on the rugby team at the college. Tim's hair was similar straight, but it moved away from the front of his head like it was skeered to get in the way of his bulldog face.

"I do the right thing in the end, though, don't I?" Guy says. John refrained from a reply.

"Johnny," Toke says, "what you need to do is fetch a hen at the henhouse."

"That or a cock," says Tim, and the two boys have a fit of boys' laughter.

"That's enough, Tim," says Guy. "Respect your brother. He's a good Christian."

"Which is another way of saying 'a Christian'," says John.

"Cain't a body be Christian without being good, and cain't he be good without being Christian?" Guy says. "In my line I seen all sorts of folks: good, bad, and indifferent. The seat you're sitting in right now has held up the rears of dozens of men I love and respect who never believed in miracles."

"Men who are smart without being wise," says John.

Guy shakes his head. "I don't know how you were born my brother. The one sin I cain't abide is intolerance."

"Is that irony or isn't it?" says John.

Guy shakes his head again, and moves for the door, bone-weary from all the holy talk. "Just close up, will you?" Guy says as he went out the door, me and Tim following close. "And keep the tap flowing as long as she's open. We're goin' to get the hell out of The Summit tonight."

Guy and Tim and I headed to The Cove. According to Guy, The Cove Theater always got the best comics and jugglers, hypnotists, magicians and quick-drawers on the circuit. Just the week before it was a plate-spinner who kept up to eight pieces of fine china going at once; that night it was s'posed to be a more elevating form of relaxation: a traveling show, the Wonders of Photographic Science. An inventor and his assistant come all the way from London, England to show off their newest Calotype. They was even goin' to photograph us, the audience, during the show.

The ushers at The Cove walked the aisles and passed around printed cards from silver trays, wearing gloves; Tim rolled his eyes, muttering a plea to the Lord that the Cove warn't goin' swanky. As it turned out, written on the cards was just a reminder not to smoke in the theater, as the equipment being used that day was combustible. We sank in our chairs, Guy and Tim and I, and lit our pipes anyway.

A mustached feller in a white suit walked through the parted curtains and down the center of the stage, to faint applause, while behind him an assistant—a long-legged lady—wheeled a table out into the middle, full of strange contraptions. For her, the audience gives a more stirring welcome, with some hoots and howls thrown into the mix.

Though he looked foreign, the man's speech showed he was Midwestern. In the end I judged that he warn't even an inventor from London, England, but a Chicagoan who purchased some equipment, trained himself to use it, and now traveled week-long tours with his pretty young wife to cities like St. Paul, Indianapolis, and Detroit, where they stayed at the Savoy and the Ritz, getting royal treatment just for throwing around a big-shot inventor's name. "Men and women of Kansas City, today you are a goin' to see some of the most revolutionary science that man has ever devised. The calotype that will one day replace the daguerreotype as the photographer's tool of the trade."

First his girl set up the camera. As she done it, he went on explaining the photographic process in the most highfalutin terms, making pictures sound like the bulliest invention that ever been inventored. Then he p'inted the camera at the audience while the ushers raised the lamps high, and he asked us to smile. When the photograph was developing on the Xylonite, they covered the lamps so the theater went dark as night all a sudden. Folks murmured and laughed in the darkness while the gentleman says how they use stuff called "bromide of potassium" in the development to reduce fogginess on the print, and to make a picture sharper than ever before.

"What about the Lord?" a man calls out from the unlit audience.

"What about 'im?" the gentleman says.

"Ain't you trying to act His part—the way Lucy-fur done—by capturing man's own image, who was created in the likeness of God?"

There was a silence first, that was filled only when the

mustached man laughed. "We are *definitely* in Kansas," he says, but hain't nobody laugh at that one. "Sir, with utmost respect, photographers have been capturing man's image on copper plates since before you or I were born. But it's our Xylonite that will make them available to everyday folk such as yourself for the first time in history."

The lamps was uncovered, and the lights come on again. I was thankful at first to be back in the visible world, but when I saw what a grizzly, toothless old feller was standing and speaking on behalf of our Lord, I reckoned we was better off in the dark.

"You cain't speak for me," the old man said. "I'm older'n photographs and older'n the nation your standing in. You and your devil science can git on back to France and stay there."

That gentleman on the stage with his brown mustache and his education just stood there speechless. I reckon he ain't knowed where to begin, since as I recall he warn't from France at-all. By and by the ushers bounced that grizzly old feller out on the street where he cain't disturb the quality, and the gentleman goes on with his show, mumbling a piece about what a lot of good his invention will do for mankind, "and womankind," he says, to try and win back a fond audience.

The girl brings out the photographs that were just developed in the dark, and passes 'em around the audience, though the ushers stick close by in case a body means to call it the devil's work and set it afire. Then, while the mustachioed feller was talking more 'a his technical mumbo-jumbo, one of the ushers takes the stage and whispers in the ear of his assistant. After the next bout of polite applause, the mustache steps forward and says, "The proprietors of The Cove Theater have asked me to make a public announcement. During yesterday's gun show, a valuable and rare Revolutionary War musket was stolen off the back of Winnifred the sharpshooter's wagon trailer. Anybody with information leading to the return of the firearm and the arrest of the man who stole it will receive a considerable reward. Now, on with the show!"

I look at Guy, and he look at Tim, and Tim look at me, and warn't any words necessary. We didn't stand up and leave the theater right off because to do so would implicate us; but I was sorely tempted. We needed to warn Toke. The bulls were after him now, and even if he sought refuge at the Summit, Guy was like to strangle the bastard for trying to unload upon him his ill-gotten gains.

Chapter XI

Next day as they set to open, Guy gathered together his family—by blood and by labor— and we all sat around quiet waiting for Trombo, who used to be a roughneck with Guy in the ironworking days before The Summit. I wondered where Lee had skedaddled to, and whether he might just have abandoned me there 'mongst the rum dums and roughnecks. "What are you up to now, Joe?" Mama Sereny says. "Here was a traveling sort who said he'd learn you to become an independent man, and now you've up and joined another gang."

"These men can learn me plenty," I says out loud, catching a rabbit-quick glare from the serious eyes of the men surrounding the rain-worn table—or, s'posing it had never been kept out of doors, the *drink*-worn table.

Finally Trombo lumbered in and pulled back a chair. When he sat in it, it looked like a doll's chair. I reckon Trombo's sort is an indispensable friend whether you work the saloon or walk the hobo trail.

"I have something to say," Guy led off. "No *one* of you is goin' to talk to the law today or any day. Even if they're offering a hundred dollars for information about that gun. It don't matter. If they ask *Have you seen a man walking around with a Revolutionary War musket in his hands?*, you just laugh in their faces. They'll get used to it. Understand?"

We all consented to this plan with nods, except Trombo, who tipped his hat, and Tim, who sat with his arms a-folded in front of his chest, which was unnatural wide for his frame.

"You ain't gonna back the bastard, is you?" Tim says. "You might as good get hauled off to jail."

"Shut your bone box, Tim. This ain't your fight," Guy says.

"I knew this business would bite you back," says John,

and then goes quiet, as though even he senses that his sanctimony has gone too far. Folks are staring at John, then at Guy, and Trombo strains to lift a heavy eyebrow.

Tim starts to pipe up, but Guy shows him a fat finger. "Take whatever you were about to say and pocket it, Timmy." Then he turns to John. "You can condemn my immortal soul to your heart's content, Johnny," Guy tells him, "but say nothing. To the law. About the musket."

Guy smacks the table twice like an applause, and we all stand up, ready to go back to work. Just then Whelan, who we hardly noticed, for he was leaving his ass's imprint on the stool at the bar's end, stands up, sober as a churchwoman, and says, "I seen that boy Toke with the same one."

It's such a shock to see him on his feet, that between the quick pace of his speech and taking the size of him, we're all of us still and silent as the shadders of houses. It ain't take much to figure that Whelan had only been possum-drunk.

"Tim, John, Trombo, go do the books," Guy says, and the rest of the men—a couple of them just boys—move to the back room and give 'em the floor of the saloon.

Standing off with Irish, Guy is one hairline short of the other man's six feet. "What're you playing at, Whelan?"

"I'm not playing at all, you old rusty guts. When you put down a month's wages on a longshot and the horse came in first place, Guy, that was your day." He breathed on his hands as though it's cold in the saloon. On his first day without firewater in so many years, I guess his body didn't know how to make its own warmth. "Today I heard somebody'd pay a hundred dollars for a piece of information that I happen to know, so today is *my* day."

"Listen to me, pecker. You didn't hear what you think you heard," Guy says. But damned Whelan fixed his jaw.

"I'm gonna walk out of that door, and I'm gonna go to the authorities. It's up to you whether you want to stand in my way," he says.

Guy stepped aside. "Go to the police. I hope you do. They'll come in here and say 'Guy, your regular Whelan said he saw the musket offered you by a boy by the name of Toke.' And I'll say, 'Sir, that Whelan couldn't see a hole in a ladder,' and that'll be the end of it." Guy grabbed the broom, swep' the floor by the entrance, and give him a butler's bow.

"Trombo!" he calls out, and the big man stepped through the doorframe, nearly filling it with his bulk. "*Bounce* him."

Trombo stepped into the room, followed by Tim, and the two of them crowded Whelan out the door. Outside the door now, by the street among the morning rushers, Trombo says, "I just wish I could see the cops' faces when the lousiest drunk in Kansas City walks in their station with his tail down and his face busted up from a bar brawl." The glass doors swing closed, and I seen 'em, but could barely hear 'em talk.

Whelan touched his cheek, as though expecting to find something there, and says, "but my face is—" It's then that Trombo gives him a nose-ender, laying him out on the street.

Tim walked back in the saloon and picked up the broom set against the doorjamb. Then he stepped back out holding it halfway down like a baseball club.

Guy was an admirable man, I reminded myself, a good man, I repeated, as his men thrashed Whelan on a public street in the daytime until his clothes changed color and his fingers quit their twitching. "Lord, Jesus Christ," I whispered, "have mercy on me, a sinner."

Chapter XII

Next morning I felt a wanderlust more befitting a real tramp than a fake one. I sought out my road-kin, and after approaching a few chinamen who turned out to be strangers, I was relieved to find Lee sitting 'mongst the chess-playing philosophers in the park, scratching away on the same sheaf of papers he'd had tucked in his satchel, not far from where we'd begun. Seeing his ca'm face and habit of gracefulness, I could have gathered the man into a hug, but for the sake of being proper.

"Where you been, Joe?" he says. "What sorter mischief have you been up to?"

"Oh Lee, I've been party to thieving and backstabbing and mob justice that you wouldn't believe in this blamed town, and it's only Wednesday morning. I thought I'd done forever with the pirate life, but here I am party to more acts of violence and villainy. I reckon Johnny Law will make it mighty warm for us, 'less we light out."

"Well I've been hunted up before, and beaten, but never caught," Lee says. "And I'd like to keep it that-a-way." I judged it was good fortune that Lee had no crimes to confess other than tramping.

"I thought you might've been gone for good," he says. "I thought I'd lost you to Van der Loost and his clan."

"But you waited!" I says. "How'd you spend your break from Joe Harper?"

"Hermiting," says Lee. "Cadging. Same as always. But now I've got a ken to see more of the West."

This plan was mighty agreeable to this geycat, so we hopped a way car at Union Station and rode the deck.

Riding the deck is how I learned that the State of Kansas was a whole lot of empty. From there atop the hindcar, I'd close my eyes so they wouldn't go dry, then open them ten miles later, but nothing would 'a changed. There was the same brown grass, some taller and some flatter, some flecked with seed on the stalks, but all the same an endless plain that buried not just the senses but the memory of senses—as though even an act of imagination warn't possible here.

Up top we was cold and wind-bitten, and the further West we came the colder and windier it got. I ain't wonder anymore why Trombo and t' other boes always piled on the gloves and scarves over their coats. I still had my poke with the di'monds in it, but I reckon I would 'a traded 'em for a wool cap.

I passed the hours palavering with Mama Sereny.

"You don't need to suffer this a-way, Joe," she says.

I says, "A man has to suffer one way or t' other," and she 'lows it's so.

"I'm proud of your courage," she says, talking the way she did when she lived, so determined that I should feel approved-of.

"You're the braver," I says. After all, I tells myself, it warn't I who had to face a hard death and the Lord's reckoning.

Then Lee says, "I'm keen on ditching this train when she slows," though he's driven to shouting to make himself understood.

"No, sir," I says, full of renewed wanderer spirit. "We are goin' to beat this line all the way to Colorado!"

Even though he was behind me and more sheltered from the direct blast of the wind, I reckon Lee was just as uncomfortable, but somehow he didn't see his pain as penance, as I did. But that's just the way it is with an old pirate who counted up more sins than treasures. I couldn't close my eyes for long without seeing the faces of men who endured my wickedness, or failed to endure it. So I savored the dry, cracked feeling of my hands as they clasped the edge of the car roof, and the tingle on my ears and lips reminding me that something other than numbness was possible in that freeze.

Then the rain came on, and I conceded to Lee that it'd be better to find a place to stay dry. But it warn't easy to move around when a body's riding the deck, so at first we tried to tough it out, until I heard what sounded like a clink of metal on metal up ahead, then another, and figured maybe we rousted a brakeman with all our hollering. But then I feel a thump on my thigh, and one on my back, and I reckoned the rain was turned to hail, and it was time to slide out. We clumb down to the rear lookout, where we was partly protected from the rain, and the speed of the train made the hail look like it was headed back East without us. We heard on the metal roof the hard clang of each nugget, from which we were thankfully sheltered.

But then the double-lock opened and out walked the shack, but instead of a hammer, he was holding a gnarly apple, pieces of which he was chewing even as he stood opposite his nemeses. "Y'all look cold. It's warm *inside*," he says, a little Tennessean, though it warn't exactly Southern hospitality. Sure enough, over his shoulder, a coal stove is in the corner and to each side, a pair of padded benches that're more welcoming than a church pew.

"I can offer you accommodations," he says, "fer a dollar."

"But the overland fare is a quarter," says Lee.

"Sure it is, and the deck is free." The shack p'ints up at the roof where the knocks hain't let up yet. "But this ain't the overland passenger, and riding the deck might cost you the nose on your face."

I look at Lee, and he looked at me meaningful-like, his already narrow eyes a-narrowing, but I cain't read him.

"What about riding blind baggage?" Lee puts to him.

"This is the short-run, the KC special, and ain't none of our cars empty," he says. "So if you try it, I'll have to ditch you."

"Well…" Lee says, making us wait an unreasonable long

time before he puts out, "How about riding the rods?"

"You're welcome to try," says the shack, "though you'll have to manage it at top speed, since there ain't any stops until Topeka."

Finally I got Lee's game; he aimed to stall that shack 'til we made it all the way to Topeka. "How about we stay right here on the lookout, not a-bothering nobody?" I says. But the shack calculated Lee's intention at the same time as I done, and he put on a grim face and take out his hammer, reluctant to do us harm but resigned to 't. Without another word Lee and I jumped the train while she's highlining, and aimed for the tall grass, though my foot catched on the buffer chain and it sent me rolling in the gravel of the road bed. When I'm on my feet again, I seen my shirt and trousers is all torn, and spots of red show up where the sharp rocks found a soft place. Lee fared better, and he helped brush the dirt off of me, though you cain't tell the difference afterward, and it raised up enough dust to send us coughing for a spell.

"Don't mind the blood," he says. "Tomorrow it'll be as brown as your shirt."

But if Lee was trying to comfort me, he needn't be. From all the stumpies I seen in the hobo jungle, I reckon I was lucky to have all my extremities intact. And besides, the sting and the ache of my body was all just a part of my penance.

We drilled the rest of the day and into the next, walking the ties without saying shucks, until we stumbled out of the dawn and into the prairie town of Topeka, Kansas under looming gray clouds.

Chapter XIII

Sooner or later on the road you find yourself hungry and mean as a badger, and you must decide awful quick whether your line is cadging, or yegging, or jack-rolling. The result has naught to do with a body's skill, but ruther it has to do with how his mind is set—his tolerance for violence, or risk, or pity. F'rinstance, Trombo would have made a legendary jack-roller, being a boxer and a roughneck and big enough besides, but he fell to cadging for food because he never wanted to lay out a feller 'less he deserved it. Most road kids, if taken under the wing of a profesh, learn to cadge because they get more attention for being innocent young'uns; but left to their own devices, many a road kid lands on yegging, though precious few can out-pace a bull.

For me, though I was born with sympathetic features— long lashes like a girl and dark eyes of appealing sadness— my pride kept interfering, and I couldn't even approach a mark to start cadging. And since I gave up pirating, the idea of jack-rolling folks for their money seemed too much of the same. So I took to yegging. My first boodle was to lift some new rags, as mine was mighty sour, and between my boots and my trousers there were enough holes to make a cork stopper for a wine-jug. Even though he swore he warn't a blowed-in-the-glass profesh the way he'd let on, I could see plainly that Lee had more experience in The Life than I had, so I fell on his wisdom once again.

"How's a bo to find a wardrobe out on the road?" I says.

"Well, some is gooseberries plucked from laundry lines—shirts and undergarments, mostly—and some is mission clothes—you can get trousers that a-way, since they'll fit you with a belt. Some is yegged from overland passengers what carry luggage and such. But when it comes to hats and shoes, Joe, you have to scrounge up a half-dollar or more."

Lee, I was learning, was the sort who liked to give answers, whether he had them or not.

"There's got to be some way a body can get shoes without buying 'em. Where'd you get your outfit, fr'instance?" I says.

"Mine?" he says, putting his hand to his chin like he had to think about it. He'd grown a wiry beard in the days since we met up, and I guessed that my mutton-chops was bushing out in the middle by now. "From a lady friend who had extra rags around."

"They seem to fit you fine," I says. "If I didn't know you already, I'd 'a thought you had it tailored. Then ran it through the mud."

Lee hardly seem to notice me talking. "She was a good woman," he says. "And I'm a scoundrel."

Lee turned distant and thoughtful, so he was no good for talk, but by and by I get my answer. Tramp around the train yard in Topeka for one morning and a body will learn precious quick how a hobo gets a hat. A working feller, his head as bare as a baby's, ran around wildly through the crowd at the station, shouting to the Lord and all his flock that his Stetson was stole from his very crown. Then, down in the jungle, I seen a whole gang of road kids sit around a fire jawing, all of 'em with hats, and none of 'em that fit.

I judged it would 'a been easy to have taken a hat off of a road kid that morning, but I reckoned from our run-in with Jersey Joe the week before that even yeggs ain't s'posed to lift from other boes. So I jungled up with t' other boes and asks, "how's a body a-goin' to negotiate some new boots?"

There's laughter, much as I expected.

I shook my head. "When a body is broke and hain't had a proper meal for two days, it ain't the time for laughing," I says.

"Bo, you just described the life of every tramp who slept out-of-doors, and it's just the time for a-laughing; what else are you goin' to do?" This bo carried a bindle, like he's ready to work at the drop of a coin. But no matter which direction you go in, there warn't any work in the jungle.

It come back to me then, how different a life it was now, when the simple comfort of warm hands, and feet that ain't sore and blistery, seemed like an impossible dream, half-remembered from long ago. Even on the high seas there's always shelter below deck, and a hot meal waiting somers to look forward to. And there was women a-plenty, which kep' me from goin' cabin-crazy for the red years of my youth, but which always sent me yearning for a dank and lonesome cave. Then, when I come home after more'n ten years a pirate and learned that Mama Sereny was gone from the world, it seemed to be the only thought I could hold in my head.

Now I was back in the company of strangers, looking on through a side-alley as a parade of workingmen dressed in glad rags walked by with their hats on straight and their boots strapped tight and their keisters full of business. A thought occurred to me that has occurred to every tramping fool since the invention of poverty and idleness: *Where are they all going in such a blamed rush?* I begun to see the stiffs the way they must look at the boes; that is, like them stiffs don't hardly matter. Only pretend-people bustle around, occupied with their daily business, while *real* folks put on their boots and go a-roving.

But here I am: broke *and* I've got no boots.

Then midst the bother there was one lady who stopped dead on the sunny side of the alleyway, whose neck tilted toward the shadowy jungle and whose eyes squinted into the dark. 'T was as though I'd been a ghost, invisible to the mass of humanity, and some gifted seer had struck upon a vision of me. Her hair was scraggled and tending to gray, and her natural thinness was undermined by broad straight shoulders from which hung a blouse that billowed out like a padded quilt.

"You hungry, Mister?" she says, with generous eyes, and

a smile that held nothing back. "My husband just butchered a suckling pig, and we have more in our pot than we can handle ourselves."

My first thought was a suspicious thought, but then when I seen her hands folded in front like a girl's, I scolded myself for such distrust. "Sounds a mite better'n another cup of mulligan," I says.

"Oh, I'm famous in this town for my apple butter pork," she says, taking my one hand in both of her'n, "and I won't take no for an answer." I turned back and looked at Lee, and he just nodded at me like there's no excuse in this world for turning down a home-cooked meal. The lady led me to a clapboard home only two blocks away on a pleasant street with young fir trees. I could smell the aromatic herbs from the street, and my lips answered by wetting and puckering, leading me forward as though tied to her tether.

Now I wondered whether the story of Bag-ass and Philly-man weren't gospel truth. Here was an American Florence Nightingale lending her tender soul to the lowliest boes of Topeka. Following two paces behind her I thought too about her tolerance for what I imagined was the rank smell of a man whom the even the most delicate nose couldn't distinguish from a real hobo.

She opened up the screened door and I made to step through, but she stopped me. "If you don't mind, I thought we could sit together and eat upon the porch." I looked both ways down the street, then up above me for good measure, but I didn't see a porch in any direction. Then I seen she meant the dusty stoop we was standing on, and I done it. Aside from her use of the "we," she never joined me in a sit neither. I guessed the only thing that mattered to me at that moment was the apple butter pork.

Finally she served me up a bowl and placed it in my hands. I thanked her mightily, then was about to dig in when I noticed there warn't a spoon. "Could I trouble you for a spoon?" I said. I was hungry enough to tilt the contents of the bowl directly down my throat, but having added up more years now as a free man than a child in his mama's home, I was still afflicted with manners. Even on the hobo road I could usually count on a ladle, but Lee carried ours in his poke. There was a sudden, brief flash in her expression that could have been disgust or pity, but she answered by stepping through to the other side of the screened door and fetching a spoon. "Sorry it ain't silver," she says, though I cain't reckon why. I ain't asked for nothin' but a simple scoop.

I dip the wooden spoon to the broth and lift it, closing my eyes and taking a minute to savor the succor. Then when I opened them again it was just in time to witness the lady pulling the bowl out of my hand. She kep' peeking down the road as though awaiting some arrival. Then she turned her attention back to me. "You poor thing, your Mama never learned you your manners, did she? Don't you wait until everyone is served until you begin, and don't you say the Lord's prayer?"

My first instinct whenever I hear Mama Sereny so maligned is to return malignancy in kind, but since this lady was doing me a good turn by feeding me a home-cooked meal, I reckoned I would keep my bone box shut, and I swung it.

"Ma'am, I apologize," I says. If I had scored a hat, I would have removed it now and held it in front of me to indicate my embarrassment. "What's your name, Ma'am?"

"Oh, we don't go on much for formalities here," she said. But she still ain't say her name.

Occasionally, a boy would rush past on the street, his hands buried in his pockets; or a maid from a neighboring home would peek out her window at us. But when a particular lady in black lace over a purple evening dress turned a corner, I guess the waiting of Mrs. X was over, because she shoved the bowl back into my hands and says sharply, 'most desparately, "eat!"

I ain't needed any more prompting than that, and I cast off modesty as quickly as a shawl on a warm day. I couldn't tell if the apple butter pork was the ambrosia she claimed, or whether my hunger made it so, but the lastingness of the flavor in that meal is almost unmatched in all my lived years. Then she laid her hand on my shoulder saint-like, a furrowed look of concern spreading from her third eye outward. Strange to see how earnestly this Mrs. X watched me, when only ten seconds before I might have been a raccoon for all the attention she paid.

The black-and-purple lady, who also adorned her head with a hat that appeared inspired by the shape of a conch—which you'd never know if you never left Kansas—stopped stiff in front of us.

"Good evening, Mrs. Winn," Mrs. X says. "Heading to the church picnic?"

"I must be, Mrs. Kriegal," conch-hat answers, "since I arranged the guests and arrayed the tables and provided the goods. Were you not invited? Lord bless, what an oversight." Then with a smirk that seemed the most natural expression of her face, she says without even peeking my way, "Entertaining a visiting relative, are you?"

"No, no," Mrs. Kriegal says. "William and I live too modestly to keep guests. But I'm so glad to hear you are still sponsoring the church picnic. It's great to feed people… even if the people you're feeding aren't hungry." Then she turns a glance toward me. "I respect your choices. The Lord has called upon me for a different purpose. I can't help my sympathy for the poor, and I can't but indulge my feeling to help out the *less* fortunate."

I had no clue, at first, what had passed between these women as Mrs. Winn shuffled away flushed and flustered, but in hindsight I reckon she'd gotten a hiding on account of hers being the lesser of two charities.

Thanking Mrs. Winn for the best meal in memory—who couldn't get rid of me fast enough—and returning to the cold shadow of the bo jungle, I laughed as I come to realize that this was my first exhibition meal. On my approach, when t' other boes heard my laughter, they looked at me like the devil's only child. So even though the sun warn't yet down, I found me a clean spot to lay out my coat like a bedroll and flop.

As I drifted off to the shadder-world, I brought up one thought after another. Unless I got lucky and could ride blind baggage from here to San Francisco, I resolved that I warn't goin' to ride another car 'less I had a hat, a scarf, a pair of boots, and some gloves. I'd had enough of the cold air of a moving train. Soon as I had this thought, though, I got a gut-tingle, like I was socked in the belly by Jack Wanderlust. The notion of giving it up brought a pain in my liver. I reckon I would 'a ridden the rods, or on deck, or somers 'tween the two, as long as I still had ears to hear the mournful call of the train whistle. I even considered for a second whether my plan to find a cave and die in it warn't the *second*-best plan there ever was.

When I rose up, the day had gone dark, and Lee was pounding his ear in the bedroll. I must've out-slep' his shift. So the first thing I done was check to make sure I still got my poke, which I had. By then I'd acquired the habit of tucking it on the inside of my trousers ruther than outside, ties and all. When I felt a bug a-creeping up my neck, I jumped to my feet and swatted it. When I did, the bruises on my collar stung again like they was fresh.

Once my eyes adjusted to the orange city-dark, I seen a couple of boes awake but most of 'em laying out around the fire. I could hear a couple of boes telling a wander-path story about some tramp who once saved a train from an accident, so the railroad awarded him a road pass—free passage on all their trains for all time—just the sort of story I'd got used to hearing and never paying my mind to.

Down the alley, a body was walking fast in our direction, and from that distance I wondered if it might be a bull coming to bust up some boes. But when it came close enough I seen it was just a street girl earning her daily bread. She was slim with puffy hair, one snaggly tooth but a lot of different expressions that she flashed quickly in and out of. Seeing I was awake and on my feet, she walked up to me and whispered, "They're rustling up the bums tonight. I heard it in the stir."

"You speaking true?" I says. I don't know how or when it happened, but I dasn't trust a stranger no more. The poorer and hungrier I got, the more I seemed to care about those di'monds I kep'.

"C'mon," she says, tugging me along.

"Wait," I says. "I need to fetch my partner."

She looked down at sleeping Lee. "That chinaman? Leave him be, bo. I reckon the bulls won't want him neither. They got a negro jail and a regular jail, but no louse hotel for a chinaman."

So, bleary from sleep, afear'd of the bugs and the bulls, and taken in hand by a street girl who seemed to offer the soundest advice, I followed this slim, puffy-haired gal to the hookshop. It was only afterwards in the cat house that I wondered whether she meant they'd leave Lee alone, or treat him to the kind of abuse he'd gotten in Kansas City, and the town of Lone Jack, and back home in San Francisco.

Chapter XIV

If I ever confessed just how ca'm and comfortable I become in a cat house, you'd think me an unrepentant sinner and worse. But that's the way of it for an old pirate. Living on the ocean is a fine life for some, but I reckon the company I kep' back then was even low-livelier than at present, and the brothels full of foreign women speaking in strange tongues was always a welcome refuge from the profane, sea-faring folk to whom a pirate otherwise indentures himself.

Now I was soaking in a bath while my clothes were boiled to get the crumbs off. As me and my rags was both stewing in a pot, that street girl—whose name was Etta—undressed for her turn in the tub, and I was surprised to see that for her slimness, there was a small, appealing pouch at her belly, and small, appealing pouches acrost her chest. "Why should you want to take in a tramp and give him a warm bath and a tumble?" I asked. "You must 'a judged I have the means to pay. How d'you reckon?"

"Truly?" she says.

I nod my head as I suds up my arms.

"Okay," she says. "I thought I'd ask. Some folks like to pretend they're special."

"I've been around the block a time or two," I says. "So spill."

"Well, I seen you stand up and check your poke," she says. "Why else would a body get up in the middle of the night and check himself? So when I seen you were satisfied with what you found, I reckoned I'd be satisfied too."

"So they ain't a-rustling the bums tonight?" I says.

"In Topeka?" she says. "Bums are getting rustled every night. But if you're wondering whether I'm goin' back out to the jungle, I ain't. You're my claim." She touched my cheek with her fingers, a bit motherly, and I wondered at her uncanny instinct for knowing a man's heart. If you want to know if a feller has a dollar in his pocket, find a street girl to tell you. And if you want to know a feller's dreams and desires, ask his seducer. They are, every one, cleverer than tramps, more tenacious than working-stiffs, and cannier than wives.

"Didn't you come all this way across the state of Missouri, and into the cold fields of devil- begotten Kansas, to get away from womenfolk?" Mama Sereny says to me, just when I least want to hear it.

"You're right," I says. "I have to get the blooming hell out of Kansas."

Etta looked at me curious, then says, "which way?"

"West," I says.

"South," Mama Sereny says.

"You sure?" Etta says.

"I have to find Lee, and get back on the road," I says, standing up and reaching for a towel. Etta took one and dried me off herself like she were a lady-in-waiting, patting it gently to allow the cotton to absorb the wet, then replacing it with another dry one.

"You sure?" she says. "Cain't wait for your rags to dry?"

Suddenly I warn't so comfortable as I was on my way in. Here was kindness such as I've known in many a harem overseas, but something in me must 'a changed, I s'pose. Maybe I was still a-mourning the loss of my Mama, and hearing her voice revived my wanderlust, or maybe I felt more keen a loyalty to my road-kin than I reckoned. No matter how I twist it, what it came to was that I suddenly couldn't abide a whore's false sentiment. Sensing the shift in the room, she walked back behind the changing-screen, covered herself up with a robe, and handed me another dry towel while turning her head demurely to the side. There was her instinct again.

"It'd be better for you, bo, if you turned around, or ran

a circuit by way of Nebraska," she says. "I've heard it from a hundred other freight-hoppers. If you want to beat a train through Salina, you're goin' to tussle with Big Sur, and if you're goin' to tussle with Big Sur, you might come out the other side of Kansas with a stump, if you come out of it at-all."

Big Sur, she learned me, was the name of a hound that was rumored to have crippled dozens of boes, maybe hundreds. The beast was trained, they said, to go for the limbs ruther than the vitals, because deaths on a train yard are properly recorded in the public ledger, whereas accidents of the non-fatal kind are referred to the hospital, where if they bleed out it's the bo's own business. But more often it leads to amputation, and she didn't ever want to see me lose my extremities.

I went over to where my clothes was soaking, reached into my poke, and plucked out the smaller of the two di'monds, then placed it in Etta's hand. For even when she learned I warn't an easy mark, she was still a-looking after my safety as I was asking for the door. Though I hadn't reckoned she'd shriek in surprise the way she done—an invitation for all the girls in the joint to pour in and croon over Etta's take. Pretty soon the word spread around until every last working gal was standing there in the room, with me a-covering up my gentleman's parts. Somehow, I kep' myself modest. It's just the way I was brung up.

All the ladies was unnatural friendly, which about tore me in two, but I found that the wander-lust trumped t' other kind. "You can keep that di'mond," I says. "But I ain't got more. So could you repay a body's generosity with some clothes? A clean shirt, trousers, long johns, boots, gloves, and hat besides?" It took those hard-working women all of sixty seconds to scare up proper men's clothes I could fit into just laying around in a hookshop.

As I made for the outdoors, walking through the low lit

hall, I passed by a row of abandoned fellers whose midnight conquests had all run into my room just to have a peek at my di'mond. One otherwise respectable-looking gentleman— nearly my height and shape to the inch— stood around with only the clothes he was born in. I reckoned his old rags was my brand-new ones, and I thanked him with a tip of his own hat. He turned away, though, too ashamed, I s'pose, to be seen in the natural among the street girls of Topeka.

When I opened the door, the sky poured in like floodwater, so thick with green clouds. They was strange clouds too, hanging like udders from a long-bred cow. I stopped short upon the threshold, 'most blown back by the sight. This was a sky for tornaders.

Sure enough a gust of wind sent me in the way I came out, and all the half-dressed and ain't-dressed men and women got thrown back that a-way too. My hat, of which I'd been so proud a half-minute before, and had even traded 'most my worldly wealth for, was swept from my brow.

I guessed it was near morning now, though a body couldn't tell for sure with them big mammaries hovering over us. I took a deep breath like I was fixing to dive in a river, and made a run through the onslaught. Wind blowed hats and umbrellers around, so it warn't hard to get a-hold of each. If I warn't so picky, and took the first umbreller that landed in my lap ruther than wait for a steel-ribbed one, I reckon I would have reached Lee sooner. As it were, by the time I reached the jungle, the sky was mostly dark, but full of sunlight yonder on the Eastern horizon, where I warn't goin'. It quieted down like there never was a storm, though 't was all around me now. This kinder night was "the night that talks not," a hobo poet once said.

A silent storm is a fearsome thing, for when the funnel cloud puts its vengeful finger on the earth by and by, all you will hear is a freight train balling the jack like a cannonball, and then you're wiped from the world as though you was never born. I raced through the alley 'til I find the place I laid my bedroll.

'Cause of the unnatural quiet, the jungle was still at rest, undisturbed by bulls or tornaders. And there was all the hoboes of Topeka, bound in an invincible, guiltless sleep! I stirred up Lee and he came to slowly, like a school-kid trying to prolong the start of his morning lessons.

"Git on up," I says. "We got to light out."

He stood up quick and ready. "Is the bulls after us?"

I shook my head.

"Who is after us?" he says, tying his trousers and buttoning his now comically ragged coat.

I p'inted up at the sky, and Lee's eye follows my finger up to the firmament, where the clouds are straining down but cain't manage to find purchase on the prairie. "The Almighty."

Staring up at the storm a-gathering, Lee says, "Is that natural?"

"Just get your blooming boots on," I says. The wind was upon us again, and t' other boes was rising with the sound of whistling and howling.

"What're you all a-riling us for?" one bo asks me—the bindle-stiff who was full of wander-path stories.

"There's a tornader coming as sure as daylight," I says.

He shook his head. "I wouldn't say there was a tornader coming," he says, and I looked at him queer-eyed. "I reckon there's seven or more."

That's when I knew for sure: I cain't understand a man who lives in Kansas. "Don't it explain why I'm fixing to leave all the better?" I says.

"Well…" the bo says, scratching his lousy beard. "Can you really *run* from 'em?"

It seemed a sad and helpless thing to say, and I was eager to shake it off, but after I took a think, I got it up again. I've met a score of prairie philosophers since then who say the same, and I cain't help but wonder if there's something to 't.

"Don't go West, boy," the old bo says as we git up to leave the jungle. "West of Topeka is where you'll find Big Sur. They say the beast has got a third eye, and with it he can see into a man's soul. So when he catches you, he'll tear off more'n just a piece 'a your body."

It 'most give me the fantods at first, when he said it, but then I was glad he did, 'cause it give me reason to call him nutty and ignore his prairie wisdom about how you cain't ever run from a tornader.

When the storm came in proper, it rendered the whole sky thick and clayey, and the sun turned pale like a full moon behind the wisps. But we started padfooting it, thinking what an easy time a tornader would have lifting up me and Lee, both of us bone-thin from too much roaming and too little food.

Then my hermit guide, old Airedale that he is, had a brainstorm that would put to shame Archie Meaties *and* Eye-sack Newton. Lee noticed that the wind was blowing West—our direction—and he reckoned there was a hand-cart in the rail yard. He'd reckoned right—it was a mighty sturdy one too—so we found us a gooseberry bush and yegged us a clean white sheet for a makeshift sail, the freshly starched fabric uncreasing with the expansion, its entire width strung to a crucifix of a mast we made from two cracked railroad ties, growing big-bellied in the wind. Then we cranked the hand-cart to get her started and let the hard gusts send us full West, with no stops, waylays, or detours.

It was not my fortune to have children or grandchildren; but if the other destiny had been mine, then this is the moment I'd say, "And so, kids, *that* was the day your granddaddy rode a tornader!"

Chapter XV

When the storm passed and the wind ca'med down, jacking the hand-cart became a tiresome business, and it was ruin on my arms you bet. We chose to give our legs a turn, abandoning the hand-cart to just padfoot for a while, and it was a good thing we done it, 'cause soon after there was a train that high-lined through, and with the quick bends and the roaring of the wind, we mightn't have noticed it until too late.

"Lee," I says, because sometimes staying mum is better than saying shucks, and sometimes it's t' other way around. "I'm tired and hungry as all get-out."

"Ain't that what you always wanted?" Lee says.

Well, Lee was right again. Just when I suspected he warn't a-listening, and just letting on he cared what I was saying so long as I kep' him company on his journey home, he comes out with a memory like that. "Sure, I s'pose. But does a body ever know what it really wants?"

"I reckon it does, sometimes," he says, taking the fabric of my coat between his fingers, to test the quality. Lee noticed my new rags for the first time, now that we warn't a-running from a storm, but this was one of the times he chose to stay mum. He prob'ly reckoned I yegged it from an honest man.

"I expect it seems crazy to you," I says, "pining for oblivion."

"No," he says. "It's just that, you know Joe, there's an easy way to meet that partic'lar dream. But now that we're road-kin I ain't want you to rise to the occasion."

"It's not any old death I'm hunting up," I says. "I don't want to hang from a rope, or jump from a cliff—"

"—or get sucked up by tornaders, or thrashed to death by a shack—" Lee put in.

"—or grease the tracks, or be drownded in the river—" I says.

"—or drink p'ison?" he asks, unsure whether this warn't the sort of death I sought after.

"No, *nor* at t' other end of rifle, in a war," I says.

This one shut us both up, 'cause in '71 warn't a body in the States who hadn't lost some body to the war. Mine was Huckleberry Finn, a boy my age from St. Petersburg who become a pariah when he growed up, for taking up with ab'litionists and turning Yankee. Even today there's some folks in that town who look back and spit and say they always knowed Huck was born wrong like his Pap, Jeb, and he only got what was a-coming to him in the end. As for me, I think different. Huck was like many a dead soldier—too damned good for St. Petersburg or the Earth.

After taking it up, I got to thinking on my boyhood years, which put me in a strange place. I was a boy who always done what his Mama tole him until I met Tom Sawyer. Then I always done what *he* tole me. Once he give up piracy, I stayed on The Oaken Bucket 'til by and by I give it up too, and thought I'd go back home and ask Mama Sereny for her forgiveness—which, as a Christian woman, she was obliged to give; but which, as a natural-born grudge-keeper, she give me reason to fear she would secretly withhold whilst professing it. But she passed away before I could ask.

"Well, Lee, it's like this. When my best friend Tom Sawyer was a young 'un, there was a time every body in town thought he was dead. We'd all ran away from home, the way boys do, and by and by we found an island, where we played pirates a while. By the time we git back, we come upon a funeral all laid out for Tom Sawyer!" I says. "And do you know what he did? He went and attended his own funeral!"

"Tom Sawyer the Privateer?" Lee says, as though he never heard the story, and missed the p'int entirely.

"Yes indeed. Though, come to think on't," I says, "the same thing happened to Huck the summer after it, 'cept folks thought he was dead a long while before we found out he only run South, and ain't any body cared enough for Huck to arrange a funeral."

We walked that whole day—another Sunday, I reckoned, since there warn't many passenger cars, and I felt all holy for going dawn till dusk without thieving so much as a free ride—so that by sundown we'd traveled 'most the way to Salina. Just after dark we hit a train yard, and I suggested to Lee that, in case the street girl and the old bo were right about a mean dog in Salina that cripples folks, we should flop in the local jungle, then take a train North, ruther than try to pass through the city. Instead of agreeing straight off, though, Lee wore a puzzled, unsettled look.

"What's a matter, Lee?" I says.

"Well, it's a bully idea, Joe," he says. "But where's the jungle? I don't see or hear any boes anywhere."

"Is that all?" I says. "It's been a-raining, so the boes likely scrounged up their dimes to stay in a flophouse for the night, and it's Sunday besides. There ain't nothing to worry about 'cept the usual... until we get to Salina."

We come upon a part of the train yard that looks sorely neglected, with grass higher than my knees and a burn barrel so rusted out it had holes in it, with ground so muddy the ties started to sink in places. "Huh," I says. "There ain't no boot prints." But without saying shucks, we both notice the paw prints at the same time.

"What'd the old bo say about a dog?" Lee says.

"Don't worry about 'im," I says. "Etta says Big Sur catches boes all the way over in Salina."

"What's that, then?" Lee says, and he p'int at a water tank with a conspicuous lack of hobo writing on't.

It's plum dark, specially for a train yard, but I can just make out the faded white letters on the water tank that says, "S-A-L-I-N-A."

Chapter XVI

I thought my legs had reached the end of their usefulness, but a big, three-eyed hound with an appetite for hobo meat was enough to cure my joints of ache, and cleanse my heart of any complaint but the present. We spaded up the dirt as we ran, the spongy earth sticking to our boots and flinging out from the sides. I practiced in my head what I'd say to Lee later. "How's I to know that Salina warn't a *real* city, but just a lay-over town with a set of rails that looks like a boneyard?"; "Could *you* tell the exact distance we walked, and all the miles we covered a-sailing on the hand-cart?"; "So *what* if we each lost one limb to a mean, hungry dog—you still got t' other three, ain't ye?"

Since we settled on running, I thought we may as well keep goin' West, so I hollered for Lee to make for the near fence. But when I seen Lee pick up his pace to pass me, I thunk what the tramps always say about running from Johnny Laws: *I don't have to be faster than the bulls. I just cain't be slower than t' other feller.*

Big Sur charged out from under a tin roof and took after us like 't was a foxhunt. Here was a hound unnatural quiet, who cain't be bothered to bark, so all you could hear was the pant of the chase. I reckoned he was saving his jaws for chewing hobo meat. When I turned around to see how close he'd come, I got enough of a glimpse to judge Big Sur was actually a drooling Mastiff, massive in a way that don't require exaggeration. And ruther than boasting a surplus eye, he was subtracted a good one, with half of his face mangled, and, though we warn't to blame for it, a body wouldn't know it the way he threw himself at us.

I was all set to make the fence—the new-fangled kind with the barbs on it—when I get to thinking about that ugly half-a-face of his, and I cain't resist taking another look.

So I turned my head around, and there it was again, like a sunflower with the petals torn off, and most of the seeds missing; irresistible, grotesque, of every hue of gray and brown. Looking at it longer than a moment made me think he was a pitiful cretur, not the supernatural terror he was made out to be. But then I tripped over a linking chain that'd been carelessly thrown down in the very path I was using to make my getaway.

It warn't two seconds before Big Sur was on top of me, and I felt what Huck must have felt when his Pap would hunt him up and chase him round like a goose for the roast. Huck warn't raised by a mother, and I warn't raised with a father, so we always envied each other's lot, but I reckon I wasted my envy on Huck. There hain't an ounce of love in an attack.

Lee, who had clumb up on the fence, was throwing pots and empty bottles and every other thing he could find in his satchel, hollering at the beast to quit his 'sault. But Big Sur don't listen, and don't mind getting showered in the debris, he was so intent on his task.

I've been a pirate since I was old enough to grow a beard, and I've been stuck in messier scrapes, I reckon, but I was brung up a thoughtful, indoor child, and I had to shake off a score of thoughts preventing me from taking action—the foremost of which was, What to make of this half-mangled dog-head. Was it struck by a train, or set afire, or chewed off by an even bigger, meaner dog than 'im?—before I thrust both my hands in the mud and shoved as much of it as I could into his good eye.

I slipped out from under the beast, by and by, but not without a couple scrapes acrost my shoulders from where his paws tried to pin me to the wet earth, and I clumb up behind Lee, where I managed to save myself from the barbs, but had to sacrifice the coat, and left long jagged tears in my good, clean clothes.

By and by a logging train come our way, so we hopped a gondola car and lay flat between the lumber and prayed the Lord they'd never load more logs on top of us. It rolled us all the way to t' other end of Kansas, and kept rolling, and kept rolling until I judged that I couldn't wait any longer for a washroom. There warn't any stops in Kansas so far, and when Lee found he was similarly afflicted, he settled that we would hit the grit ruther than soil the car and risk getting sniffed out by the shacks. The train she never slowed though, and by and by she started balling the jack. She picked up so much speed it left only the one option: crouch off the side of the gondola and empty our dirty leavings wherever they dropped.

Lee unbuckled his fancy trousers and got right down to the deed. But the way I was brung up made me unnatural modest, and I couldn't bring myself to finish that a-way without a leaf or cloth or something to clean with, even on the hobo road. So instead I clumb to t' other side of the car and just pulled out my pecker to piss in the wind.

If I offend the reader by exposing him to the ruck and the filth of the tramp's life, know only that it is, at such times, an even greater offense to live that life. As I drained my overfull bladder with delight and relief, I happen to look left and there was the shack on my side of the hind-car, getting caught in the spray!

"Hit the grit, you crum-bum!" he says, maneuvering himself toward us, but unable to dodge or shelter himself from the deluge. I'd been a-holding it in 'til it hurt, and was nowise ready to stop now. "Hit the grit!"

"Lee!" I called over my shoulder. "Bo chaser on the hind-car!"

Lee came up on my side and spotted the shack a-crawling onto the gondola, not ten feet away. "Well, Joe," he says, "what're you waiting for? Let's blow!"

"I cain't stop!" I says, a-holding my pecker with one hand and the tie of my trousers with t' other.

Noticing the hammer in the shack's hands, Lee looks all about him for a stick or some other tool. "P'int it at the shack!" he says to me, and soon as I catched his meaning, I turned my body East and waggled the spout to give as much as I can to the wind. The onpour made the shack grimace and pause, but it ain't seem to have any effect other than to rankle him. By and by the stream ca'med down to a trickle, and the shack charged forward faster and fiercer than before. Though the spray had done him no harm at first, his haste was such that he slipped on the slick logs and took a spill worthy of a circus acrobat, barely keeping himself from tumbling off of the car.

Our good fortune was that she slowed up just as Lee and I was ready to ditch. The conductor hadn't gotten any signals from the brakeman—'cause he was occupied with bo-chasing, and presently trying to pull himself up from a stack of wet logs—so they stopped feeding her coals 'til they heard boo from their man on the train. Ditching a train car at a slow pace is nothing like hitting the grit when the firemen are balling the jack, and we eased ourselves down to the roadbed like fish into water.

Though we left him a-soaking in the foam, I reckon that shack was up there now celebrating another victory over his nemesis, the law-breaking vagabond.

Once you ditch, and the train steams on yonder, it leaves a body feeling naked, or melancholy, or both—all a body knows is that he's missing something important, like his rags, or his mama. Then as you pad the hoof around, things seem to stay stock-still even as you move. Whatever you see, it don't change fast enough, and whatever you hear, it ain't near loud enough.

I kep' talking to Lee to relieve that feeling, chewing his ear with stories of how I'd nearly gained an Amish wife in the Lone Jack stables; and how I'd nearly abandoned the hobo road *and* my hermitage in a cave to shack up with a saloon-keeper and his family. Though I warn't about to confess it, either fate seemed welcome to me now and then, especially now, with my joints sore and my head dizzy.

"Everywhere we go there's bad roads," I says. "Ain't there a place somers where boes is welcomed, like at the temple of Zoos?"

"It's a myth, Joe," says Lee, with more acid than usual, which I reckoned was due to his being dis'llusioned on that score. "And a rotten lie of a myth too."

Lee's sinking mood 'most drowned mine 'long with it. "Maybe they's just stretchers?" I says. "I judge nobody got turned to trees, but that don't mean some poor folks never opened their home to strangers and built a temple somers to honor the god who came a-throwing his feet at their door."

"Ain't you just the gulliblest sumbitch the devil ever knew?" Lee says. I cain't say I recognized his bitter tone. P'raps he got so used to being called the Airedale he reckoned that getting ditched by the shacks but once would ruin him. "You believe everything you hear, ain't you? You think that Dutch gal Ruth keeps a candle lit for you, ain't you? And you think Guy van der Loost was fixing to invite you to live on his charity for the rest of your natural life, ain't you? I reckon you think gods is still walking the earth."

"Warn't it you, Lee, who believed gods was walking the earth?" I says.

"Least I can learn," he says, "but your head's too thick."

There warn't a lot of blowing in those days about feelings and such, but a body cain't mistake such a silence for an absence. My nerves burned at the thought of Mama Sereny in the ground so that all I could stand was to dream about rotting in a cave and being left alone with my grief. I could see right as day that it was Lee expecting to be offered some kind of welcome from Van der Loost and his boys, but even a man known for his boundless charity wouldn't welcome this Airedale into his saloon if he was a chinaman.

As for Ruth, I reckoned that I warn't such a fool to think she kept a candle lit for me. Course, Ruth never said anything good about me, but in the moment we had together, she did talk rot about other men. Folks is always speaking cross-wise, I reckoned. Fr'instance, when a body says "I'm not one for tea," that usually means they run to coffee, and when a body says, "I don't care much for cats," they usually run to dogs. Here was Ruth a-going on about how she never want to marry Abram Hershberger, so I reckoned p'raps she meant that she ran to my sort.

"I may be gullibler than most," I says. "I cain't say for certain. But it don't make me thick-headed. I'd know as much as you do.... If you'd learn me."

"All right, Joe," he says. "I'll learn you this much: you should 'a stayed home and made a life in the osage plains o' Missouri."

"That's swell," I says. "We've already left Missouri behind, and more'n halfway through the dreary plains of Kansas." As I turn around and p'int in the direction we come from, I spied a body following us along t' other side of the rails, from the looks of him, another bo who'd been ditched by that horstile bo chaser.

When he gets close enough to me and Lee opposite us on the road bed, we see it's the same deafie, covered head to foot in rags, who rode with us into Kansas City a week back. "Hey there," I call out, "Deafie!" before I realize how I just proved to Lee how thick-headed I am.

Stepping up on the tracks without even looking East and West for the next line, the deafie takes down the gray hood and says, "Hey, Joe Harper." Then I seen it ain't a deafie at-all, and it ain't a *he* neither. It was Ruth who stepped down from the road bed and into the company of the smilingest couple of boes that ever wore a rope for a belt. I stood speechless as she made her leisurely way, still covered neck to ankle with layers of robes that served to keep her warm and hide her natural form, but above the chin was a halo of unkept and unwashed hair like the mess of hay she once sat in. To Lee, she seemed to step out of a myth where folks goes around in disguise as tramps and proved without a doubt that unbelievable strange things go on in the world.

Chapter XVII

Lee walked a pace ahead of us, in that determined way he always strode. Instead of a bindle, or a poke, he carried a satchel at his shoulder like he was ready to board a liner. I have to hand it to the chinaman—it warn't easy to bear a load all those miles, and it makes me weary even to think on't.

"You're a runaway now!" I says to Ruth. "Ain't it likely to cause your people grief?"

She had her hood pulled back, and I seen her cheeks flush from the cold. "I vould alvays run avay, ever since I vas a little one. Only dis is de fardest I've gotten," she says. "Tanks to you."

I knowed I didn't do shucks, but I warn't shy of taking the credit. "Whenever I run away as a boy, when I come back my Mama would whip my behind until it don't work no more."

Ruth shrugged her padded-up shoulders. "My Ma and Pa never vipped me ever."

"Not *ever?*" I says. If it was true, she'd be the first soul—man, woman, or child—I ever met who never felt the bad end of her parents' hand. And if it was true, I wonder why she should be so hell-bent on running off in the first place.

"My people are pacivists," she says. "Ve believe dat God vorbids violence of any kind." But the way she says "God" sounds the way normal folks says "good."

"Well, how clever you are," I says, "stowing away on our boxcar, bluffing you was deaf and dumb so nobody'd hassle you."

"It makes everything easy ven you don't say a vord, and volks just pity you like a stray. Dat vay dey'll throw you a bone." I confess it was hard to imagine Ruth cadging at all, proud as she was.

"You're sure to be safe 'long as you ride with me and

Lee, I reckon. But how'd you beat the trains this far?" I says, my own pride injured a bit, I won't lie, by the way Ruth was able to get as far as me and Lee, and just when I was starting to fancy myself a blowed-in-the-glass profesh.

"Vell, I vollowed you on de virst one, on de vay car. Den I noticed dat de brakemen alvays checks up top by de lookout, and checks in de cars at every station, but only looks underneath once or twice during his shift. I vigure it was safest to ride de rods."

I couldn't help slapping my knee while I laughed. "Lee, look at the hoboette who beat the shacks! She's the true Airedale, ain't she?"

Lee had grown considerable less comfortable about Ruth being on the trail with us since she first showed up, and was growing less comfortable by the mile. "A woman don't fare well on the wander path," he says. "No matter what, if you live on the street, they'll call you a street girl, and they'll treat you same as a street girl."

"Then I'll let on I'm a man, as I have done, and a deaf one," she says.

"You aren't the first to pull that graft," Lee says. "Being a deafie might make you an object of charity for the marks, but it'll make *you* an easy mark for any jack-roller who was born without an organ for pity."

"Aren't you de great protector?" says Ruth, a bit warmly for such a close cut. "I don't expect I'll ever need de advice of a track-laying chinaman."

"Now," I says, cutting in, "Lee's got a mean streak, but he's got just as many streaks of gray-haired wisdom. Don't you, Lee?"

Lee grimaced like he just bit into a sour apple. "That's right, Joe. I'm wise as all get-out."

"Vise like a fox," says Ruth.

I start to hear Mama Sereny chattering away, but I dasn't answer her with Ruth a-walking right beside me. In truth,

Mama said the meanest and hurtfulest things about Ruth that I cain't even answer her 'less I reveal them.

By and by we come upon an old ghost town that used to be set up for traveling miners and tracklayers back when Kansas had use for 'em. The sun was downing and the buildings looked all the more ghostly for the long shadders they cast on the prairie. There warn't but four buildings, and two of 'em half-sunk into the earth already. None of 'em was fit for living in, but I judged they'd do all right for a night's shelter.

I mosey up to the one that seemed to keep its shape better than t' others.

"Don't go in there," Lee says.

"Why?" I says. "What's to hender me?"

"Nothing," says Lee, "except the haints."

I looked wide-eyed at my road-kin Lee and just laughed. "You'd sooner convince me it's a beehive, Lee. Least that'd give me the fantods. I been at sea more'n ten years. I know all the fish stories."

"I ain't telling you a fish story. There's haints in there sure as you breathe. Look: you can tell by the dust on the threshold," he says, p'inting to the traces of fine white powder scattered on the boards at our feet. "That's where the last tresspassers, soon as they tried to cross the perimeter, was evaporated on the spot! And take a sniff of the air here. If that ain't the smell of death, I'm a flounder. I tell you, Joe, this house belongs to the haints."

I stand with my palm on the door, but never push. Ruth stands by wearing a look half amused, half concerned. "Wait a minute, Lee," I says. "If living, breathing folks like us is evaporated on the spot soon as we cross the perimeter, and there ain't no corpse that's left behind, how come it smells so like death?"

Somehow this conundrum don't settle anything as far as

Lee was concerned. "It don't matter if they has bodies or no bodies. That's the smell of rotten soul."

"You ought to try the door," I says. "Just to prove it to yourself, that there's nothing to be a-feared."

"You prove it. You're the scientist," he says.

"Exactly," I says. "So there ain't no reason for me to prove what I already know to be true."

"Then do 't just to show me you're the braver," he says.

By and by Ruth shoved me and Lee out of the way and pushed that door wide open. After all my blabbing about science and superstition, I'd no choice but to go on in after her. But before I done it, I repeated in my head the words I seen on the water tank when first entering Kansas City: "Don't Expect Much, Joe. Don't Expect Much."

It *is* rank-smelling inside after all, but that warn't any proof it was full of haints, I reckoned. Ruth stepped acrost the threshold like she was walking into her vestibule.

Once our eyes adjust to the half-dark room—its windows was all boarded up, but for torn pieces and gaps between boards, which let in rays of sun one at a time, and a great big hole in the ceiling that casts a misty white glow—we learned it was a flophouse for tramps like us! There they was, laying about in a one-room house, sleeping on the boards side by side, some of 'em propped up 'gainst the wall and others leaning on the furniture never-minding the cobwebs. I judged they was night-shift, 'cause here it was past noon and those boes were so droopy they ain't let the sunlight bother them at-all.

"Hey, boes," I says, and set down at the table, which warn't occupied. Lee takes a chair, though still hesitating.

"You sure they ain't dead and rotting?" Lee says.

Ruth takes a closer look, and when she does, one of the boes take a-hold of her ankle. "I ain't touched the skin of a lady in seven-year," this one says. Lee and I stir up from our chairs, a- feared that we'd have to defend her honor. But

Ruth she bring her fist down hammer-like on the bo's head, knocking him back into the same pose he started from.

"Hot dang!" I says. "You seen that, Lee?"

Lee nods approvingly. I believe Ruth finally won his respect.

A couple other boes had woken up at this p'int, and one long-bearded feller shaked his head and says, "that lady done took care of Hardpan Lou."

"Took care of 'im?" I says. "She wrecked the bastard. Our girl Ruth put the 'fist' into passifist!"

That bo took a disinterested glance over at the concerned party and says, "I s'pose she did."

"Any one of you want to try us?" I says, standing next to Dutch. But they was still all laid out on the floor, even the ones who'd waked.

"That Hardpan Lou had it a-coming a long time," the one bo says. He starts to cry all a- sudden. "He never knowed how to treat a lady. I had a wife once, and she was an angel, like my mum was an angel."

"Them's all angels," another bo says who sit up for the first time. "Every one."

I ain't mentioned the fact that they just seen a lady leave her knuckle-marks on the head of one of their own. Or the fact that I just come from boarding at an establishment for ladies of the disreputable sort. Or mention all the sisters I growed up under, any one of whom was 'most as wicked as a man.

"Not like my mum," says the first bo. "There ain't a woman ever born like her. It was her nature to despise evil and give charity to the poor and the afflicted."

After he take a pause, t' other bo says, "Where'd you say she lived again?"

Chapter XVIII

The bo that just stood up in respect for our Ruth, who was called Boonie Don, kept running his p'inter finger acrost his lips like a harmonicker. It was a curious fidget, and I've seen some fidgets. One feller I knew on *The Ragamuffin*, where I was first-mate, had a way of stretching and scratching everywhere. He'd stretch out his arm and scratch it, then stretch out and scratch t' other, then go for his neck. Between the two fidgets, I reckon Boonie Don's was the stranger.

By and by I notice that a couple 'a those boes had that same fidget! If this warn't a mystery, I don't know what is. The next one I puzzled over was how the sleeping hoboes twitched, kicking with their legs like they was a-riding a horse, and making throat-clearing noises that sound a mite like the warbling of a tree frog. It warn't long before I spot other clues: the smell, which I reckoned now was the result of stomachs a-heaving, scarcely bothered them; the way they lay about, dead-like, was idler than the lowliest bum in a jungle; the wide hole in the ceiling, from which a drizzling rain trickled in, warn't bothering 'em with its endless drip; the white powder, not just on the floorboards, but on their clothes, and... on their fingers!

"Lee," I says, "don't be alarmed now, but I think these ain't haints at-all, but they may as well be: they's opium eaters!"

"You think I ain't know an opium eater when I seen one?" Lee says. "I judged they was opium fiends before I set a foot inside." I ain't believed Lee when he says it, but I 'lowed him to have his way.

Upon hearing our palaver, Boonie Don says, "You must 'a confused us for gentlemen," he says. "Opium will cost you more'n gold ever since Lincoln's war."

"So, what then?" I says.

"Big-Belly Rob got a-hold of enough Po-bro to choke an elephant," Boonie Don says. "And it feels mighty good, though it's a week we've been without food."

"What's Po-bro, bo?" I says.

"Po-tassim Bro-meed," says Boonie Don. "The salt of heaven."

I looked around at all those smelly boes getting rained on and thunk, it ain't the way I pictured heaven at-all. 'T was a sight more like t' other place.

"Potassium Bromide?" I says. "Ain't that the fixture photographers use to keep a picture sharp?"

"The same," says Boonie Don. Lee raised an eyebrow at me like I warn't expected to know shucks. But I just proved myself equal to the monicker of scientist, and I cain't help but give him a knowing wink.

"Here," Boonie says, holding his chalky fingers out in front of me. "Give it a lick."

I says no thanks, as pleasantly as I knowed how.

Lee and Ruth says no thanks too, and the boes perked up all a sudden, like they's noticing us for the first time. One bo, who a body could see plain as cabbage was the one they called Big-Belly Rob, lumbered over and took a seat at the table with us. "There a problem with it?"

"It's just that I ain't had a proper meal today, and the kind of salt I go fer is the kind I can sprinkle on a ham hock," I says.

Big-Belly Rob was the big-belliest hobo I ever seen. His arms and legs was thin, but his belly stuck out in front of him like a baby, giving an outline that was spidery, and it spooked me you bet. By and by I start in with the questions, 'cause that's what a nervous Joe Harper does. I ask him why nobody ever calls him Big-Belly Bob, just for the ring of it, and he squint at me over his mustache. "You think Big-Belly Rob is a kinder joke?"

"No, sir," I says. "I'm serious."

"If that's the way of it," Big-Belly Rob says, "how come I can hear your brain a-laughing?"

I counted this question among the hardest I'd ever been called upon to answer in my 35 years. I reckon a body can be called to account for his own mind, but how's a body s'posed to account for another feller's—one who says that he hears your brain a-laughing?

"Sometimes," I says, "I think I hear a body laughing off somers, and it turn out to be the wind a-rustling a curtain."

"Is that right?" he says. "Well, there ain't any curtains in *this* flophouse."

"Oh," I says. "Now that you mention it, wouldn't curtains be swell? Maybe glass on the windows besides?"

"Bo," he says, jacking his thumb behind him while he speak slow and ca'm. "I will lay you down like a lame colt, as I done to Dead Ernest."

I look down at the place where he p'ints his thumb, and there's a feller laying stiff as a pole with his eyes open.

"Why ain't you a-laughing now?" he says.

I swallow hard, trying to conceal the fear in my eyes the way a body does with a wild animal. "Now I knows you ain't making jokes," I says.

Big-Belly Rob shakes his head. "That one *was* a joke, and a rip-roaring one. What's that feller's name? It used to be *Dakota* Ernest. Now it's *Dead* Ernest. You mean to tell me it ain't funny?"

I smile wide and sudden, though I bet my eyes was as wide and skeered. "Sure it is," I says. I turn to Lee, but he looked about as unsettled as I feel. Ruth was wise and found a spot to linger near the door.

Big-Belly Rob drops a tin of that Po-Bro on the table and says nothing. I could 'a grown a second beard in the time we sat there in painful long silence, staring at his rusty tin crusted over and flecked with white powder.

Now and then I'd try to meet his eyes, thinking to search

them for an intention, but his unchanging stare deflected me. It warn't long before I reckoned I knowed his intention, but I hid it from myself as long as I could manage, since I never wanted to taste of the stuff that turned these boes into such senseless sleepers.

By and by I scooped up a pinch and brung it to my lips.

"You'll want to start with a mite less," Big-Belly says. "Just use the pad of your finger and it'll be candy."

I dropped most of it back in the tin. Then flicked the tip of my tongue on my finger like a rept'le.

"Yeah, save some for the rest of us," says one crippled bo who just stirred up and cain't stop kicking the air with his one good leg.

Big-Belly nodded toward my road kin, so I passed the tin to Lee, who gets a tad on his finger same as me, then passed it along to Ruth.

When Ruth took her fingerful, Big-Belly let out a raucous laugh, which threw me back a yard.

"That's funny," I says. "Now *I* hear a brain laughing."

When he's done amusing himself, Big-Belly says, "You boes are okay, I reckon."

When I set back down at the table I worried that I warn't ever goin' to leave that house again. It seemed the forlornest place for a body to spend the rest of his days, and surrounded by such a close crowd. As far as the house being full of haints, I reckon Lee was partly wrong and partly right.

Chapter XIX

Staring up into the hole in the ceiling, I started to feel like I was at the bottom of a deep abyss. It warn't a bad feeling at-all. I forgot I was surrounded by the smelliest bunch of boes who ever skipped a meal. I forgot how Big-Belly had wrassled me into sampling his Po-Bro. I forgot that I ain't have a bedroll, though the sky turned black and cold, and was growing blacker and colder, and begun to let down rain that froze on the ground where it landed, which our bodies warmed into slush. All of us was buried in the admixture, and I reckoned it was okay.

Why, this warn't much different from a cave, I reckoned. In fact, 't was a sight better than a cave, 'cause to fetch water all you need to do was open your mouth and drink the downpour.

Lee was off in another part of the room, but I call out to him. "You thirsty, Lee? There's enough water here to slake the devil," I says.

"I see it," Lee says. "Go on and enjoy."

I was in a strange place, and Lee seemed to be talking straight into my head, the way Mama Sereny does, and that gave me to wonder why she warn't there. Was she still dead? I ain't remember any kinder funeral, so it ain't ever seemed to be real.

"So what's in your satchel, Lee?" I says. "You been hauling it all this way, and I never asked you what-for."

"I cain't say," he says. "What's in your poke?"

"I cain't say," I says.

I looked over at the bo next to me, one with hair as orange as candlefire and an overbite that pulled back below his lip like his chin had been carved away, who kep' a stained-up bindle next to him in plain sight, where any body might yegg it. "What's in the bag, bo?" I says.

"Don't ask him," says Boonie Don.

"Careful now," says Big-Belly Rob, who was laying prone once again amongst the boes.

The orange-headed feller sat up and looked down at the intoxicated bo at his side, which was me. "I'll tell you," he says, good and slow. "But what's your monicker?"

"Mutton-chop," I says.

The bo frowned back at me. "I wish I hain't ever asked," he says. "Now I's hungrier than I was before."

"You can call me Missouri Joe," I says.

"All right, Mutton-chop," that bo says. "Everywhere I go they call me Head-in-a-Bag. But it ain't always been that a-way. I started out a bindle-stiff like every other stiff you ever laid eyes on. Jack Wanderlust never possessed me much. I seen The Life as my temporary lot, and planned to make it pay until I could own a piece of land and start a proper life on a farm. I even worked the coals as a fireman on line twenty up in Minnesoter. I wore them dashboards and everything. But just after the war the controller come down hard on all the boes that was coming out of Chicago in those days, and when he learned I warn't ditching 'em, he ditched me instead.

"So with a year's wages tucked in my bindle along with a pan and soap and you-know-what-all, I padfoot it south, thinking I'd find somers fertile to get an early start on planting. One day I come by a farm house where a good German couple set me up with a heavy meal of taters and sausage, some Christian words, and enough bread and jam to last me a fortnight. I give them as many blessings as I had, and go on my way. I never meant to be a burden to nobody.

"By and by I reckoned I was due for another night spent in a proper bed, so when I find myself in Indianap'lis, I find a jungle and ask where's the best flophouse for a working bo, and a couple of hungry-looking boes send me to a place they say is comfortable and cheap. But when I come upon the hotel, I seen they was charging twice what I'd expect to pay in

Minnesoter, and it warn't a proper bed at-all but a hammock in a room with five other hammocks, a bo to each. Well, all right. Now in those days, bo, jack-rolling warn't frowned upon the way it is today, and for lots of boes it was their main line. Around midnight I hear the door creak open just before I reach sleep, so I stir up just enough to see what was a-goin' on. These same boes from the jungle who'd sent me to the hotel was sneaking into the room, making to rob me blind!"

Though I was delirious and barely-there, I brought my hand down to my poke and held it by the strings. "So what'd you do?" I says, with a gulp.

"What could a body do?" he says. "I warn't a palooka. All I got is my bindle full of things and my horse sense. So I hold on tight as I can to the hoe—this was back when we was real hoe-boys, all of us just out-of-work farmers looking for a way to get back to our place on the earth—but they meant to untie the knot and release the goods. It's dark, and I cain't see how many they was. So all I could do was lay there and pretend to be the kind of sleeper who holds on tight to his bindle.

"They's working the knot, which was doubled, when all a sudden they quit. All was silent for a long spell, until one of 'em says, 'Oh my God. Oh my Lord.' I peer over, where in the half-moon light from the window I can see that bearded bo stepping back, horrified, until he trip over the feller in the hammock behind him. That startles him up, and that startles the rest of the boes, until one of 'em lights a lantern and they all seen my bindle, puddled red at the bottom and hairs a-sticking out from the top where they'd manage to loosen the knot, and as the yeggs run out they's a-crying out, 'There's a head in the bag! He's the murdering kind! Run for your lives!'

"Now all t' other boes take the measure of the scene before them, and judge it best to light out. It was just the can of jam that broke because it warn't packed well, and the

97

horse-hair brush I yegged from the Lutherans. But the word spread all around the jungle, and *every* jungle, since Wander Path stories grow faster'n ivy. So ever since, when boes seen my pointy red hair, and a red stain on my bindle, they knows right away it's Head-in-a-Bag, and they'll keep their distance."

"So you never keep a head in the bag at-all?" I says.

"Well," says Head-in-a-Bag, "Now-a-days I have a reputation I got to uphold." He shrugged, and I reckoned I wouldn't press the matter.

By now everything felt warm, tingly, and strange. There's a pleasant throb to my face, to the room, to the earth.

"So what happened to all the money you made, since it warn't ever stolen?" I says.

Head-in-a-Bag sniffs, and his eyes water some, and I cain't tell if its mournful tears, or another twitch. His gaze drifts to the mass of bodies all round us. "I've known Big-Belly a long time," he says. "A long time."

I fade out and fade in and fade out.

—

Rain on the ocean is a vain thing, an act of self-love on the part of the Almighty. And the Old-Testament God who seems to write my destiny will boast of His own power at every hazard.

On the day Tom Sawyer left me to die, taking *The Ragamuffin* and her rowdy crew with him north to the Mediterranean, discarding me like a rind on an uninhabited island off the Ivory coast, the heavy sky drizzled a fresh coat of superfluous rain on the indifferent Atlantic. If I'd suspected that that lonesome hump of an island might become my crypt, I'd have gathered the large-leafed fronds of the palm and laid them out on the sand like so many buckets to collect the pure water. The last evaporating droplets of the evening shine even brighter—blindingly so, each one containing a small sun—in my memory.

My mind spirals and wheels endlessly around that moment when Tom shoved off the island on the connector boat, and I realized he warn't coming back. His silent smile said all that needed saying. I had failed to live up to the name Joe Harper, Terror of the High Seas, and this was my education in manhood. He was too far away already—almost all the way to the suddenly massive silhouette of The Ragamuffin—when I started shouting after him, "Least leave me a raft! Least leave me an oar!" I waved my arms, and leapt in the air as high as I could go, and danced the jig, but Tom never so much as stood, and if he ever said shucks, 't was overtaken by the swell of the tide which, even as it retreated, made the sucking sound of a breath.

My sojourn on the island was positively the first time I had met my own solitude, and though 't would last a mere fourteen days, that one fortnight drove me to petition God for a rescue, how I would return home to take care of Mama Sereny in her dotage, and make a good life for the woman who made me, and do what I could to please the Lord she loved. He kept His silence, but communicated instead through the *chip-chip-chip* of angry insects, and the mockery of strange birds; I asked for Mercy but was answered with demonstrations of Fear; The Lord warn't done showing me His power.

For the first three days I was a society unto myself. I kept Joe Harper company through carrying on conversations with him, but I had already lost much of my power for civilized speech during my sea-faring decade, and my talk soon turned to palaver, and then my palaver fell into babble. On the seventh day is when I first heard Mama's voice inside me, and I would calculate that this date corresponded with her natural death.

In the end it was Mala the corsair who saved me from exile. Mala, the soil-dark North African goddess, whom

I already loved unrequitedly, now become my savior. Tom warn't with her. I understood then that all his balloon juice about the nobility and honor of a pirate was a lie from the get, and I'd wasted more'n ten years pursuing another man's whimsy. I was so grateful to the physical embodiment of grace in the woman who was my rescuer, and so indifferent to the past and the future, that all I brought with me on the boat were the two di'monds I kept on my person by accident. If you should ever undertake a treasure hunt, you'd do well to start your expedition on the driest, beatenest islands off the Ivory coast.

The only memory I have that is equal to the memory of Tom's abandonment was of the first time I awoke on Mala's ship, The Oaken Bucket, and seen the near-full moon on a cloud-clear night and heard Mala's voice crooning a most sublime song of her native country—though her coarsely beautiful features was lost to the backlighting—and felt the drip of water on my lips from a wrung rag. I wished I could stay helpless forever, until my senses returned with the sun, and I resolved to make good on my promise to the Lord to be a good son.

When my words come back, I asked Mala if by undertaking my rescue she sought secondary employment as an angel of the Lord, and as she brung out a fresh rag for my head she says, "There ain't no Lord but death, and He needs no assistants."

This one stumped me, since I never knew a body to deny the Lord, not even the rottenest pirate on the ocean. "If I believed that, I'd have given up long before now," I says. Of all the parts of me that survived the scarcity of island life, the part I least expected to meet again was pride. I endeavored to sit upright, but I warn't ready yet, and the ache turned to a burning feeling, and sent me back down on the seal-fur.

"If I believed that there was a master overseer in the sky," says Mala. "I might have accepted the yoke of slavery 'stead of making my own way in the world."

Mama Sereny says, "I wish you'd make your own way in the world, too, Joe Harper."

"What way is that?" I says.

"To take back from the empire that robbed the soul of Africa," says Mala. "It isn't much, but it is my life's purpose."

I peered out of the slats of the cabin. It was another pale and cloudy sunset. I come to notice that there was a loyal crew of North African and Mediterranean pirates, so silent in reverence to their corsair captain they might have had their tongues cut out.

When we made shore in Morocco, I asked Mala, Would you come with me to St. Petersburg and become my wife, and Mala says, No, Joe, for never will a man or nation claim me until I die. That warn't the last time I proposed to Mala, but it was the last time she answered. For here was a woman whose worth was plain, and she let her silences sing.

—

It warn't yet daylight now, and the first thing I noticed was that the moon was shining straight down through the hole, and all around it snowflakes look like stars being shed off of it like crumbs from a pie. Instead of freezing rain, it was soft touches everywhere. When my nerves start to return to me, I feel only half there. "Whats'it," I says.

Lee and Ruth bid me quiet as they lift me up by the arms and support me on their shoulders, dragging my limp body out-of-doors. "What's the matter with me?" I says. "I cain't feel the left side."

"Shh," says Lee. "You're frostbit, that's all. I reckon your feeling will come back to you once we get somers warm.... But when it does, you may not want it to." That's just the way it was on the road. All you have to look forward to, some days, is a time when you ain't so numb that you cain't feel the pain.

Chapter XX

When I came back to my senses, Lee and Ruth was hovering over me flapping like hummingbirds. I waved my hand to show I'm okay, and then I noticed that I warn't okay. My whole lower back, all the way down to my hind parts, felt like it was being pinched angrily and constantly, everywhere. When I extended my left arm, it felt loose and empty, like the limb of a manikin. And when I tried to stand, 't was as though a fish had grown legs and found them flimsier than a tail.

"What's happening, Lee?" I says.

"You've been out of your head for days, Joe," he says. "We've been flopping here at a goods shed since we cain't seem to get you far on our own."

When I lifted my head, I saw one endless brown Kansas field upon which was cast the light of a late Autumn sun, though my eyes were sheltered by what looked less like a goods shed and more like an outhouse. Just the act of looking strained the nerve of my eye, and brung back the sting that made waves from my neck to my arms and lower back. That sort of wracking pain, I reckon it ain't ever gonna be gone, but once it's kinder familiar, I started to notice something else. I says, "I'm hungry, Lee."

"Ain't none of us eaten for three days," Lee says. "I walked some miles North of the track, looking for a farmhouse, but... it's just a whole lot of Kansas out that a-way."

I looked around at the flat colorlessness with the chill and the sun, and I thunk about the desert island where Tom once'd left me, and I felt a sudden dampness on my cheek.

"But that ain't the worst of it," Lee says. "Ruth and I decided to roust you because I was a-spotted by a brakeman, and he swore to high heaven he would be back with the bulls to throw us in the stir for being rotten, no-good tramps."

That brung me to my feet for sure, though it warn't long before the weakness of my body overcome the strength of my will, and I collapsed again on the hard floor. In Ruth and Lee's faces I seen the same defeat that I felt down in my gut. My insides, the only warm thing I'd got left, was crying out, "Give it up, bo! Give it up!"

"Go on, Lee," I says, "and take Ruth with you." Fresh from the memory of my island exile, I either wanted to redeem my wickedness as a pirate, or to repeat history by suffering their abandonment. I was in such a state of mind, I cain't honestly remember which.

"That's an all right plan," says Lee. "But where'd a body go?"

The autumn crickets answered, and a half-hearted wind.

When the brakeman came, he brung a bull with him as promised, but neither man showed any boast when they pinched us, the way city bulls would do. Out there in the county, folks recognize a pitiable sight when they see it.

"It's all right, bo," Lee says to me. "At least they got food in the stir."

"You'll take care of Ruth here?" I says to the men. "She's not a low-down tramp like us. She's a proper lady who's lost her way. I don't want her to regret ever setting foot in Kansas." But they never gave us an answer.

"It's where you've been headed a long time," says Mama Sereny. "But it's up to you whether you face it as a man."

"Why is it always a woman teaching me to be a man?" I says, "And why is it a heathen teaching me to be a Christian?" But Mama Sereny had gone quiet. Her voice had been softening into a murmur for weeks, until it was nearly gone.

After the bull ties us on to the wagon, he throws a cloth over us, and grateful for the bit of warmth, I was off again to the shadder-world.

When Lee rousted me, I found myself in a corner cell shared with the local drunkard—and two chipped walls that was covered in unfinished pleas, treatises, and the most acrobatic feats of profanity I'd encountered since I lived at sea. The ground was lumpy, and it poked into my already irritated back. By and by a bull comes down the hall with Ruth behind him and opens up our cell. My lungs swell with relief, but the bull says, "You stay put," to me, and takes Lee out. Lee looked resigned to his fate.

"Psst," I says to Ruth. "What's Johnny Law up to?"

"I talked to de men, and dey agreed dat if a Chinaman vere too stay in a regular prison, dere vould be violence," she says.

"So they're just releasing him?" I says.

"No," she shook her head. "He'll be put in de lady's prison."

That struck me strange, but I ain't question it, since it was all the better for Lee, who wouldn't have to do the hard labor of a chain gang.

"What's goin' to happen to me?" I says.

"Lee is coming up vith a plan, and ve vill rescue you," she says, putting her hand through the bar so I could hold it, which I done. It brung back the day we met and she helped me gather up my poke, and without meaning to, we held hands.

"How come you and Lee warn't affected by the Po-Bro? That stuff nearly knocked me off the earth," I says.

"Lee guessed de fat man's intention, and he sneaked a bit of regular salt onto his vinger, and passed it to me to do de same," she says. "But it was too much attention on you, Joe, vor him to sneak it into your hands."

"That's all right. I may be a-hurting in my joints and limbs, but I'm more worried about you. I don't ever want any harm to befall you..." I says, and worrying that I'd over-stepped the natural bounds of affection, I added, "being a lady."

"Oh, Joe. How are ve going to get out of this mess? Vat is going to happen to us?"

Just then, as if in answer to her question, a man with a rebel uniform and a proper pistol walked in the door. His chin was broad, still slick from the barber's razor, and his hair was cropped angular, giving the overall impression of a box. It fit perfectly atop his boxy frame. He introduced himself to the room as Quentin Blutes, as though he were addressing a crowd ruther than a handful of hoboes and some bulls he already knew. His voice was bassy and sucked inward when he spoke, as though he could swallow all the air in a room.

But just when he was finding his rhythm in the speech, he broke it off and set his eyes on me through the bars. "You ain't belong here," he says.

I p'int to myself. "Me, sir?" I says.

"That's right. You ain't from here, and you stick out like a scarecrow. You must be an eastern boy."

"Well, I'm from Missouri," I says, "if that's what you call eastern. My name is Joe Harper."

He hardly paused. "If you was heading West, Joe Harper, I s'pose you saved us some trouble, since that's where we'll be a-sending you. But I'm goin' to wire ahead so they'll be expecting a stranger in their midst."

I ain't asked him what he means by a stranger, and he ain't say. I never used the wire myself, but as a boy I heard Mama Sereny read the news when the first-ever telegraph went out, which went down in the history books as these four words: "What hath God wrought?"

"What's goin' to become of Ruth?" I says, as she and Lee is walked out of the station flanked by two serious men.

Quentin smiles for the first time I seen him. "That pussycat? Oh, you'll never lay your eyes on *her* again."

It was Quentin Blutes who led me West in irons, and it was Quentin Blutes who kep' me in irons when he throwed me in the stir. He even overseen the chain gang where I was made to work, among which the men called him Cubie, after his unnaturally square head. It was all negroes, plus me. I'd never seen so many negroes, and I hadn't even known there was so many in Kansas. We was working just along the rocky border of Colorado, where Kansas had its share of gypsum quarries and quartz mines, and there was rumored to be silver. Compared to the flat and endless nothing of Kansas that I'd coasted over from atop a train car, these modest rocks made for such variety of shape and color that I judged their beauty superlative—an opinion I overturned as soon as I was made to split them.

"What landed you in this mess?" I asked a bearded mullatter next to me named Farley, who worked a pick like it done him wrong.

"It warn't what I done, but what I was: a runaway slave," he says, surprisingly soft-spoken for such a strenuous worker.

"Farley, you are having a bit of fun with this ignorant stranger, ain't you?" I says. "I may be foreign to these parts, but I knows that the slaves has been 'mancipated."

"Is that what you know?" he says. "What d'you call it when a man is told that he owes his old master a half-dollar for boarding ten days between the time he's 'emancipated' and the time he learns of the emancipation? Then, since he ain't ever had a cent of his own before, has to go to work for his master to pay off his debt? But meanwhile he has to keep boarding at the old master's house and eating the old master's food until he's in such debt that the only way to keep out of prison for what he owes is to sign a contract with his old master to work for him four years? And when four years is gone, he's told that in all that time he's run up even more debt? So he runs away and gets snatched before he can get as far as Colorado, and put in chains and made to work for free?"

This one give me such a shock I cain't answer right off. "I s'pose I'd call him a slave," I says, "like you said."

"That's *exactly* what you call him," Farley says.

Now I look out on the work team, full of black bodies and black faces that become less strange to me by the hour. "Is they *all* runaway slaves?"

"Every black man in prison in Americy is a runaway slave," he says, and no matter how I twist it, I cain't argue.

That night, on the upper bunk in a former barracks—which never saw any use, but just grew old and dusty until it was employed for a prison—I nursed my sore feet and back, hurt at the bone, and hurt at the skin, like a bee-stung palm, and listened to the soulful song of a suffering brother a-laying down in his bunk. I released to sleep, thinking on Huck, and what he must a' seen and done in his years to turn Yankee.

Cubie rousted us before sun-up by banging on the metal frames of the beds and hollering, like it was a proper barracks. Following t' other inmates, I judged I was expected to stand at attention, and I done it with as much pep as any aching soldier. I reckoned Cubie had been a private in the confederate army as a younger feller, aspiring one day to be a general, and dreaming the next of retiring to a plantation and becoming rich enough to own a score of slaves, and his position as prison-master was a way of fulfilling the two dreams at the same stroke.

"It's time we got started with the real work, boys," he says.

"What d'you mean, the real work?" I says, afeard that my frostbite had left me too impaired to survive whatever came next.

Cubie answered me, but not before he swatted me with the butt-end of his stick, leaving a new purple welt on my temple, one to add to the colorful collection of marks adding up all over my body. "All you nobodies have done so far is loosen a few rocks. But now all them rocks need a-moving. We won't waste another week breaking 'em up, since we have such a pack of strong-backed creturs like yourselves. Now git in line!"

Since it was only fifteen minutes in the morning before we got clapped in the chains, it was always a restless quarter-hour during which I entertained notions I never would have hit on before, or any other time in my life: rabble-rousing the crowd, starting up a riot, taking a hostage, ambushing old Cubie and staging a break. But it warn't hardly a week of this before I began to accommodate myself to the life I'd fallen into. The food was foul, but less foul by far than hunger. I missed my road-kin Lee and that dear girl Ruth—as much as a born hermit can miss a body—but the company there was friendly and no longer strange. Ever since I ran with Van der Loost I had become a hound for tobacker, and could sniff it out anywhere, which was both a terrible vice and a great convenience since I always carry it on me, and I could trade it for 'most anything. I begun to walk with a limp, since frostbite and hard labor made me favor one side.

But on the hardest days, I would go see the overseer, risking another of Cubie's beatings, and beg him to send me to a white man's prison where they don't work a body so weary that his bones want to part ways with his skin. "Your bones want to leave, do they?" he says. "Well, I'm goin' to teach them bones a lesson." And he's back to thrashing on me again until I beg him to let me stay.

"Don't expect much, Joe," I says to myself, laying in bed at night, thinking how no one—no one—was a-listening. "Lord, Joe Harper, don't expect much."

Chapter XXI

By and by the gang found itself hauling rocks from deep within a supposed silver mine, though none of us seen any ore to speak of. I judged that if we did find valuable minerals of any sort, that's when the trained labor would take over. But here was a member of a chain gang carrying around a di'mond in his poke—which was tucked safely next to my gentleman parts—made to scrape rock all day long on the chance it would shine underneath. It occurred to me now and then that I might bribe Cubie and get out that a-way, but I feared once he'd seen it, he'd nab my di'mond and choose to work me to death anyways.

So I kep' hauling rocks with Farley the mulatter, and Harold the minister who used to work the underground railroad, and Dominique the Haitian. It was Dominique who learned us the technique of rolling the big rocks, pushing from behind and passing it to the next feller in the gang ruther than taking turns hauling each rock on your back, where you have to wait because every body is chained to another. It was a relief on our legs to manage this a-way, and the work got done faster, but we still never got a break, and at the end of the day a body felt a powerful pulsing in his chest from pushing boulders all day long, which felt the same as a pain in the heart.

Though it was now officially winter, Cubie ain't let Harold wear a shirt. I asks him why, and Harold says it was on account of the way he'd dressed when he'd been pinched, which was in a minister's robe. It was further punishment upon him for being a man of God and a man of learning, and for dressing that a-way.

"Don't it make you bitter?" I says to Harold, once I'd looked around to make certain Cubie and his men warn't around.

Harold gave it a long and silent thought, so that I 'most give up on an answer. "There was a time in my youth," he lets out, "when I was completely against God, and there have been times when I endured great suffering upon His will," he says. "But somehow they have never been the same times."

"This is penance, ain't it?" I says. "All our troubles in this world will be the thing what saves us in the end, won't they?"

The Reverend Harold took a pause again, and this time I took a pause with him. "I don't know," he finally says. "But they'll help us to keep striving."

Harold's assurance made me feel tolerable proud of my hardships, and though I ached everywhere, I held my chin up.

"Don't listen to that nonsense," Farley says. "The Reverend is trying to make the best of a bad situation. If you ain't bitter on a chain gang, then you ain't alive. This is no smithy for a man's soul to be forged in. It's hellfire, Joe. We's *in* the pit of hell."

I look around me, and thunk to myself, "Ain't it a deep, dark cave I's been a-looking for all along? Why cain't a body appreciate his blessings even as he counts his suffering amongst them?"

That same afternoon a group of men rode in on horses— not just any horses neither, but show-horses in palamino and chestnut—and for the first time I seen Cubie shuffle over and shake a man's hand. "What kind of progress are we making here, Quentin?" the man says, who wore a shiny gray suit that could have been made of silver itself.

"Things are moving along, sir. They might be no more'n dogs, but I learned them to roll the rocks so the clearing-out would go quicker, and they managed to adopt my method," Cubie says.

"Who told you to train them?" the man says. "I didn't recruit a man from Salina, Kansas for his brain."

"Yes, sir," he says. "I won't instruct them any more, sir."

"That's all right, Quentin. You may be a blockhead, but you run a tight ship, and you know what a penny's worth."

Hearing Cubie called a blockhead straight to his face, all of us held in a laugh, but for Farley it come out a squeak.

Cubie does an about-face that only served to strengthen my belief that he once'd been a soldier. He seized Farley by the scruff of his neck and yanked on it. "D'you think I give you permission to laugh? D'you think you are a man? You ain't nothing but a girl, and if you don't believe me, I'll bring you back to the guardhouse and prove it to you."

Every man of that chain gang stared at the ground like it was full of pretty pictures.

"That's all right, Quentin," the man says. "I'm glad to see you still have a firm hand. The reason I came down here, though, is I heard you had a white man working with the negroes, and I wanted to clarify the rules, in case there was a lapse somewhere in your understanding."

"No, sir," says Cubie. "I agree that this man looks white, but he told me himself that his mother and her whole family is black as they come. He's what they call an albino negro."

I had the urge to holler, but I wisely held it in. Growing up in St. Petersburg, being called a son-of-a-negro was the ultimate insult you could ever lay on a body, though I s'posed, now that I knowed a few, that it warn't much of an insult at-all.

"I appreciate that," the man says. "But it's appearances, you understand." He waited for a response from Cubie, though he looked like he warn't about to wait very long. By this time, I had mustered the will to peel my eyes from the ground and look at the horse-riding man who held my fate in his uncalloused fingers.

"Well, you can take him," Cubie says. "He's a lousy worker anyhow."

"Of course," the man says, and Cubie gave me one more

scowl while he unchained me from the group, and sent me off tied behind a horse.

I was mighty pleased to be free of his watchfulness. No, pleased ain't the right word, but unburdened, like a great rock was being lifted off my chest. Which, of course, it had been.

Chapter XXII

We walked as far as the ridge, past the jailhouse, going silently, and when we could no longer see the mine, the man turned his horse around and all the men stopped with him. Kansas had turned rocky, and here we was stopping outside a cave on a cloud-covered day. The air was wet, but it warn't yet raining—it only promised relief from pressure in the atmosphere that never came.

"Joe Harper, you're free to go," he says, as one of his men untied me.

I feared for a moment that this was a sabotage—if the man weren't just a sportsman looking for a body to hunt out in the mountains, or a mercenary hired by folks who wished me harm.

"You have a friend out there," he says. "And your friend is waiting in that cave."

I mumbled "thank-ye" and stumbled over the rocks to the mouth. When I got inside, there was a drip from an old rain, and a bit of light from a lantern set up on a flat place, and it was surprisingly warm on account of a hot spring, which I'd learned crop up all around those parts. Sitting in the flicker, though I could hardly see her in them dark, Dutch clothes, was Ruth. Her light hair illuminated the space around it like an aura, and I felt a kindred glow in my chest when I made her out in the darkness.

"How vould you like to live in a cave like dis someday?" she says.

"Ruth!" I called out. I cain't help running up and taking her hand in mind and kissing it, just as grateful and improper as I can be. "Oh, Ruth. If I lived another hunnerd years, I'd never live in Kansas. Partic'larly the part of Kansas where I'd been kept in chains and thrashed like a mule."

She laughed a lady's trilling, musical laugh, and the sound

was welcome strange. I 'most forgot myself and kissed her on the mouth, but my horse sense kicked in just in time.

"How'd you get out of your fix, and have enough ketch-on left over to spring me? And where's Lee?" I says, looking further into the cave, in case he was still a-hiding out.

"He indentured himself to dat man, who is named Pendleton. You never recognized Lee because dey fit him in a new suit and hat."

"You mean Lee's out there 'mongst that rabble, and I never noticed 'im?" I says.

"That is right, and ven ve vere tried, Lee settled through a lawyer dat de both of us vould go free, ruther dan sit a month in jail, and dey'd find a vay to get you out, if he vould vork vor de big prospector in town vor five year."

"Lee's to work the mine?" I says, imagining him chained up alongside Farley and Harold.

"No, Joe. He'll be a house-servant. In de million-dollar circles, having a Chinaman as a house-servant is a zymbol of high status," she says.

"Well, that ain't right!" I says, standing up.

"Joe," she says. "Lee has done this for my sake… and for yours. You can barely walk. Another month in the mines vould kill you."

"What d'you reckon it'll do to Farley and Harold and Dom and Thomas and Barry and Walt?" I says. She looked empty-eyed at me then. She never say it, but I reckoned she knew who I meant. "They's being kept as surely and unfairly as any slave, and here I thought slavery was a subject for history-books."

She was painful quiet and looked down at her feet before she spoke. "Ven my people first start to vorship together, hundreds of years ago in the old country, they had to meet secretly in a cave near Wappenswil, much like dis one. Dey could be thrown in a jail or killed vor vat they believed."

I was tugged between the anger I nursed while working

on a chain gang and my affection for Ruth. "I don't know Wappenswil from Timbuktu. What should I take from it?" I says.

"Oppression is everywhere. You still have to take care of yourself. It is better to survive," she says. "Unless you are defending your life, violence is never the vay."

"I ain't sold on your passifism for a second, Ruth," I says. "Didn't the whole nation just fight a war that ended slavery?"

"But," she says, "you just said that slavery vas still alive in the mines."

There was a bit of quiet, until I struck on a thought. "You and Lee was tried? In a court?"

"Of course," she says. "Didn't you have a lawyer?"

"Cubie stopped at a building on our way to the mine, where a man pronounced my sentence..." As I told it, it became clear that that *was* my trial, though it were just a row of hoboes like me standing out in the cold and none of us 'lowed to speak.

All a sudden I felt an itch, and when I go to scratch, my hand came back with bug-juice on it. I was bit by a blood-sucker! Without waiting to see who'd come with me, I ran out of the cave at the same speed as if I was a-falling, as though I warn't lame in the leg at-all.

"Mo-skeeters!" I shouted, and there was the men all a-horseback, just the way I left 'em, except I noticed Lee this time, clean-shaven and dressed primmer and fancier than before. They ain't scattered the way I expected, but just looked at me with strange, pitying faces.

Lee catched one of the bugs that come out the cave after me. "It ain't a mo-skeeter, Joe," he says. "They's just gallinippers."

Hearing Lee correcting me after more'n a month was a pleasing sound to my ears. "What's the diff'rence?" I says.

"Well, both of 'em lives near a swamp, but only one of

'em wants to feed from ye."

Lee gave me a look, and once again I reckoned he was trying to communicate a thing with his eyes. But paint me red and white and call me a barber pole if I knew what he meant.

"I'm sure you misspoke there, Lee," says Pendleton. "There's no swamp in this range. I would know, since I was with the team that surveyed it. You're thinking of the hot springs that crop up in the low parts."

"You're probably on the nose," Lee says. "But it's what *I* call a swamp anyway. Still water three foot deep, fifteen foot wide, murky so you cain't see the fish?"

"Fish?" Pendleton says, and laughs. His men follow up with laughs of their own. "Now I *know* you are playing games."

Then I finally struck on Lee's gambit, and eager to prove my cleverness, I threw in, "Huh, now it makes sense."

Pendleton turned to me, his pointed eyebrow yanking upward like on a string. "What makes sense, hobo?"

"Well, Cubie—I mean Mr. Quentin Blutes—would run off on a Sunday morning—I always thunk he went to church—but by noon we'd all swear we smell fish a-roasting on a fire somers," I says, in a performance worthy of Buffalo Bill. "I couldn't puzzle it out, since the nearest market warn't less than ten miles away, and he warn't hardly gone three hours."

By and by Pendleton aimed to prove that he surveyed the land accurately, to prove me false. So he asked the three of us to lead him to what we s'posed was a swamp. Ruth, Lee, and I headed into the same deep and winding cave where I'd just run into the skeeters.

"What d'you reckon, Lee?" I says. He ain't answer, just walked his purposeful walk, but then he slyly handed me a tube, like a hollowed-out piece of wood no more'n an inch wide. I wondered what he meant it for. It looked like stiff straw, or a thin flute. Was it music? Was it food?

As we moved into the recess of the cave, the darkness became absolute. If it warn't for the one lamp Pendleton carried a few paces behind us, we would have been shut off to the world. "Why don't you move ahead of us?" I says to Pendleton. "That way I can see more'n just my own shadow."

"Not a chance I'm letting an albino negro and a sneak-thief get behind me," he says. "Here, you can light a brand from my lamp." He handed me a sad little root that was now flickering on one end like the last ember, and pushed me forward into the blackness.

Though he had the view of my neck, now and then I found reason to glance backward. I noticed two things about Pendleton: he warn't shy of getting dirty, unlike other rich folks I seen; and he was too proud to say when he'd surpassed his natural limits. Soon we used this fact to get a considerable advantage in distance, and Pendleton never asked us to wait or slow up. When we came to a slope that led down to a deep place, Lee a-sudden called out, "let's go!" and slid down, somersaulting a bit but coming to an abrupt stop with a bit of a groan added on the end.

"Put out your light, and come on quick!" he loud-whispered, and Ruth skirted down like it's nothing to tumble down into darkness.

I clumb down half the way before gravity took over, and sent me tumbling down the way it done Lee, and the brand I carried extinguished itself. I raised up, supporting myself by the wall of the cave, and I noticed by feel how even the stone was a-sweating. The heat down there was a relief. There was but a little light from Pendleton's lamp coming up further behind us.

"It ain't a swamp, but it's a hide-out," Lee says, and he sank into it like a bath. Then— though I could barely make it out in the faintest reflection on the surface of the water—he took another wood tube, stuck it in his mouth, and lay down with the tiniest spout sticking out so that you couldn't see that any body had ever been there at-all. Even the ripples disappeared, and it was still water.

Then I reckoned that's what the straw-flute was for! But I never says shucks, only Ruth and I take our own tubes and do the same as Lee. As I was getting ready to immerse myself, I heard voices echoing from up where we came from. I s'pose Pendleton had gotten back-up, because these were rowdy voices calling out, "Shouldn't we tie 'em up?"; "Why? Where're they goin' to hide?"; "They's been living as tramps who knows how long. They could just light out on the next train"; "There ain't no train a-coming at this hour." The rest of this dispute was lost in the muffle of sound when I felt the water fill my ear channels and plug my nose, and the only cavity that warn't stoppered was the spout that sprung up from my lips in the form of a wooden tube.

Then it was a job of waiting. The only thing I heard was the sound of my own breath, and it seemed so durn loud I was sure they'd discover me. But the time just passed, and nothing happened except the slow-cooking of Joe Harper.

—

In Marseille the sky bloomed differently. I had gazed for so long upon Atlantic clouds that I had made a science of them—their gray masses, like brains scuttling slowly on crab's legs across the stage of the horizon, seemed to turn purple in the sun and bear fruit, only to be smudged by the heaviness of air, dragging them down into elemental forms. But in this windless city they went nowhere but folded in on themselves, hatching curious forms you could spend lifespans ciphering out.

As soon as we disembarked from The Oaken Bucket, Mala insisted that we find French doctors for my proper care. And though I protested—for all I'd suffered and endured in the pirating line, I never had cause to lay in a hospital bed—my deprivations were numerous enough to leave me constantly dizzy and weak, in need of good mothering, which Mala, in her restlessness, was loath to continue. She deposited me at an open-air building near the Mediterranean shore where, I soon learned, the quality of Northern Europe would travel in order to convalesce as close to the equator as they dared go. Then Mala says not to worry, she'd paid for a three-month stay and she would visit by and by to ensure my proper care. Then suddenly she was gone and I was in a room with a dozen other sickly men with an open window as my nearest companion. 'T was another island of solitude, I thought, without Mala to bear me up. That first day, the open window was a near-irresistable temptation to a malingerer.

If I had arrayed all my doubts about French medicine in a mental column, assigned them numbers according to the severity of my suspicion, then used the sum to measure the degree of my objection, it was the introduction of a petite French nurse named Cléo that caused me to reset my mental arithmometer to naught. Her hair was straight and brown but coiled as it passed her shoulders, turning faintly golden-red on the very tips from the duration of exposure to the Mediterranean sun. Her delicate neck and perfect knob of a chin were typical of the French breed, but the slightly ample roundedness beneath her chin as it receded toward her throat, and the versatility of the movement of her lips (neither perfectly flat nor perfectly rounded, but given to sudden variation according to mood and expression) were her own. Adding to this equation the lingering cat-like eyes and perfectly pointed nose yielded a sum that guaranteed a full three-month recovery for Joe Harper. For there was now an adjacent column with her name:

Cléo
Cléo
Cléo
Cléo

Cléo

Cléo

To my everlasting good fortune Cléo turned out to be training herself in my language, and she soon apprenticed herself to this ailing American, though she found my manner of speech strange and frequently rebounded to the phrase "speak slowly, please." She was assigned to our room most days, and would bring in French books and try to translate them into English as a way of passing the dull hours. She would read aloud the passages as she imperfectly transcribed them.

In this way I "read" a book by a famous French writer named Dumass—about a proud sailor named Dantes who, I gather, takes revenge on his captors and everybody else. One night she left the book behind, and I spent the night trying to learn French by looking at her translations in the margins and ciphering out which words corresponded to which.

Next day she pretended to scold me for stealing her favorite distraction—I feigned hurt that she didn't regard me as such—and she planted her wrists on her hips, pushing the white fabric inward at the middle, creating the vision of a complete woman that clinched it. Though it struggled mightily with her beauty, the modesty of the nurse's uniform turned out to be no match for her natural form.

On a day when a sunken-cheeked and sallow-faced old man in our room began to groan in distress, then in agony, crying out "M'aide, Maman, m'aide!", Cléo rushed in to administer a dose of morphine with a hypodermic syringe in hand.

Holding up the emptied syringe she says, "Thank god for the American Civil War," as the man's convulsions settled into a twitch, then ca'med into an infant sleep.

"I don't think you'd say so if you was a born American," I says.

"Maybe so," she said, "But without your war, many

around the world would suffer."

There was a vast and unclosable chasm between the feeling that good woman had for suffering men and women the world over, and my own hand as the instrument of that suffering. I tried to muster my imagination to achieve the care she had, and I hit upon my earliest memories as a boy in St. Petersburg wanting nothing more than to escape. I knew not whether any of my boyhood friends other than Tom survived those years, but I suspected that the town of St. Petersburg was now about as empty of young men as my household was. But it hit me for the first time that this was a tragic fact ruther than a neutral one. I wondered whether Joe Harper had anything in him to call a soul.

In error I had assumed, upon my arrival, that the city of Marseille was a dry and windless place, an accidental city in a desert whose only charm was a fortuitous view of the Mediterranean. But that was before I met the Mistral and the Sirocco, the northerly and southerly winds who were to be my new companions in idleness. They turned the genteel drama of hatching clouds into a clash between gods. The firmament became a gray ocean and the clouds swum about like confused ships caught in a sea-fight, and when those vessels met, rain came down like a thousand fallen sailors.

I told Cléo what I'd seen in the sky, and she laughed, saying she s'posed every sailor who spent his life at sea looked up at the sky and just saw another ocean.

By and by Mala fulfilled her promise to come back and rescue me again from another island of solitude, which had now grown mighty comfortable and familiar. She strode in, clad in a buff jerkin and doublet, saber at her side, as though she was ready to take sail at that moment. "We're shipping out," she grinned. "I received word of a British merchant ship weighed with so much cane it could rot the teeth off a shark."

"I cain't go yet," I says, unable to look up from the patterned quilt in my lap.

"What do you mean, you can't?" she says. Mala warn't used to being disobeyed by her crewmen, especially one whose bony body she hoisted on her back and drug to shore. But we warn't yet trodding upon the boards of The Oaken Bucket.

"I cain't."

She stood. "We'll wait for you three days," she says. "If you come to your senses, find us at Vieux-Port, dix-huit."

I nodded solemn, but said no word, my voice choked with too much to say that was hidden.

I never seen Mala again, for the three days she waited for me were three days too many—the authorities caught her and hanged her. And Joe Harper's weekend? T' was occupied by a belief that love would catch between a French nurse and one of her dozens of patients, a candlefire fantasy that was snuffed out by a light wind, as her shift changed to another ward.

Chapter XXIII

It was only when the water started to pour through the hollow of the tube that I shook awake and sat up. It was deathly dark and quiet now, but for the splashing noises I was making. I felt around until I found Lee and Ruth, then all three of us crawled out of the hot spring, the sound of sopping clothes slapping against itself filled the cave, echoing out.

"They'll be gone by now," says Lee in a whisper. "They reckoned we got out of the cave by taking a circuit and doubling back. So they've gone a-chasing after us."

"Dey don't even tink to look in de spring?" says Ruth.

"Why would they?" says Lee. "They don't know about the bamboo, do they?"

"Is that *bamboo*?" I says, holding the length of tube in my hand that kep' me alive while I was underwater. "That was lucky. But… Lee! Your satchel!" I says, realizing he'd left it out there with the pack horses.

"It's okay, Joe," he says. "It was all personal things, which I no longer need." I didn't ask him why he carried it all this way if he was just goin' to leave it behind, but I wondered.

By and by we seen a light, and we made our way by feel until we got close enough to the entrance to see, then stumbled out, sheltering our eyes from the intensity of the sun, which was still in full blaze, though the world it shone upon was cold. We all breathed freer when we seen there warn't any men or horses in sight.

"So, now we have to go spring the men on the chain gang," I says. "All of 'em was put there by Cubie, which means none of 'em got a proper trial."

"Nohow and noway, Joe," says Lee. "Now that Pendleton knows we escaped, he'll round up a posse, and it's a good bet your man Cubie is already in pursuit. You and I warn't soldiers, and we ain't heroes, so there's nothing for us to do but cut."

"That's your plan, Lee?" I says. "Just high-line it some more until we run out of track?"

He nods. "It's the only plan for us, in the spot we're in."

"What about hermiting?" I says. "We could hide out in this cave, and sneak in the prison every morning like Injuns, and steal the men one by one."

"Joe," he says, putting a hand on my shoulder. "You're goin' about hermiting all wrong. Firstly, even if we managed to steal all them prisoners, we couldn't be proper hermits with a crowd like that, could we? Secondly, you don't run off and live in a cave when winter's a-comin'."

"But you don't git it, Lee! It's the cold of the cave I'm looking forward to!" I says. I wished I had the silver tongue to explain to Lee how a body could long so after its own injury, but that story would have to start on the day I was born, and how well my sissies learned me that a sinner gets what he deserves, and run through a catalog of all the sins I'd added up in my years as a pirate, ending on the day Mama Sereny died, leaving no body to absolve a lost Joe Harper.

We both of us stood as still and silent as the shadders of houses, and I kep' trying to find the proper words. But then I sensed Lee was coming around to my way of seeing things, and I didn't want to interrupt the flow of his thoughts in the proper direction.

"If anyone is goin' to be set free, then we sure ain't a-goin' to crowd 'em into a cave," says Lee.

"So what's your holt?" I says.

"There's only one thing they won't be expecting from us now," says Lee, "which is to hit 'em before they get back on their feet. If Pendleton is using every one of his men, including Cubie, to scour the range looking for us, then they won't have more than a man or two overseeing the mine, which means an easy getaway for your chain gang."

"Now you're talking, Lee!" I says. "So let's not dawdle."

"But there's something you're missing here," says Lee. "Fr'instance, how're we goin' to get those men out of their shackles?"

'T was a simple question, but I couldn't muster an answer.

Ruth puts in, "Ve either get de keys, or cut de chain."

"I'd reckon," I says.

"If we want the keys, we need to take it from a guard; and if we want to cut the chain, we need to have the right equipment," Lee says. "Otherwise, we're stuck with a plan and no exit."

It warn't hard to rule out cutting the chain, with nothing but rocks around us, and the only ones large enough to dent metal was too large to heft, and even if we could find a man strong enough to lift it high enough and drop it hard enough to make an impression on iron, it would take us 'til kingdom come to break them all that a-way.

"There's only one way I can see outta this," I says, and I lift my bamboo chute like a pistol, close one eye, and drop my thumb like I'm about to shoot the chute.

Reconnoitering the scene at the entrance to the mine from a far promontory, I reckoned Lee was partly wrong and partly right: there was only one man guarding the cave mouth, but that one man happened to be Quentin Blutes. My heart sank, and my head started to sweat. What chance did we have of saving these indentured men forced to work the mine? And furthermore, what obligated me to? Warn't they arrested for actual crimes, despite what Farley says? Here was the only member of Pendleton's gang who could positively identify me—why didn't I follow my instinct to hop a cannonball West and never turn back 'til Kansas was just a rumor?

From the edge of a rock face with a full view of the scene below, I stood literally on the brink. 'T was as though

I had to decide whether to turn away from these men for good, or to jump into their midst and risk falling terribly. In that moment I learned that anger was more powerful than fear, and when I spied Cubie my eyes fixed upon him as though he were in the sights of a sniper's rifle.

I crept around, using the outcropping to mask my sinister intention. I was as much an animal as a man, and when I found myself ten paces away from my captor, before I ever get the chance to doubt my plan, I closed the distance and stuck the bamboo chute against Cubie's neck from behind and I says, "Don't turn around or I'll shoot ya!" And indeed, if he did turn around, I would have had no choice but to chute him.

"Boy, you don't know what you done," he says, grinding his teeth but never turning around. "It's nearly suppertime, and you're the meat."

"Nevermind all that," I says. "Believe it or not I'm here to help you, Cubie."

I hold out the di'mond to the side, so he can see it out of his peripheral vision.

He turns his "neck" slightly, and at the sight of the di'mond his eyes go wide and spirally like Franz Mesmer. "You are goin' to hand the keys over to Lee, and you and I are goin' to go into the mine shaft and wait until he's freed all the men in your charge. Soon as every last one of the men has moved on to points unknown, you'll walk deeper into the cave where there ain't no light, and the rest of us is goin' to catch out. As I'm riding West, long as there ain't any men a-following me, I will toss this rock off the side of the car onto the roadbed at the next switch, where it'll wait for your discovery. And that's the last you'll ever need hear of Joe Harper."

"How do I know you'll honor your word, boy?" says Cubie.

"I could shoot you now," I says. "It ain't the first time I

done it." This detail, though calculated for persuasion, was sadly, sorely true.

Cubie breathed loudly, but he handed over the keys promptly, which I passed to Lee, and I led him at chute-point into the threshold of the mineshaft. At the place where the dark dominated the light, I pushed Cubie forward to make a little distance between us, so I warn't touching him with the length of bamboo. Then I says, "keep moving."

I was standing just on the dark side of the border, with Cubie dwelling in its deepest shadow, where I listened to him panting heavy like a hungry bear. We stood this way for a long time—I cain't say how long, because the hole in our plan was that none of us carried watches, and even if we had, I could scarcely see my own hands in the darkness of a mine—and felt it more and more likely with each passing minute that he'd change his mind, or get wise to our deception, and leap out of the bowels of the cave and sink his teeth into me, or let fall his dreaded club upon my skull.

I whispered to Mama Sereny, "Many's the time I wished I never left home, but if I can make it to the other side of this adventure, and onto a Westbound train taking me to a better cave than this one, I'll have no more regrets." But no answer came.

Cubie never asked me what I was mumbling about, or why I cared about this chain gang, or what my story was. He just kept on breathing loud and animal-like. I begin to wonder if it warn't an animal in the dark there after all; if I'd been in the cave so long now that the beast had already et Quentin Blutes and was waiting until hunger come again so he could make a meal of me.

At long last I heard Lee's whistle, and as I backed away into the light, I says, "Remember that di'mond, at the next switch West on the road bed, and don't you send any men after us."

I stepped out of the mine and followed Lee to the tracks,

hopeful that I'd seen the last of violence and misfortune. Ill-luck had so far sent me into the hands of bulls, shacks, wild dogs, bo-poisoners, and chain gangs. I'd been ditched, scratched, drugged, and beaten so that the thought of dying alone in a cave seemed more and more like paradise.

When we seen a slow-moving train creep up on us Westbound, and before we ever find any covered siding to wait, I decided my luck *was* a-changing for the better, and things was finally a-goin' my way after all.

But then, in among the usual howl of the engine, the hiss of the steam, and the clacking of the wheels, there was a sound I never expected from any train: a lion's roar. Unmistakable, that sound, though I'd only heard it once, when Mama took me to the St. Louis menagerie. Sure enough, when the train came close, along its side we seen these words: "P. T. Barnum's Grand Traveling Museum, Menagerie, Caravan, and Hippodrome."

We watched in silence as the cars passed us full of the orneriest bunch of camels, zebras, giraffes, ostriches, and the such-like. For all her pluck and toughness, Ruth gasped when she seen the tiger; and for all his 'loofness, Lee he couldn't stop going on and on about the elephant. But the one that struck me was the ugly, horned rhinoceros. He seemed to be all flank, bone, and crinkled gray skin. The lumbering elephant was an ungainly big thing, for sure, but the rhinoceros looked to be one single muscle whose only purpose was to bore you with its horn—there warn't nothing nervous about him.

My eyes followed the rhinoceros car long after it passed, fixing on the bars, the blur of color from the mural behind him, and the afterimage of that one moment I'd witnessed in the life of this rare and noble cretur. That hunched boulder of a beast just shuffled one leg forward, and at that moment, there was a terrible shift in me. I warn't sure anymore what the difference was between the living and the inanimate. If a piece of earth like that could hold blood and walk around, what's to stop the trees? What's to hender a train from running off the rails, growing a hundred legs, and prowling around of its own will?

When the freshly painted caboose came around with the words "Caravan of Monsters" on its side, I looked at Ruth and she looked at Lee and he looked at me. All of us must have figured out at the same time that here, finally, was a train where we belonged, and if we got ditched, the ride alone would be worth it. "Hop the waycar?" I says. And it's just what we done.

The curious part, to think on't, was that, having slept one night amongst the good-dead and near-dead boes of Salina, Kansas, and having spent a month with the rank, hot breath of Cubie hollering in my face—I ain't mind the smell of elephant dung at-all.

We was several miles into our journey before I realized that I forgot to drop the di'mond on the roadbed as I tole Cubie I would, and could now expect that rhinoceros of a man to hunt me acrost the blamed world.

Chapter XXIV

I cain't get worked up about nearly dying as I once'd. It begun to happen so frequent it was just the way of things now. If I warn't being chased by a dog with half a face, or thrown from a train, or drugged by rapscallions, or beaten by a bitter old rebel, then I was in an uncomfortable peace, like a babe in the woods. For some folks, that's how they aim to live. But for me 't was like the green sky before a tornader touches, and I'd ruther be lowered into the earth than get blown away by an ill wind.

It ain't bravery, I know, but it ain't weakness either, for a man to covet his own early death. Some days, whether I was on a boat, or an island, or a cell, or a barracks, the only relief I could get was from the thought that ends all thoughts.

It turned out there was already boes on the waycar, amongst the circus workers, and unless you was one or t' other, you could scarcely tell which was which. After four months a tramp, though, I reckoned I knew the breed. It warn't just the bindles they carried or the fact that they was dressed too warmly even for winter; but the eyes that always pleaded or threatened or scolded but never relaxed into anything like comfort.

When they seen us on the perch, they let out a general shout and opened the door of the caboose, welcoming us into the cabin. A dozen names was thrown our way, but only a few of 'em stuck: Trotter, Tomlin, and Twee Gary. 'T was the first time since I met Lee that I was invited inside any place. With most folks, when they offer you a meal, it's an exhibition meal. You sit on the stoop so that the church-going folks can see you taking a meal, then go on and spread the word about their neighbor's habit of Christian charity. But riding with the circus was the bulliest time we'd had yet. Soon as we set down our rears, we was drownded with drink and food and song—the first such surplus I'd known since I stepped onto the cinder trail. It warn't riches they had, not hardly, but a fairness and inborn generosity that give them license to act on't.

It was about a dozen folks in all, plus us, and we squeezed in the benches and used the close crush of bodies as a furnace to keep our road-kin warm. There was six of 'em who carried fiddles, banjoes, dulcimers, and mouth harps. Among the rest there was just a rhythm they carried out in boot-stomping and a-knocking on the frame of the car with their curled left hands—t' other was in most cases carrying half a bread-roll.

Trotter, the one who led the band, had the longest and run-downiest beard I ever saw. It gnarled and knurled and poured forth in wavelets that would have fit upon the trunk of an oak. For a tree he was powerful animated, full of kick and swerve. He ventured to stand up on the cluttered, rocking floor of that caboose and hollered his song at such a volume that the devil'd take notice.

The men turned every story they knew into a tune. There was many a wander-path story I'd heard ten times before that sounded jumpier and livelier in a song. When I gave up waiting for a break in the general amusement to throw in a word, eventually I just shouted out, "Sing a song about Head-in-a-Bag!"

There was a quiet moment, in which I wondered if I hadn't stumped 'em with the morbid request, but then Trotter turned to Twee Gary and says, "D'you remember the key?" and Twee Gary says, "Yessir, key of E." And they proceed to pound out a jolly rhythm, and the rest of us stomped along.

When they was finished, I never gave 'em a breather before I says, "D'you know one about Big-Belly Rob?"

"Yeah," says Trotter. "I know a few, but I'm bored with bums like Big-Belly. There's a star in the sky for every tramp who fancies himself the next Jesse James. Just 'cause you rob a train and share your loot with the boes you hide out with, that don't make you *Jesse James*. The truth be told, Jesse James makes for a good clapping song, but I doubt the real man's ways would agree with ourn."

"What about Mutton-chop?" Twee Gary says.

A murmur runs through the group. "Now there's a tramp I can stamp my feet for," he says, and he starts up a thrumming rhythm. I thought it peculiar that there should be another bo who shared my monicker, but I said nothing about it in case this other Mutton-chop turned out to be a partic'larly unlikely namesake. In fact my whiskers had grown wild and everywhere since I started out on the road, and since I could no longer claim it accurately, I figured it was just as well that that name belonged to another feller.

But when he begin to sing, I slumped down and buried my face in my scarf for shame. 'Cause it was my own story he was a-singing! I kep' my ears just above the cloth, in case I misheard and it warn't me at-all. In fact, it was a sorely inflated account of my travels, filled with stretchers, but it could hardly be mistaken for another bo's story. This Mutton-chop was a young pirate who give up the pirating life, resolving never to kill or steal from an undeserving soul. He returns to his boyhood home, only to find it changed past recognition, and all his old friends and family dead or moved on. So he decides to go find a cave to wither away and die in; on the way he meets an old Chinaman ("I ain't so old," Lee a-whispers) who reveals that off in California, in the city of San Francisco, there is a cave so deep that it goes all the way to the center of the Earth, and even further, to t' other side, to China! So Mutton-chop he hops a train and sets off for the center of the Earth and was last seen digging his way through a mountain being hunted by some bo chasers who aimed to send him to the stir, or down to hell.

When it was over, the men lifted a cup and drank a hot mug for Mutton-chop.

"How d'you know that's the way it was?" I says, when the men was all warmed up and the singing had all cooled down.

"We knowed the story of Mutton-chop for weeks now—it's been around every jungle West of the Mississippi—so everybody has heard of the tramp a-looking for the center of the earth. Then suddenly here's a rich man who has been hassling boes and asking questions about a man last seen with a pick and a Chinee…" They noticed for the first time that Lee was as Chinee as they come.

"Say, bo, what'd you say your monicker was again?" says Tomlin, a scraggly-haired, well-fed, mustache-wearing feller.

"I didn't," I says. "It's Mutton-chop, and he's Lee the Bo, and this'n here is Deafie. … He ain't got a proper name, on account of his deafness."

The reverent silence that followed was the most respect I ever got in my life for all I've done, and it was worth passels more than the fear I once'd witnessed in a sailor's eyes when he seen us fly the jolly roger.

The caravan climbed a mile and some more to the city of Denver. From our vantage, it looked like a tower atop a hillside atop a mountain, and we was still just winding around its toes. It was sunset now, and on the very peak, there was a fan of sunlight splayed out behind it like a raging fire, and not far to the right, an ember of a moon in the darkening blue. The starkness of color—in angular patterns of red and blue and yaller—rose out of the nave of the city like a stained-glass sky.

Tomlin poked his head up to the lookout next to Lee. His eyes was red-streaked, and the smell of rum was heavy on him. "She ain't afire," he says. "It's a trick of the light, where the buildings sparkle and glow like amethysts," he says.

"You familiar?" Lee says to Tomlin.

"This is my homecoming," Tomlin says. "Say, boes, why don't you let me show you around my city?" Lee, Ruth, and I agreed that we hain't have a better plan.

When we reached the fairgrounds, the four of us got off and circled the train, taking a last look at the rare and unusual beasts in the menagerie before we moved on. "Which one is your most favorite, Tomlin?" I ask, privately seeking confirmation that I'd chosen the best cretur in the caravan when I favored the rhinoceros.

"My most favorite?" he says. "I cain't say. It's a bully bunch." He speaks up louder, with the authority of a man just arrived in his home-town. "But I can say for damned sure which is my least favorite. The *bloody* peacock."

"Vhy so?" asks Ruth, to my surprise, though Tomlin either forget that she's s'posed to be deaf, or he's already too deep in his drink to notice. I reckon she didn't care to travel much further pretending to be a deaf-mute in front of a man who was no longer a stranger.

"Because the peacock," says Tomlin, "is over-loud, and over-proud, and has never done a body in this world any good."

"It's not enough to be beautiful?" says Ruth. "Ven it comes to animals, I mean, if you can't eat dem or keep dem, dey should be a pleasure to look at."

"If you want to know why the peacock is a waste of birdseed, I can show you proof-positive," Tomlin says. "C'mon." He waved for us to follow, and we started tramping north of the station.

To our surprise Tomlin drew us away from the caravan, up to a part of town far from the railway, where there warn't any jungle, the street was lit with gas lamps, and rich men promenaded with their accoutered wives all night without ever worrying about being swarmed by road kids. My first thought—shaped by the habit of a road-wanderer, stricken with hunger and discomfort—was that this was virgin territory that an ambitious tramp could plunder. But it was my second thought to which I gave voice. "You're goin' to get us pinched, Tomlin," I says. "There ain't a jungle in sight, and not even an alley to light out from."

He shook his head and waved off my concern. It was partly drunkenness, and partly indifference, but Tomlin was blind to the stares and sneers he received from the quality. Odd for a tramp of any stripe, he looked like he never cared to ingratiate himself with any of the local gentry, if even for the purpose of throwing his feet at their doors. Instead, he took us past a hedge to a wrought-iron gate, that led to a courtyard for a mansion so fine it brung to mind a Turkish palace or a Sultan's castle—which I used to marvel at in the illustrated pages of *the Arabian Nights*, and once slept in at the peak of my pirating days.

Then, to my considerable surprise, he strode up to the side door and rattled the latch, which was fixed by means of a knob on the right-middle of the door. Once he jangled his keys and found one that fit—I reckoned it must 'a been a skeleton key like a profesh would use—he turned the knob, which operated as a sort of lever, and it swung open, leaving room for Tomlin to stumble in with this rabble behind him.

Strange, but I felt even colder and ghostlier passing the threshold of this well-lit mansion than I felt lingering at the doorway in that abandoned track-layers-town in Kansas. Tomlin sneaked up the stairs, us following close behind, until we come to a room filled with just clothes. It was a closet, but as large as any room I ever slept in. "Is this where the peacocks are kep'?" I says.

"Put these on," he says, throwing some glad rags at me, and some at Lee. "We'll take care of Miss Deafie in a spell."

I threw mine on the floor. "I ain't goin' a step further, Tomlin. Lord knows I ain't a high-minded stiff, but you're taking an unreasonable risk, yegging from rich folks who may be stalking around in this big house as we speak. Don't you think they'll notice so much clothes gone missing and other fine things?"

Tomlin, red-faced not so much from shame as from liquor, crouches down to pick up the clothes I just throwed down, and hands them back to me. "I know for cold, hard fact their owner won't miss 'em, because they's mine."

"D'you mean," I says, "that you ain't a proper tramp at-all?"

"You can keep the clothes, and boots to go with 'em, long as you don't tell a body where you got it, especially not Trotter," he says. Tomlin teared up, and his mustache twitched sorrowfully. "I love that man, and I love the Life, and if they learn I'm just a hobby hobo, they'll never treat me the same."

I tell 'im it's okay, but I cain't help thinking what good Wanderpath music his bo story would make. And somehow I cain't muster the sympathy he asked for. "There's plenty of folks who could get themselves used to *this* life, too," I says.

"Is that right?" he says. "Well I ain't one of 'em. Just put on the clothes, and I'll show you what a peacock is worth." Tomlin sniffed, then wrinkled his pink-drunk nose. "But first let's get all of yous a bath."

By and by Lee and I was suited up more finely than we'd ever been, with gold embossed cufflinks and a puffed collar like gentlemen, but now that we was powdered and cleaned and clothed, I start to notice other deficiencies, like the ache in my leg, and the itching everywheres. I couldn't keep from scratching at my pits and my neck and my thighs, and in between my thighs. "I done picked up the fleas," I says to Tomlin. "I'm afraid you won't want these clothes back."

"That goes for the both of us," says Lee, though he warn't scratching at-all.

"That'll do, I reckon," says Tomlin. "Those gladrags

you got on belonged to my father, who ain't in the world anymore."

"I'm sorry to hear it," says Lee, then turning to me he says, "But did you know, Joe, that catching fleas is lucky?"

"Lucky? I thought you was on *my* side," I says, "and here you are speaking out in favor of the enemy." Tom Sawyer always used to say that fleas was the champion of bugs, though you wouldn't know it the way folks is always using 'em to lay an insult on a body, what with the *flea-brained* this and the *flea-ridden* that.

"Fleas and moskeeters is all just parasites, Joe," Lee says, "which means that the food they eat don't die. Ain't that a better way to feed from a body, if you think on 't? You and me have to kill in order to eat, but the parasites just take a biteful and leave you alone till they feel hungry again. I wish folks would learn better how to live from fleas."

"Okay, I take your point, Lee," I says, "but here we are taking our very clothes from the dead. What does that make us?"

"That makes us scavengers too. Ain't nothing wrong with the life of a scavenger neither. The dead is already dead, so really, bo—What else is you a-goin' to do?"

Ruth stepped into the room then, set up in a collar and shawl like a society lady. Though her blush was applied too thick, and her hair was just starting to dry in a way that puffed out at the top, the effect of the change was uncanny. The three of us stood in a state of awe for so long it went from flattering to inappropriate.

I ain't ask Tomlin why he keeps ladies' clothes on hand, 'lowing that he lived there alone, but on the question of how a lady might find herself in his mansion in need of clothes, I reckoned I could use my imagination.

Chapter XXV

If I had to work from memories of St. Petersburg alone, I would think that public dances were formal, somber things. There would be a tent set up on the fairgrounds, with only the gals attending, nervous and puffed up with false expectation. Mama Sereny meant to trap five husbands for her five daughters, but as the night would plod on and no young men showed up, she insisted that I dance with each sister in turn, just in case a proper feller walked in and was too shy to start up the dance on his own.

One result of this was to make Joe Harper a compliant, but not a capable, dancer. The other was to create a shock in him when witnessing, for the first time, a proper dance in a proper ballroom. It turns out St. Petersburg had been missing a key ingredient in the social ritual of cavorting to music: whiskey, which, now that I think on 't, would have been a great draw for the young men of St. Petersburg as well. But if the rich young men of Denver, Colorado ever wondered where they would get theirs, they needn't have gone far.

When we first stepped on to the balcony that over-looked the scene of the dance, Tomlin waved his arm to encompass the whole scene, putting on a sneer as though we were meant to share in his general disgust. But soon as I looked down and seen the close-trimmed men and the long-necked women cradling each other in ways less than vulgar but more than polite, I 'most cried to think how far I'd come from the fierce and unrelieving grip of Quentin Blutes. "It's a bloody beautiful thing," I says.

Tomlin looked at me, then back at the ballroom floor. "From a distance," he says. "But let's have us a closer look."

Lee, Ruth, and I started following Tomlin down to the ballroom floor, but then Tomlin spun around halfway down the spiral stairs and says, "Not you, Lee-the-bo. You cain't blend in with the quality. Why ain't you sit on the balcony and act like a bored servant with nothin' to do? That's a better ruse."

Lee says it ain't far enough from the truth to keep him interested in the subterfuge, but he done it—though not before reaching over the banister and grabbing a plateful of creamy pastries from the ballroom to take with him onto the overlook.

As we walked down the ivory stairs curving towards the first floor, guiding Ruth on my arm, I felt such a warmth I never knowed before. It warn't in my heart at-all, and it warn't in my head, but it filled up and tingled in my ears, my toes, and my guts. In her Dutch get-up, Ruth had been a beautiful silhouette cut from dark paper; but in a frilled dress of French style and a sere shawl, she seemed more real than anything around her, and ten times as pretty. I knowed Tomlin's heartfelt intention was to show us what a rotten thing it was to be rich, but for me it was the bulliest adventure we'd had yet.

Tomlin begun to introduce us as Dr. and Mrs. Sartin from St. Louis. He reckoned that this crowd knowed all the rich folks in Kansas and Colorado, so it was safest to say we was from Mississippi River country, and if we was said to be educated in the arts, it would excuse every one of our eccentricities. But after meeting the quality of Denver, Colorado, I judged we shouldn't worry too much about our own oddity. There was a feller who "bred horses" and occupied himself earnestly with the bedroom business of animals; there was a lady who wore long gloves and avoided any sort of touching, and another who et only vegetables; there was a couple from Boulder who loved to walk up mountains for fun and swore they seen God up in heaven when they reached the peak. Ruth and I spent a good half an hour standing across from this wide-eyed pair, named the

Collinses, as they had a peculiar habit of never stopping in their speech—when one of 'em would pause, t' other would fill in the gap—and a peculiar belief that no subject could be of greater fascination than putting one foot in front of t' other when you's goin' upward.

Mercifully, Tomlin pulled us away, making no apologies about it, and says, "They's just humdrum, but I ain't bring you here to see the boring rich; I brung you along to see *the terrible rich*." As he guided us through the crowd by one hand, Tomlin held a half-full jigger of whiskey in t' other. His walk was a bit fast, and his grip was a bit firm, so we was tugged along to wherever he decide to lead us, which was between a wall-sized oil painting of Napoleon and a man who had been staring up at it admiringly.

"Dr. and Mrs. Sartin, let me introduce you to Paul Windham, oil baron," Tomlin says.

Paul Windham laughed a whinnying laugh. "You'd best forgive Tomlin," Paul says to me in a thick and raspy New York accent. "To coal men, we're always 'oil barons.' But it's a misnomer. These Barons are relics of the past, and oil is the fuel of the future. Maybe we should start saying 'coal barons' instead?"

I shrug. I judged there was more goin' on to this scene than coming up with clever names for leaders of industry. Tomlin belched with purpose.

"And... you are *Mrs.* Sartin? You sure about that?" Windham says to Ruth with another pleasant laugh, and an eyebrow lifted at me. "Young lady, you look young enough to debut."

"You are very complimentary and kind, sir," she says.

"She speaks as a child speaks," he says with feigned wonder and failed discretion, impressed at his own courtesies and platitudes. "Like a new-washed babe." I shifted in my suit, suddenly uncomfortable in the collar Tomlin had fitted for me. Meanwhile Tomlin took a few steps toward the wall, lifted his front flaps, and relieved himself on the potted ficus in the corner.

"Perhaps we should get him home?" I says, trying to look appropriately shocked, though it were no surprise to a tramp.

"Men like Tomlin do what they please," Windham says. "They own this city. So who are we to say this dance hall isn't his wash closet?"

As if to answer this question, a man stepped into our conversational circle, wearing a vest that boasted fancy silver buttons, a silver watch chain, and silver pins, and who's triangle face sported a mustache and pale hair that was made paler by its scarcity. "Is that fool Tomlin dragging his bottom on the floor again?" he says. "The dog."

Windham, the only one present who might have made a proper introduction, retreated with a bow for Ruth, and used his window of opportunity to move on to loftier company—a trio of painted ladies who poorly imitated the fashions of Paris. Tomlin stumbled and recovered, taking his place at our side, intending to fulfill his duty of introduction, but seeing that Windham was gone, thought he'd better rip on the absent feller instead.

"So what d'you make of that big, stinkin' phony?" Tomlin says.

"He was a mite proud, I reckon, but I'd judge most of the folks in this room have something to be proud of," I says.

Tomlin gave me his blank, kinder Russian, pink-cheeked face again. "Not a one of them has shucks to be proud of. They're all thieves and beggars worse than I ever seen in any jungle. What d'you reckon, Ruth?"

"Truly?" says Ruth. "I s'pose he vas charming."

With her powder on, I cain't tell if she's made to blush, but just in case I threw in, "Now that you mention it, he was a mite arrogant."

"Are we still talking about Windbag?" Silver-vest says.

141

"What's so interesting about him? Oil men are all the same. In ten years he'll be so fat his cheeks will swallow up his nose, and he'll die of suffocation from his own excess."

"Selling oil is like selling anything. What's so special about silver?" Tomlin says.

Silver-vest stiffens and takes an imperial tone, "Silver is a malleable precious metal, so trading it is always a matter of quality. Have you ever heard an oil man speak of *quality*? Concerning his oil, or anything else?"

I couldn't help but be impressed with the ease of this man's speech and manner. Looking closely at Silver-vest now, I couldn't help but think I'd seen the man somewhere before, perhaps in a photograph from a newspaper I once slept on. "I reckon he got you on that score, Tomlin," I says. "Oil and silver is two different substances, and it takes two different sort of men to sell 'em."

Tomlin shrugged. "Oh, I've been rude. Dr. Sartin, Let me introduce you to Carl Pendleton," he says, and I was struck dumb in an instant. "Say, wasn't you s'posed to be out pursuing fugitives rather than goin' round to society balls?"

Pendleton looked like he warn't goin' to answer Tomlin, but finally he says, "The albino negro and the chinaman were heading to Denver—the street girl with them—and I've got eyes on every freight train leaving this city, so I can relax and make friends... maybe the sort of friends who'd like to buy an interest in a mine?" He p'ints his eyes at me like a double-barrel. When he sees the skeered look on my face, he was blessedly mistaken as to its origin. "Oh, I'm not truly trying to sell you an interest. There's already too many who want to buy in, that I couldn't possibly let go of a share even if it were to for my own mother."

Tomlin leans in to my ear as though to whisper, but he don't whisper. "This is where you're supposed to say, 'Pretty please can I buy an interest in one of your silver mines? Now that I seen there's such a demand for shares, I want a hundred!' Pssht! Here's another wind-up toy who stops for naught but sleep." But all I could think about was how I better not turn around in case Carl Pendleton remembered what the back of my neck looked like, from staring at it as we walked down into the cave that was our getaway.

"Oh, I'm not too keen on sleep either," Pendleton says. Then *he* pretend-whispers to Ruth, "For men who have inherited all their worldly wealth, like our friend here, salesmanship is a vulgar art."

Ruth nods, but she dasn't answer him, since Pendleton has heard her voice before, and though he ain't recognized her all got-up in lady's clothes, it warn't hard to miss an accent like hers.

Tomlin takes me and Ruth arm in arm, turns his back to Pendleton, and says loud enough for the room, "I wouldn't know shucks about being vulgar," then farts even louder as he leads us away from the nose-wrinkling odor.

Chapter XXVI

Up on the balcony, we reunited with Lee, who surrounded himself with every kind of food that was ever offered him by a servingman. There was tea-cakes and buns with jam just as you'd expect, but there's also nougat, sugared figs, and exotic fruit skewered together in an aesthetic and aromatic arrangement. I reckoned his hour was considerably better spent than ourn.

By and by the four of us retreated to the roof, which had a widow's walk with an iron railing plated with nickel. The mansion overlooked a park and a cemetery. The park was flat and the cemetery was an entire hill covered in marble tombs that jutted up from the ground and showed angels and cherubs, and well-groomed grass that riffled slightly with the wind, with lamps and wreaths and ornaments that sparkled and dangled and all of it suggesting the flourishing of life where there warn't any.

As always happens with such a view to look out upon, we started speculating about the dead. Tomlin came out right off and says that he don't know about dead folks in general, but he reckoned these partic'lar dead rich folks is just as grasping now as they ever was in life, and not a one of 'em is at peace.

Lee says he judged heaven would be a place where the unredeemed are finally redeemed, and it serves as a correction to all the error that one makes in this world. I 'lowed this was about as good a way to imagine heaven as any. Only the Lord keeps the number of my sins, and I dreamed that one day He'd see fit to burn the pages on which they was written. Lee never says what, but a body cain't help but wonder what unredeemable sins *he* was fixing to erase.

"My fader would alvays say dat heaven is a large velcome place but dat few souls ever make it dere," Ruth says, looking at the floor, having acquired, I reckoned, a habit of humility in all spheres including matters of the spirit. "But dat's not my belief."

"Is that why you run away?" I says, still not satisfied that escaping a suitor was a good enough a reason to leave a place forever. "You ain't believe what your family wanted you to?"

She looked stunned, either because I was so off the mark as to be shocking, or so close that she was surprised to find me capable of such a keen observation. "I believe in de same God my mudder believes in, but I don't vant to be like my mudder; I never vant to be ashamed of vanity. I don't tink God punishes us vor veeling proud," she says, then turned toward Tomlin when she says, "and I don't tink peacocks are a vaste of seed."

Tomlin answered back, but he warn't exactly talking to Ruth in partic'lar. "The shit of it is that that fool Pendleton is right. I've been running the same coal operation since I was old enough to take orders from my Pa, and the only reason I cain't get rid of it is that there are near five hundred families in this town who depend on my solvency."

At the name Pendleton, Lee flashed me a look, and I could only shrug.

Tomlin went on. "I never wanted for anything as a boy, so I was never hungry the way these men are hungry: Windham, Pendleton…." At this second invocation of our pursuer's unholy name, Lee give me another look, and this one I read better—and what I read in it was blame. "After the war, my Pa gave money to families who lost their sons, so that there'd be no bitterness toward him for never sending his own boy."

"Well that was noble of 'im," I says.

"Is it?" Tomlin never looked scornful or sad, just tired as a man could be.

I thunk on't for more than a moment. "I believe so. You'd be surprised what money can mean to folks who hain't got it."

"I s'pose," he says.

"The thing is, Tomlin, I know you won't hardly remember tomorrow anything I tell you today, but I come to think that you're a superior sort of man. You made your p'int about peacocks, and at first I thunk you was being unnecessarily hard on a helpless bird, but I seen what you mean now. It ain't wrong to have more feathers than you need, or even so much that you could make five birds out of the surplus, but the better sort of bird don't need to remind you all the time of the feathers you ain't got."

The door leading down from the roof opened up then, and three bona fide widows stepped up to the railing of the widow's walk, where we was comforting the sour rich man who wished he was born a tramp. It was 'most uncanny the way they shuffled upwards in their get-ups, looking about as much like peacocks as I s'pose three ladies ever will. There was feathered hats, fox-furs, and snake-skin belts. From the cosmetics running at the sides of their eyes, I reckoned they'd just had themselves a good cry in the powder room, but from the silver and jewelry they wore, a body could see plainly these warn't war widows such as I met before. Each one curtsies and says her name in turn:

"Alexis," she dips.

"Morgana," and she dips.

"Temperance," and she dips.

The first thing these ladies did when they reached our perch on the roof was to sweep their eyes over the shape of Ruth who, at half their age and twice their natural grace, molded the air around her into one fluid curve that was either inspiring or terrifying depending on which of the sexes you belonged to. Alexis, Morgana, and especially Temperance fought hard to keep their eyes from bugging wide and skeered at the sight of this country beauty. Lee and I introduced ourselves as Dr. Sartin and his man, and Tomlin just stood there like they must've already knowed his name.

It was Morgana who first succeeded at pretending that Ruth warn't there. "How fitting that three ladies should climb three flights of stairs to find three gentlemen waiting at the summit!"

They seemed to be in the same state as Tomlin, though Lee and I, having been slower to imbibe and nowise afflicted, could not as easily return the sleepy-eyed stare that Morgana sent in our direction. "Don't forget Mrs. Sartin," I says, gesturing at Ruth. "Three gentleman *and a lady*." Having thus protected myself from reproach, I found further refuge by nudging Ruth forward a step in front of me.

"Oh, I do wish Ms. Doucet was here," Alexis says, dabbing her eyes with a kerchief. "She is such a legend among us improper ladies."

"Yes, our society is positively scandalized by her," says Temperance, feigning boredom but with a genuine excitement underneath that neither artifice or drink could fully mask.

"If she were here, *she* would know what to do with Mrs. Sartin," Morgana says, with a crude wink, now that it was no longer possible to ignore Ruth.

"Do you mean that she is sapphic?" Lee says, with a bluntness I'd begun to think of as fundamental to his nature. Even his deceptions are straight-forward, I seen now.

"I mean," says Morgana, "that Ms. Doucet loves every kind of person, and knows all the body's arts. Why? Are you a moral philosopher?"

Lee shook his head. "Don't let *me* interrupt," he says. "You were saying, she knows 'all the body's arts'?"

The three ladies crowded us into a corner now, and there warn't any escape unless I clumb over their heads or sneaked under their dresses, with each alternative lending itself to a different misinterpretation. Morgana leaned in and drunk-whispered, "Ms. Doucet never married because no gentleman could ever satisfy her."

"So she turned her attention upon lonely ladies," Alexis put in.

"—Then took up with gentlemen *and* ladies," Temperance added.

Morgana got in close enough now that her furs tickled my neck uncomfortably. "She's still never found a man or woman could please her, but she's learned ways to give pleasure to a man that will paralyze you—Leave. You. Empty."

Lee give me a look that says, "let's cut," and I give the slightest nod so he knowed I was along with the general idea. Holding Ruth's hand now, I flopped down on my hands and knees, scurrying under the poofiest dress, which was Alexis'. The wine had slowed her down so that we was all the way on t' other side before she let out a yelp and a chuckle. Poor Lee had thought instead to navigate through the crush of bodies, and found himself squeezed between two furry, feathered, perfumed, and powdered fashionable ladies.

Well, I couldn't leave 'im stuck there, so Ruth and I linked arms and used all the oomph we had to tug him all the way through. Bad as I reckon it was for Tomlin, we never turned back for fear of his captors. A cathouse is one thing; a nest of black widow spiders was something else.

When our feet was finally planted on the ground floor, and had gained a good distance from the crazy rich folks, at last I told Lee about Pendleton, who had men all over town watching the trains come and go.

"How're we s'posed to light out of Denver without a train to hop?" he says. "We cain't padfoot it all the way to San Francisco."

"You warn't listening properly," I says. "It's the *freight* trains they'll be a-watching. Pendleton won't have eyes on first class."

"But that don't change the fact that I'll be the only chinaman at the station," Lee says. I smile in answer because for the first time on our adventure we found ourselves fitted with new rags, new destinations, and new identities to match.

"But you *ain't* some chinaman anymore," I says. "You're Dr. and Mrs. Sartin's man. All you need is some snapper rags and a ticket."

Ruther than having his eyes light up the way I expected, Lee looked down at the front of his suit-coat.

"What's biting you?" I says.

"Nothing, Joe," he says. "Only there's a rule; a profesh never pays for a ticket to ride."

"Is that all?" I says. "D'you ever hear me say shucks about *paying* for a ticket?"

Ruth, Lee, and me sat on a low wooden bench at the station, hands folded on our laps like 't was Sunday and this was a pew. I looked to Ruth on my right, then I looked to Lee on my left, and I thunk what a well-mannered crew we was. Although this was our first boodle, and we was there at the railway station for the sole purpose of yegging the first easy marks we could find.

"Vhat about dis one?" Ruth says, p'inting in the direction of a feller with wet black hair and a skinny neck, toting his luggage on his back like a tired youngster.

"No sir," says Lee. "I won't hive from a man who's too poor or too proud to employ a valet."

"S'pose he's just cheap?" I says, thinking we'd be hard up to find an easier mark than him.

"S'pose you're just lazy," says Lee. "We need us three overland tickets besides. What about them fellers?" Lee gave a slight tilt of the thumb to the station entrance, through which walked a crew of college football players, Ivy league men headed West to spread the gospel of the game.

"Now Lee," I says, "you already know I'm after a hard life, but while I'm *on my way* to the hard life I plan to live, does a body have to make everything so difficult?"

"One of these days I'm goin' to learn you about synonyms, Joe," says Lee.

I looked at him with disapproval. "I've had enough sin in my life already, Lee, without any of your *sin on 'im's*. Ain't regular sin bad enough without sinning *on* a body?"

Lee sucked in a breath and was about to let out a harangue, when Ruth leans over me and says to Lee, "Gimme a slap."

Ruther than a slap, Lee gives her a pained look.

"Slap me right now," she says.

When he refused, Ruth slapped him across his cheek, and left a pink mark on his high cheekbone. Lee's eyes registered surprise ruther than anger, so when he raised his hand to block, I mistook the gesture for an attempt to return the favor, and jabbed Lee in the ribs instinctively to lower his arm. Then Ruth she slapped me for the interference, for it was her aim to provoke.

Just then the Ivy league men come over saying, "hey hey hey," and "are these two bothering you, Miss?"

Ruth immediately ran over to one of the men and tucked against his side like a wad of chaw. It happened so fast that I nearly called aloud, "What's our holt?" since I scarcely knew what Ruth's aim was, nor what part I was meant to play in the drama.

Apparently neither did Ruth because when the men repeated "Are these two men bothering you, Miss?" she stood still as a statue and said naught.

But Lee picked up the fumble and shouts out, "If you insist upon leaving on that train, as Mr. Sartin's lawyer I must insist that you leave behind all possessions belonging to Mr. Sartin, not excluding any gifts material and saleable, such as the very clothes on your back."

"Hold it, Chang and Eng," the biggest of the three fellers says, waving a stubby finger in the air menacingly. This was the strangest insult I'd ever had laid on me. Did these men earnestly mistake me for a chinaman? "If you're fixing to take everything the lady owns, at least leave her her clothes.

Otherwise you're a villain."

"We can negotiate on the clothes," says Lee. "But her purse and hat and jewelry were all gifts from Mr. Sartin, of a considerable sum."

The smallest of the three had active eyebrows that showed how much he enjoyed the art of instigation. "You aren't going to let a couple a' dirty chinamen tell you how to treat a lady?" With my wide eyes and pale English skin, I wondered what spell was cast over them that they made me out to be Lee's kin.

The big 'un stepped forward and hulked over us both, pointing in the air again, his fat finger raised up like a club. "The lady keeps her clothes, her hat, her purse, and everything else on her person. Got me?"

By now we had begun to draw the unwanted attention of strangers, passersby, and bystanders. I begun to feel the eyes of Carl Pendleton on my neck, and was eager to move along to the next holt.

"It matters none to me," I says, affecting the New York voice I remembered from Paul Windham, "since Mrs. Sartin has no money to buy herself a ticket." Then I turn about and walk t' other way out of the station, with Lee close behind.

Ruth she made a show of weeping and a-carrying on until the men consoled her with a ticket. *But didn't they know that she couldn't go anywhere without taking along her two little darlings—Jem and Lucy?* Pretty soon Ruth had three tickets and a warning to stay away from chinamen.

Chapter XXVII

As a pirate, I followed pirate law—which is something Tom made up, as otherwise The Life was just a bunch of mischief and lawlessness, and Tom believed it was rules that kep' a body alive. Fr'instance, even though I was called first mate, the bosun and the navigator formed a bloc and outranked me. As the only man who knew how to properly prepare a fish, the cook settled disputes between officers by default. Even the lowly cabin boy could have judgments overturned if he petitioned the captain, which he once did, when a bad angler fish didn't agree with my stomach—a result of a prior dispute with the cook—and I was forced to empty my sick in the crew's quarters, and I decreed that as the only witness the boy must keep the identity of the guilty party to himself. He tattled on me to Captain Sawyer, after which I sentenced the cabin boy to solitary confinement, which Tom subsequently pardoned.

I had my own rules, too. Fr'instance, I would never laugh when a body was sent over into the drink. Killing a man is bad enough in the sight of God, but to scorn His creation is an invitation to the devil. But I'd bet my last di'mond that there's a gallery of angels up in heaven a-watching and a-laughing at our follies and foibles all the way to our graves.

When I first took up the hobo road, I aimed to heed a new set of rules, but now I was on my way to breaking every one. I cheated folks, stoled their food, false-witnessed them. Now I'd yegged some poor travelers' means of passage. It didn't seem right, yet was all done in the name of survival.

I'd tell myself, *At least there warn't a need for murdering*, then instantly I'd feel like a good man again, and I could always go on feeling righteous and proud. 'T was like smearing my lips with po-bro, this feeling; it gave the world sense, and everything took on a golden hue. For all the murdering I *ain't* done, I was a saint.

As we waited to board our first legitimate passenger train, Lee seen it in my face, the way I was struggling with the path we found ourselves on, though he mistook the origin of my grief. "Don't fret about Tomlin. That bandicoot has added up so many years in the good life, I reckon he can take the hit."

"I s'pose you're right, Lee," I says. "We've seen plenty of men worse off than Tomlin."

"Don't 'Lee' me," he says, whispering like the old folks next to us was really bulls in disguise with nothing better to do than gather information on our conspiracy for a free ride.

"Just relax," I says to 'im. "Act natural."

Lee put on a face that was deaf to reason and blind to mercy. "Suffering fools gladly ain't *my* natural."

"And you ought not to be so friendly vith de valet," Ruth says to me, the curl of a smile appearing at the corner of her lip. I used the ruse as an excuse to take Ruth's arm in the crook of my own, and looked out into the middle distance like I was a man with inner vision too vast to be contained by this view. We boarded the train as the first whistle sounded over the crowd.

"Could you believe that a young boy from St. Petersburg would grow up to be a captain of industry, with his own mining interest and a thousand men in his employ?" I says to Ruth, playing the part a bit too thick, even I could tell. I pulled her in closer to me, but she turned her head.

"A robber-baron is more like it," Ruth says, and while it made me warm inside to think on her as a wife, I concealed my disapp'intment that we'd moved so quick from being strangers to being married to being quarrelsome. "Dose men need liberty much as dey need a job."

All right then. I knew my part. "I'll 'liberate' every one of 'em, just as soon as all the precious ore is separated from the worthless rock, and I've moved on to the strip-mine the next virgin mound." We let out the wicked laughs of the wicked rich.

"Scuse me, sir," says a skinny old feller whose Stetson was stuck tight to his crown, and who never had a head of hair underneath it. He was just about the oldest, pock-markedest man I ever seen. "Did you say St. Petersburg, Missouri?"

"The same," I says. "D'you know it?" I was curious at first, but then I remembered our ruse, and the whole adventure we was on, and turned away like I warn't awaiting an answer.

"I once'd been a resident there," he says. "Though it's 'most forty year since I've set foot in it."

I warn't looking in his direction, but then he moved himself into my view.

"Can I ask you a question?" he says.

"Well, it ain't a crime," I says, though I only wanted him to leave us be. Ruth and I had struck on a couple of new personalities, and his air of desperation was an unwelcome odor on our happy little stage.

"D'you know my boy, Jeb Finn? How is he?" he says, forcing his face into a gap-toothed smile. "Still running with the Catholic girl? Mary, is it?"

When he seen me look down at the floor, he cover up his mouth with a withery hand.

"Is Jeb still alive? Is my boy still on this Earth?" he says.

"Pap? ... I have no news of him," I says, though it were already too late to say so and mean it. "Sorry, old feller."

He warn't inclined to move, so Ruth and I done the moving, Lee carrying an empty luggage-box for each of us— the ones I'd stole so we'd look the part of legitimate travelers of leisure. At the rearmost car, we stopped, watching the city of Denver fade into the clouds like Olympus.

"You know him?" Ruth's hand had been inside mine, and she let it slip out and fall at her side.

"I knowed his son, and grandson," I says. "But only the

Lord knows them now, I reckon."

"You should have lied to dat poor man," she says.

"It's better he remember Jeb as a boy, and think him dead," I says, "than for me to let on he's alive, and have to explain the kind of man he became."

Ruth looked to Lee for support, but he shrugged. "I'm for secrets *and* lies," he says. She scowled back at him. *Poor Lee,* I thought. *He can't do a thing right in the eyes of that Dutch girl.*

The train sailed down, down through the brush to the deserts of Colorado and the plains of the Yutas indifferently.

Chapter XXVIII

Of all the fine-dressers on this passenger car, the cleanest and most faultless was a group of close-cropped, sandy-haired men traveling together in a pack. At first I reckoned they was traveling musicians or a singing group, but that didn't square with what I knowed about the West, the country where we was headed. They were so set up in their manners and dress that I got to talking with 'em just to be reminded of the way polite folks talk. At first they described their journey east all the way to England, from which they was now returning, but it warn't long before they give a regular accounting of their personal history, and then the history of the Yuta territory, and pretty soon they was talking about the history of how God made the universe.

These men was all Morons, and Morons believed that the events from the bible takes place in Independence, Missouri—where I met up with Trombo and Toke and Red-Eye and the rest of those boes—that the trainyard there and everything around it is called Zion, and that's where the son of God is goin' to return one day to redeem all us sinners.

It was all recorded in a couple of tablets, just like Moses'—'cept these ones warn't plain stone at-all, but actual gold! Why, it seemed all the holier somehow, to have their sacred text carved not in rock but in precious ore. When they dropped this detail on me, it seemed to pull up a memory from way back in my years as a schoolboy, a part of the Moses story involving gold, but I never struck on it.

Finally they came to the part of the story where they learned me about today's Morons. Their President was such a beloved feller he had fifty wives like a Sultan, of all natures and moods, and of all ages; so the Morons they call him Bring'em Young. Bring'em Young lived true to his name, as the youngest of his wives warn't yet fifteen; though he balanced things out by taking widows as wives, some of whom was older'n sixty, so that the average between 'em equalled one lady of marriageable age.

As it turned out, this group of proper young men was likewise headed to Salt Lake City, where our journey with the stolen tickets would be terminated. I asked what-all the city had in its environment other than a salty lake, and they replied that there was all manner of rocks—strange formations of rocks, rocks of rare and uncanny colors, even rocks that seemed to be spiritual in origin. In every rock there was a story, and the author of every story was said to be God.

To me it sounded like Native religion, and I says as much to the men, but they didn't hold to 't. They says that the Indians was a different lost tribe of Israel, called Laminates, one that went astray and become uncivilized, and it was only the Morons who knew the true path, and that path was known through both scripture and the holy Book of Moron.

I told these men that I took no stock in holy books other than the Lord's Bible, but in fact their gang sounded like they had the bulliest time of all the churches I knowed. Regular Christians had tablets that was plain stone, and marriages with just one wife, and a holy land that was far away in the land of Israel. It seemed to me, I says, that these folks got it right when they says that God was next door in Missouri, and he owned fine things and didn't judge a man for his carnal sins. Here was a people who warn't skeered of pleasure, and a feller could indulge his saturnalian desire and ask for forgiveness the next day, or not.

The intensest and eye-browiest of these young men, named Mordecai, set me straight right then and there. Morons don't go in for every pleasure, he says. They had plural wives because the Lord *ordained* it, because He valued marriage so much He wanted everyone to partake in it. And it was decreed, fr'instance, that they was never to imbibe the spirits, or smoke tobacker, or have any kind of hot drink, cider included.

I wondered why the Moron God didn't let his people drink cider, but then I neverminded it, for we were now approaching the Great Salt Lake City, and could see the walls of the sandstone temple looming on both sides like the arms of a giant as though to embrace, or herd together, those who approached it.

"Looks like a walled city," I says. "Like in picture books."

"Like ancient Troy," says Lee. That made me think on the ten-years war that was fought over a part'cularly handsome gal.

"Well who's a-goin' to let us in?" I says.

"We'll be your guides," says Mordecai. "But you must remember you are guests in our city, and if you find our customs and beliefs strange, just recall that it's *you* who are the stranger."

We come to the gates of the temple, which was so vast that it could have housed an army, and sure enough 't was an army of women and children who welcomed us. These were the family of Bring'em Young, and that is just how Mordecai introduced them, for it would have taken the rest of the winter and into the following spring to make proper introductions with 'em all. This was the only family who lived on the grounds of the temple, and that land, in all its vastness, still seemed insufficient for their number.

After being brought inside, however, we warn't treated as strangers, but like family. In fact I wondered if some of them just reckoned we *was* family, since every day they had to be introduced to new members of their own clan anyhow. The only one with any hint of caution in their nature was President Young himself, whose dinner was interrupted by the sudden uproar. Still he welcomed us at his table, and we settled in and gave as many thank-yous as we could muster. President Young wore a close-trimmed beard, and he had the same buckled eyebrow that Mordecai had, which made me wonder whether these two warn't also kin.

"So, you're Dr. and Mrs. Sartin from St. Louis?" he says.

"That's so," I says.

"And this is your man?" he says, p'inting a fork in Lee's direction.

"Yessir," I says.

President Young's eyes measured his company as a father might measure a suitor to his daughter. I was inclined to put his mind at rest by assuring him none amongst us was after marriage, but then I recalled the ways of his people and thunk he might take offense if we *warn't* there to marry anyone. "What're you a Doctor *of,* Dr. Sartin?"

This was as blameless a question as he might have contrived, and early on I had made a good study of the character I was meant to inhabit, but ever since we left Denver I'd forgotten my craft, and was left a-floundering. "Philosophy... of Art... History?"

"Oh?" President Young looked interested, though I meant to pick a thing that would bore him away from the subject of my supposed expertise. "Dutch? Italian? English?"

English was the only language I knew, so I judged it was safest. "English, mostly, though you know, us doctors, we're all just men of letters."

"Of course," he says with the first, quick smile that hid back into his whiskers just as fast as it came. "So what do *you* think of John Ruskin on modern painting?"

After a moment, I catch myself staring blankly at the wall opposite, which was papered with a gold pattern.

"I don't think he should, frankly," I says. Now it was Young's turn to look blank and confused. I let lapse a pregnant pause like I'd known folks do who're full of knowledge, then says, "If John's riskin' on a thing, it ought to be *old* paintings ruther than *modern* ones. Any living person with a brush can make a modern painting, but old paintings was made by folks who're dead and cain't paint no more. Therefore the old ones is worth more, and it'll be less of a risk for John to put his money on 'em."

"Oh, I see! That's delightful!" President Young let out a hearty laugh, and all was merry at the table for the main course. But when dessert come, he took up the subject again.

"You know, Dr. Sartin, I'm usually in favor of the *modern*, because our nation is a modern one, and I'm for everything American. But in this case I have to agree with you," he says, and we nod at one another over our cobbler. "I much prefer a Turner to a Whistler."

"Amen," I says. When I seen he expected me to say more'n just "yessir," I push my chair back and stand up to hold forth again, this time finding my stride a mite quicker'n before. "In painting—and I mean *any* painting, whether it's modern or old or ancient—the thing is this: you cain't paint anything but what you see. Because a painting, it don't have sound and it don't have smell, and it'll be a rough time for the man who tries to paint a picture that *does*. So I maintain that a man who wants to be remembered for his paintings must never paint whistlers, because you cain't hear 'em anyway, and a man purses his lips and looks funny when he whistles anyhow. On t' other hand, with a turner, he might be moving too fast to catch with a painting, but even if the feller cain't keep still, a photograph will get 'em."

After I set down, I reckoned I must have impressed the quality of Great Salt Lake City, for they were rendered speechless, and we passed the rest of the meal in silence. Now I seen what Tomlin meant when he says it warn't hard to act like a learned man if you make yourself out as eccentric, because here Bring'em Young was asking me all about turners and whistlers, and what John's riskin' and so on, and it made as much sense to me as a feeble-minded bo a-ranting about cats that live on the moon.

But then, as the men were leading us forcefully back out to the courtyard, Bring'em whispered a thing to Mordecai which I could hear because I was used to listening to Lee talk above the roar of a train. "These look like good, clean people," he says. "But I reckon my nose can judge a man's character better'n your eyes." And he shut the gate, leaving the three of us and Mordecai, our guide, outside.

There 'mongst the desert flowers—cactus, milkweed, and mariposa—with the winter sun already tuckered out and gone down for the long night, it started to feel cold for the first time since we arrived. Once having given myself to the gentle life, I nearly gave up sleeping out-of-doors.

Since Mordecai and his fellow Morons had made such a show of hospitality, I asked if we could stay with 'em while we was visitors in their city, and after he asked whether we would join their church brethren and we said no thanks, Mordecai graciously invited us to stay at the methodist church on t' other side of town.

Chapter XXIX

With but one lake in their fair city, and nothing to drink but rain, it's a wonder the Morons ever settled upon the rite of baptism. The Evaginicals was a sight more practical; they determined that all a body needed to do to get right with the Lord was proclaim a personal relationship to His son, the savior, which warn't hard to come by out in the red desert where water was scarce and visions was a penny a pound. However, the Moron way of life held one attraction that seemed to outweigh the opposition by a considerable margin: they had houses with walls, and in the shade 't was warmer in winter and cooler in the heat of the day. Laying out there in our bedrolls as the half-hour sun rises over the mountains, the first thing we notice was that we warn't the only boes who slep' under the stars that night; and the next thing we noticed was that there warn't any Morons among 'em. I reckoned all the Morons had roofs to sleep under, and if somehow they didn't, they'd go and marry someone who had.

"Say, bo," I says to another feller nearby who'd woken up with the sun, and who had a beard that sculpted down to his neck, and a redness to his gaze that look like he was born with tears in his eyes. "How's a body to get his grub around here?"

He looks at me with the same pacific look he used to drown himself in the glow of the Eastern horizon, then turned his gaze back upon the lake. "In the Great Salt Lake City, there's just missions. Though you have your pick of denomernations."

"What's the difference?" I says.

"Well, to get grub from the Methodists, you have to make a show of poverty. You and your rich friends in those glad rags ain't a-goin' to get far. At the Mormon church, you purdy much have to become a member. As far as the

Catholics go, they won't even look at you 'less you're a heathen Injun and they can bring the light of civilization to you. So Evangelical is your best bet; all you have to do is talk a lot about knowing Christ like he's your kin, and act like you knows about scripture."

"How much scripture does a body need to know?" I says, sheepishly. I'd grown up hearing His holy book read to me every day, but it was a long time since I had a refresher.

"Well, with this bunch you can purdy much skip to the end," he says. "D'you know Revelations?"

"Just what I hear in church as a boy. I never get that far when I read it," I says.

With a deep sigh, he started out like a tired papa talking to his children. "So, there's a scroll with *seven* seals, see, and—"

"—What d'you need seven seals for?" I says. "Ain't just the one enough to seal a scroll with?"

"It don't matter what-for, that's just the way it is," he says, then goes on. "And when each of the seals is broken, a horseman appears, who together brings death and destruction to the sinners of the earth... and an earthquake too."

"From a scroll?" I says. "Is it just coincidence, or is the scroll *causing* the horsemen and the earthquake?"

"It's just the order of things, bo," he says. "And when the last seal is broken, seven trumpets is blown by seven angels."

"Seven trumpet-playing angels?" I says, and I begun to suspect that this whole story was thrown together by a man who just loved the number seven to distraction, and wanted everyone else to think it was the best, most perfect number there ever was. "Who's holding the scroll now?"

He coughs and looks down at his feet. "A lamb with seven horns and seven eyes."

Bodies was stirring up now. The full morning announced itself with a blast of sunlight over the bluffs. I tried to imagine a world where a simple scroll—some dried-up strip of hide with marks on it shaped into letters which formed into words which strung together into phrases—had the power to end all of life on the earth. Then my belly rumbled.

"A body's willing to do some strange things to be fed," I says.

"I reckon you're right," he says, a-rising to his feet. "Come to think on't, I could use some breakfast myself. Why don't you 'low me to come with you."

"Lead the way, sir," I says. He took to it like a habit, and he soon learned me why: he was a coach driver before he ended up in Great Salt Lake City, and was used to leading around poor lost lambs like us.

"I'm Zeb," he says by way of introduction, holding out his hand. Zeb was balding in front, exposing a shine on his brow, but at the peak of the oval of his head, hairs stood out in every direction like a mottled mane, and a down-turned fish-mustache made him look civilized ruther than rough.

"I'm…" I tried to suss out whether right then I was Joe Harper or Missouri Joe or Muttonchop or Dr. Sartin. "…Joe Sartin," I says.

He looks at me funny for my undue hesitation. "You sure?" he asks.

"Yes, I'm Sartin," I says, and he claps me on the back.

By and by, Ruth, Lee, Zeb, and I went over to the Evaginical church. It warn't a fortress, like the Moron church—which Zeb learned me was really called the *Mormon* church, and they didn't take kindly to being called Morons, though that were the name of the angel who first revealed himself to Joseph Smith. Ruther the church was clay-built, like the native structures down in old Mexico, which they called adobe. With its arched hole of a doorway, it looked as much like a cave as any building ever made by a man.

As we went inside, there was an uncomfortable moment when we were judged to be strangers to the congregation, which was followed by a general welcome, having an earnestness that was unfeigned, for this denomernation had been losing bodies to the big church across town for years. The result was a crowd that was small but could hardly afford to be provincial in the fashion of many another small church. The service warn't set to begin for close on an hour, and before the Lord's business could be taken care of, there was a quota of talk-about-town that needed to be satisfied, and the gentlemen and ladies assembled there warn't shy to meet it.

Meanwhile a tall, straight-backed feller with tightly combed, ear-length black hair came up to us and greeted us half-way down the row of pews like he knowed us. He had an up-turned and pinched way of smiling that made his lip look like a thin, painted-on mustache.

"Hello, friends," he says. "Welcome to Christ Church. My name is Fermat. This is Desmond"—he gestured to a smaller, thicker man with a shirt that was more shiny than frilly— "and this is our congregation."

"Oh," I says. "Are you the pastors?"

"Yes, sir," Desmond says, guiding us past the lectern, as though to hide us from the congregation, or they from us. "We divide the duties of the church between us. Today I give the sermon, and Fermat will show you the grounds."

And show us Fermat did. Not only all the meeting rooms, but the fig orchard out-of-doors, and the straw huts nearby where Injuns once'd lived. It almost seemed to me, for a flash, that the man warn't trying to recruit new congregants to his church, but to solicit a buyer.

These pastors was unusual young and unusual friendly, but they was also kinder unusual *unusual*, though I never suspected they was devious. I'd grown accustomed to all manner of odd behavior on the road, and could scarcely tell the difference anymore between what local folks called a normal and what they called an eccentric.

As we come back inside from this tour of the grounds,

Lee stopped just underneath a threshold that boasted a wooden cross, upon which was attached a heavy-lidded Jesus with his head tilted to the side, looking more tired than crucified. Lee was momentarily made religious by the nearness of his savior, and folded his hands in a way that was four parts guilt and one part piety.

Not one to be outdone in an expression of gratitude to the Lord, Fermat stood across the ways and folded his hands too. I warn't sure whether 't was the custom here to pray when there warn't food nor a table upon which to set the food, so I did the same. To this gesture Ruth scoffed.

Lee opened his eyes and lines formed between his eyes. "What has any man here done to earn your scorn, *Mrs. Sartin?*"

"I vas just tinking of scripture," says Ruth. "*Ven you pray, do not be like de hypocrites, for dey love to pray standing in de church to be seen by odders. Truly I tell you, dey have received der reward in full. But ven you pray, go into your room and shut de door and pray to your Fadder who is in secret. And your Fadder who sees in secret vill reward you.*"

"So it only matters if it's done in secret, does it?" says Lee.

Ruth stiffens. "To the Lord, according to His vord."

"His what?" says Lee.

"His *vord*," says Ruth.

"What if…" I put in, "a feller goes into his room and shuts the door, and there's a body at the window looking in he don't know about? He thunk he was praying in secret, but he warn't really because now he's seen by a stranger *and* the Lord. Does he still get his reward?"

"According to our Ruth," says Lee, "that ain't good enough."

"A sincere faith," says Ruth, "*is* de reward."

"So they's different rewards?" I says, puzzled afresh since I thought I got a handle on it, then lost it. "The hippo-

166

Christ prays standing in church and gets his reward, which is the respect of others. Then I go in my room and shut the door and pray, and then the Lord will reward me with what?"

"I don't tink," says Ruth, "dat you appreciate de message. You cannot see de forest for de trees." She tucked her chin low, and I swore I seen a tear form at the corner of her eye.

I open my mouth to question how I could see the trees and miss the forest, but Ruth seemed to be in a state that no reasonable speech could penetrate, so I shut my trap.

In the church office, which was a room about as large as the fellowship hall, Fermat shut the door behind us and asked if he could speak frankly. I gave him a shrug in reply, and Ruth stood by coolly while Lee put on his smirk, which was nearly the same as his regular smile.

"From the moment you walked in the sanctuary," he says with a lip-pinching grin, "I knew what sort of people you were."

Lee and I stiffened—having been hunted all across the state of Colorado, we reckoned we knew the score on how hoboes came to be knowed out West—but brave Ruth's neck stretched an inch or so higher up on her shoulders, and she asks, "And vat sort of people *are* ve, do you suppose?"

"The sort who're wealthy and lost, looking for a new adventure," he says. "Maybe you ran into some trouble with families, or locals?— It's all right with me, I'm just speaking plainly."

Well, it was a relief to be thus accused, I admit. I hung my head like I'd been found out.

"Am I right?" he says, putting on a ministerial gravity, but poorly masking his joy at "discovering" our ruse to be respectable.

"That's the way of it," I says.

"So why not settle here and stay amongst good Christian

folks," says Fermat. "Ain't it worth trying? We may not have the largest or most well-funded congregation, but we have a wondrous perch from which to view the Lord's work, and the good will of good neighbors, and we don't go hungry."

This was some advanced missionarying he was up to, and I didn't know if I had the will to resist it. My belly ached from the bread it lacked.

"I'll make you this offer now," he says. "You can sleep here in this church for as long as you like, but while you do, you must study the scriptures. Meanwhile I've already asked Desmond to introduce you to the congregation as apprentice scholars studying for the pastorage."

"And what do *you* get out of it?" I says.

He winced, almost invisibly, at the suggestion that his motives for recruiting us was less than pure. "Just the peace of mind that comes with turning another soul toward the righteous path."

I thunk, then, whether this warn't the cave I'd been after all these years. It was dim and caverny, colder than you'd expect. It was dry, so there warn't a thousand bugs a-swarming round us. In the background I could hear the thunderous roar of Desmond a-riling up the crowd. That was the matter, I says to myself, they's too many folks already tethered to this cave. Sooner or later Pendleton and his men would catch me.

As though he'd already walked on the same roads my thoughts a-wandered on, Fermat says, "Whatever crime or disgrace you left behind in Chicago, or Minnesoter, or Saint Louie, the law could look for you a hundred years or more and *never* discover you in an adobe church across the Great Salt Lake. And even if they come here asking, none of the local folks know your real names. And *even if* they discovered you here, they would bless the Lord for showing you the righteous path and turning such sinners to a life of the pastorage."

Fermat sensed we was a-running away, and although 't was an accurate conjecture, he never expected that we was harboring a chinaman who was indentured to the prospector of a silver mine.

"Tell you what," he says. "Let's have a drink tonight. Then you sleep on it. Desmond'll talk to the congregation, I'll entertain, and tomorrow you'll decide."

Lee told Fermat that a drink sounded mighty fine, and our first toast was in his honor.

Chapter XXX

Next day, Monday, when Lee and I git up, we seen that Fermat had laid out fresh clothes for us. They was all somber black clothes, same as he worn. We rose from our beds—the first such beds we'd slept in for time out of mind—and geared up like widows to a funeral. Since it was a holy house, Ruth had slep' in a different part of the church entirely, and I reckoned she warn't awake yet.

The sun shot straight into our window, so I judged it was mid-morning. Soon as we stepped out, an old woman with sunken cheeks and a flowered hat came down the hallway and says, "Are you ready, Pastor Smith?"

By now it was my habit to say yes when called by another name than my own, though I wondered why Fermat bothered to give me a name that belonged to most of the Morons in town. So I followed her down the hall to where I guessed Fermat was waiting. But then she jinked left and took us to the fellowship hall, where the whole blamed town—it looked like—had come out to meet the new pastors-in-training, with the pastors themselves no where in sight.

The lady with the flowered hat directed me to the pulpit and says, "Good luck." That's when I reckoned I understood what had happened during our powwow last night. We'd been hoodwinked into playing the part of new pastors to the town so Fermat and Desmond—if that were their true names—could light out. That Lee and I was both pastors was a fact as plain as day to this congregation, for here we was in church vestments standing at the pulpit.

Lee reckoned same as I reckoned, only a second quicker. "Go on, Joe," he says, before I could goad him.

"Speak for The Lord?" I says. "Ain't that plain heresy?"

"Not if you read from scripture," he says, and handed me a Webster's bible, of which there was several upon the pulpit and the lectern.

So, without any other plan, I opened up the Webster's bible and scanned the contents page until I find a book called "Numbers." Well, I reckoned that one would be the easiest to read and explain, so I flipped open to the middle—sure enough there was numbers on all the lines—and hit upon one where it was fit to begin a sermon.

"So Balaam rose in the morning, saddled his ass, and went," I read. "And the angel of The Lord stood in the way for an adversary against him. Now he was riding upon his ass, and the ass saw the angel of The Lord standing in the way, and his sword drawn in his hand: and the ass turned and went into the field: and Balaam smote the ass, to turn her onto the path."

I paused at this juncture because I never remembered hearing my pastor in St. Petersburg sermonize about ass-smiting and was expecting something ruther different from what I heard fall from my own lips. So after a deep breath I took it up again, only to discover this happened twice more in succession, with Balaam's ass being blocked by the angel of The Lord and stopping in its tracks, then being smote by the impatient rider. Then something happened that I never expected, even if I lived to be older than Methuselah.

"And The Lord opened the mouth of the ass, and she said to Balaam, 'What have I done to thee, that thou hast smitten me these three times?' And Balaam said to the ass, 'Because thou hast mocked me: I would there were a sword in my hand, for now would I kill thee.' And the ass said to Balaam, 'Am not I thy ass?'"

When I stopped right in the middle of my sermon, the congregation stirred uncomfortably, and waited while I re-read the passage quietly to myself, since I could hardly believe that what I just read was a man a-carrying-on like that with his ass. When Lee nudged me, I quickly finished up the next couple of lines, where The Lord appeared to Balaam

171

and scolded him for smiting his ass, who only ever wanted to avoid bumping into the angel.

"So," I says, shutting the book a tad too loudly for a silent, echoey room, "a lot of folks wonder what this story means." My eyes dart all around the room just in case there were some clues in the corners where the spiders lived. "I cain't say I blame 'em."

Then I spotted Zeb the bo in the front pew, looking as anxious as I feel, and when he seen that I seen him, he started gesturating wildly, though I cain't puzzle out what he means. He just looked like a fool making signs with his hands, all boggle-eyed. Just then I hit upon a thought. "But there's only one question you need to answer when it comes to this story. Are you Balaam? Or are you Balaam's ass? The Lord *knows* that none of us is an angel, so they's only two things you can be in the story. You can be Balaam, blind to The Lord, beating up on others who heed His presence. Or, you can be Balaam's ass and *see* The Lord yourself and speak up in His defense, and run the risk of folks fixing you with a funny stare and shouting, 'Hey, look at 'im! A talking ass!'"

I was finding my stride now, and I ran with it, in spite of all Zeb's gesturating. "Look within yourself, and every one of you will find a talking ass. Hain't you been whipped *at least* three times by some master or another? Hain't you been told a *hundred* times that there's no angels, nor any Lord of the angels?"

You wouldn't believe the outcry of amens that come at me then, and it was no longer a question of whether I could pass as a preacher, but whether there was any poor sinner out there who could resist my powerful sermonizing.

Was I channelling His will? I cain't say for sure, but it warn't my own, and that was as good an explanation as any I could divine.

After I spoke there was a line of congregants waiting to shake the hand of the new preacher, who was me. I'd reckon

I shook more hands in an hour than I had during the rest of my 35 years. For all the practice I was getting, I begun to vary the grip: the pressure, the position, the duration. Zebediah stood by waiting for an opening to jump in and give me his news, but I reckoned at least it could wait for all the good folks of Great Salt Lake to touch palms with their surrogate savior.

Finally, when the line had dwindled to none, and even the old ladies had been talked out (even when I ain't wearing vestments, I'm the sort of feller to whom pious old ladies love to talk), Lee turned toward me and he shook my hand too, so impressed was he at my ministering.

"I have to hand it to you," Lee says. "That was one strange sermon, but you made me a believer!"

"Maybe it warn't the worst thing in the world that those rascals skipped out and left us a church to run," I says.

Zeb couldn't hold it in any longer. "Them boys ran off and took the church coffers with 'em, *and* your lady!"

I was still high from my performance on the pulpit, but this punctured the veil of my pride. My stomach and heart switched places, so that the former felt throbbing full of blood, and the latter felt empty. "They got Ruth?"

"Sure did, and they was gone before the first light of dawn."

"Why didn't you say so?" I says, scolding.

"I tried, bo," Zeb says. "But you cain't run now, not when the whole town can see you go. If you duck out in the daytime, they'll tar and feather you as impostors. This crowd loves a righteous cause, and there ain't no cause that's more righteous than chasing the devil out of the Lord's house."

I looked to Lee for his advice, but he'd gone quiet, his face as pale as an albino hare.

Zeb was always anxious to please, but in his twitching

nervousness he did no such thing. Zeb smiled and looked at you expectantly, like the sort of feller who waited and waited for a tribe to come along that he could belong to—even if that tribe was just two hoboes out on the road.

In the pastor's office, Zeb laid out a map of the U.S. territories west of the rockies; the three of us huddled around it as though 't was a hearth. Lee drew circles and lines on the map with his finger, like Napoleon 'mongst his generals. San Francisco was our aim, and Lee's home, but he warned us that between us and our goal was the lawlessest, gunslingingest, unfriendliest country we was ever likely to trudge through, and since the conductors all knowed it, there warn't a single train that stopped anywhere but the capitol, Carson City. And when they do, they should expect to be robbed as sure as you'd expect a receipt at the greengrocer's. So it'd be wise to travel by carriage for a stretch, at least until we made Silver City, not too far out from Carson. It was there, we gambled, that the rapscallions had taken Our Ruth.

We lit out that night under the glow of the same bright desert moon in which we'd arrived, so the impression that Bring'em Young and Fermat and Desmond and Pastor Smith had all been part of a long dream was strong. But then the memory of Ruth's abduction would renew itself, and I'd feel a keen cut in my side and a roiling in my gut. This sense of purpose brought a clarity to things that made my dreams of dying in a cave feel small.

As fortune had it, Zeb was a coachman and the Evaginical church had its own coach, but we had to yoke it to some strange horses. The first was lumpy and spotty, with a feathery mane that would have been excessive on the head of an old lady, who in addition to his neigh and whinny let out a nasal bleating now and then that was so peculiar it sounded like a sheep and a pig after coupling—a sigh that was satisfied, sad, and disgusted all at once. The other one was a small, dark mare—I would wager my last diamond that these unimaginative folk named her Midnight—but proud of bearing, and made no sounds at all. If they warn't the saddest pair of horses this country has seen, I'm a pooka; but in my Injun-warrior fantasy, our idle theft of church property was a horse-raid worthy of Geronimo.

But if the shocking-bright desert moonlight leant a Romantic hue to the proceeding flight, for us it only meant sleeplessness and worry. As if to balance our good fortune with the bad, Zeb turned out to be—in the lamentable tradition of Western coachmen—a compulsive storyteller with a stock of anecdotes that changed in scale but never in kind. If Slade, outlaw of outlaws, had shot ten men the first account, the next time Zeb told it, old Slade was sure to have plugged twelve. But you could count on Slade, in all his adventures, never to hunt up the perfect spot for a nap, or take up the fiddle, or find himself beset with guilt over all the Irish and Injuns and Chinamen he'd ended.

Chapter XXXI

Lee and I was riding in back like the quality, the vast yellow earth and endless white sky cut down to a sliver in the curtain, through which we surveyed our wild surroundings. The carriage road ran along the railway line, slightly downhill, and wrapping around a mountain ruther than plowing through it. I catched myself stealing coy glances at the train as it passed, with all the power of a charging rhinoceros, menacing the land all the way to Silver City. Marveling, from the inside of a slow-moving carriage, at the speed of the train, I wondered whether we'd ever catch up with the men who took Ruth.

The further that stagecoach crawled into dusty Nevada, the more of a cloud it raised up. The red sands of Yuta were far behind now and settled there on the hard earth with no one to disturb it, as still as a photograph.

Lee found distraction in reading, then began to compose a letter—for his family, I reckoned. As for me, watching the wheels kick up dust was just what I had a mind to do, and I done it all the sunlit hours of the day. It turns out, when you ain't huddling in the dark of a boxcar or clinging on for dear life to the rods of a train, there's all manner of idleness with which a body can occupy itself. I spent my idleness thinking on Ruth's absence and pondering the joys of hobo life I was missing from the back of a stagecoach.

Once I'd exhausted the engine of my imagination-maker, I started to number the memories I'd had on the hobo road. They was mostly unpleasant, but nowhere in all these memories could I locate the kind of misery I deserved, but I was glad to suffer one way or t' other. I counted them up like coins, until they began to feel heavy, and I sank under their burden.

—

That night my dream was the same as a memory. It was my early years aboard *The Ragamuffin*, and it was one of the miserablest nights I can recall—mournful and moonfull, drouthy and windy so that the hull chopped the waves and the waves chopped back with the same force, heaving her up in the air and down at every cut. We was every last man-Jack one of us bored and queasy. By and by on our journey we came across a vessel that just sat in the water like a buoy, making no reply to our signals nor fleeing at our approach. An abandoned schooner was good medicine to relieve doldrums, but the ship looked empty, and it appeared to have already been plundered by quicker or more industrious pirates. I boarded first—I never board first, since I am loathe to kill on account of my Christian childhood, but when it comes to occupying an *empty* boat, I am as full of as much bluff and bluster as I have air in my lungs. I carried a flintlock, though it was as clean and shiny as any pistol whose muzzle-end had never met black powder. I ball-loaded it and funneled-in the powder, as proof of my readiness to kill.

Standing on this lugger, with its torn-up mainsail and fishy stench, I started to shout out the usual threats. If a man surprises me, I says, I'll use his skin to make a drum. But if he come out straightaway, I might even leave 'im with his clothes on. Every second that goes by without a man showing himself, I says, is another toe I'll chop off and string on my necklace. There's just the rocking silence of a boat on plunking water.

Then all a-sudden the top of a fish-barrel pops open, but it's a man who pokes out. His arms is raised, but I'm so startled, I p'int my flintlock and fire. There's a cloud of smoke, but I either missed or misfired, since he climbs out and rushes at me with intense eyes and grasping hands. O evil instinct! O devilish nature! He should have cried out for mercy. He should have begged for another minute of life. I should have done anything other than unsheathe my saber and jab until my arm tired, until it was a mass of flesh in front of me that could have been a fish as much as a man.

Another pair of eyes looked back at me from under the lid of the barrel, and they belonged to a boy. I turned back and cried out to my comrades to go back, for these men were diseased, ridden with the pox. It was mercy that the crew heeded me, though 't was my very ruse of an exposure that led to my quarantine on a lonely island off the African coast.

I wish my dreaming mind had seen fit to alter this moment, even slightly, but it cursed me with the fresh memory of it, and it was a bully thing to be awake and on land the next morning, though my jaw was sore from all the grinding I done in my sleep.

—

By and by our coach came to a full stop somewhere in the desert, and I stirred up and seen that we was stopped nowhere near a town, but down in a ravine. I volunteered to peek my head out of the curtain. There a horned bull stood righteous proud, like a monument fixed in our path. The horses stamped, and Zeb whistled, but the bull neverminded the horses or the driver, just blinked.

After an hour passed, Zeb determined the only way to move the beast was to fire off a warning shot, which he done. When that didn't inspire the result he hoped, but only agitated Old Lady and Midnight, Zeb shot at the bull directly, which act led to the predictable: instead of a live bull blocking up our path, 't was a deceased one.

"How're we goin' to catch up to Ruth and the rascals who took her *now*?" Lee says, looking anxious as I feel, and I thunk what a generous and forgiving soul Lee must be to earnestly look after the fate of a woman who so seemed to despise him.

Zeb insisted we were stranded, and he occupied himself by setting up camp in the road. Lee stirred up a fire, and I gazed upward. From this vantage, we seemed to be in a trench that coiled around and around a mountain, riding inward. The sky was the only surface that changed in this landscape, as the mood of nature changed with the weather. I never thunk before how pleasant and welcome a thing a cloud was—not only for the water it emptied upon a dry earth, but for the relief from utter repetition of color and form the desert vista afforded.

If I ever doubted his worth as a companion, Lee increased the value of his stock now by skinning the bull, carving out the best cuts from the flank and the loin, and covering it all with paper for us to feast on that night. The smoke from the fire rose and joined the lighter fog of the cloud, to make a conversation between the mists. Old Lady sighed his awful post-coital sigh, and Midnight said nothing at all.

Zeb mistook the silence for an invitation.

"Did'ya ever hear about the time old Slade held up a whole platoon at gunpoint?" he said.

I reckoned I had, and said so, but when I saw Zeb's face fix sadly on the flicker of the fire, I was sorry for depriving him of the pleasure of telling it. "Got any stories without a Mexican standoff?" I can remember a time when I delighted to stories of shooting prowess and adventuresome outlaws, but life at sea and on the road had raised my standard so that I could hardly abide another tale of toughs acting tough in a tough fashion. Give me a bo story any day.

"If it's a Western story you're a-wanting, you ought to brace yourself better for gunslinging and lawbreaking," Zeb confessed, "...unless its Shortie Bigler."

This was a strong enough enticement for me to revise upward my estimation of Zeb's gift for tall tales. "Who's

Shortie Bigler?" I says.

Zeb's face lit up brighter than the full moon *and* the campfire. "Shortie was the worst gambler the Nevada territory ever saw, which makes him the worst gambler any place."

"Worst as in *worst*?" I says. "Or worst as in most born-to-it?"

"No, bo," says Zeb. "He was the plain *worst*. Listen: Shortie started out a 49-er just like Henry Comstock. He left behind a mother and five sisters in Virginia with a promise to make them a fortune in gold. He made it all the way to San Francisco by selling shoe leather, and if he'd a kep' up that business he may have made more of himself some day than a cautionary tale."

Lee and I traded a confidential happy look, our dusty faces and tooth-rot accentuated by the orange glare of the campfire. Even amongst boes, it occurred to me, the three of us were now in competition for the beardedest.

"But when he git there, he start panning, and he pan up North and down South, and the only nuggets he find was rocks, and it warn't quartz neither. After months of plum nothing, and practically starved, he set himself up at the bar of the saloon and begs the proprietor to take his day's yield for a bowl of grit, though none of it were gold. The keeper looks down at the shells Shortie'd laid down on the bar and says 'Why, Shortie, was you panning for gold *in the ocean*?'"

That line performed its job admirably when it came to Lee, who was so tickled he nearly fell over and spilled the pan of sizzling fresh beef onto the dusty road—then there'd a' been mulligan again tonight for these boes—until his laugh wore down to a chuckle slighter than the crackle of a fire. As for me, I wanted to laugh too, but the memory of cadging at the Lone Jack Saloon stayed me. I reached under my coat and rubbed the diamond back and forth in my fingers through the leather of my poke. Come to think on't, "panning for gold in the ocean" is what I'd been doing for ten years at sea.

Zeb, mistaking my grim silence for literary criticism, took up the challenge thusly: "So Shortie figured he was beat, and he quit panning for gold. How was he a-goin' to make his fortune and make good on his promise to look after his womenfolk? Well, like many another failure, he took up speculation in the market. He sold enough shoe leather to get back to New York City and even bought him a proper frock coat and a pair of trousers so he ain't look like he was living on the street, which he was.

"On the American Exchange, Shortie specialized in war industries. He speculated in Shipbuilding & Engineering, but nobody told Shortie the war between the states would be fought on land! Just like that, his shoe-leather money shrunk to where it could fit in his hand. He used what little was left to invest in munitions—figuring armies always need ordnance—but as it turned out Shortie'd picked the only firearms manufacturer in the nation still trafficking flintlock pistols, which nobody needed except maybe to play pirate. So now Shortie had to take out a loan to buy 100 shares of U.S. Steel, sure that this was the safest investment for a nation at war; then the slaves was freed and all a sudden folks didn't need so many shackles."

This was said too soberly for drawing a laugh, but Zeb calculated this would put me off guard, and he warn't wrong.

"Pretty soon the other speculators got wise to Shortie's curse, and they learned to short stocks as soon as Shortie bought in, so investors made heaps of money on his predicament, but he could never make a dime for himself that a-way. Even when he tried to go against his own instincts and pick a thing to invest in at random, Shortie could never get around the fact that it was still *his instincts* which was telling him to pick at random, so it'd always fail. It was as though proving that Shortie Bigler was a blamed failure were a matter of principle for the good Lord.

"Destitute and demoralized, Shortie went for a walk, thinking to put an exclamation point at the end of his sad life's sentence by jumping off the New York to Brooklyn Bridge even as it was being constructed. He would have been the first sorry soul to have thus taken his own life, and gotten his fame that-a-way, but even that quest proved a failure when he survived the dive into the cold East River and washed up like driftwood on the shore of New Jersey."

"Come on, Zeb," says Lee. "You're ribbing us now."

Zeb just shook his head and looked at us cold and earnest as the moonglow and the firelight grew dimmer.

"What'd Shortie do then?" I put in.

"He was on the New Jersey shore! Standing just a stone's throw from the lousiest crew of sharps and hustlers, what *could* a gambler like Shortie do? Shortie never stood a chance. First thing he heard when he came on dry land was a couple of beach bums laughing about how a thoroughbred named Mama's Pride was set to race that day. Shortie Bigler had traversed the country trying to make his own mama proud, so he took it as his destiny to bet on this horse. The Lord had spared him so that he could live out this very moment. *And* why not *trust my instinct?* he told himself. *What else has a man got, anyhow?*

"Well it was ten hours at the races before Shortie found himself so far in debt to so many different gangsters that they fought amongst themselves for the privilege of finishing the poor man's botched suicide."

"It's true," I says. "We run across a bo monicker of Jersey Joe, who tried to yegg our pokes. You'll find dishonest folks 'mongst them, sure as your born."

Zeb shook his finger at me. "But the gangsters never git 'em. Shortie was so riled up from no sleep and losing everything he had over and over again, he stomped over in his soggy boots, a-ranting and a-raging at the jockey who'd been riding Mama's Pride. Shortie and the little feller had such a knock-down, drag-out bout that all the gamblers and gangsters from here to Timbuktu gethered round and start taking bets on a winner.

"For all his failure in every sphere of life, Shortie could hold up his end in a tussle, but his misfortune was that the little feller scrapped like a bulldog. Though he were half a regular man's size, 't was as if a regular man had been squeezed down to his shape but kep' his weight, so he struck like a thunderclap and kicked like a mule. The rider of Mama's Pride also had a taunting way about him, squeaking out so many condemnations of Shortie's blood and family and name that it made grown men blush."

Here Zeb stopped and seem to just stare into the campfire, and we answered his silence with the obvious questions. "So who win the fight?" I says.

"Well, who d'ya think?" he says.

"My money is on the scrapper jockey," says Lee.

"I'm with Shortie," I says.

"You'd both be right," Zeb says. "That jockey spun around like a fighting chinaman and swept the legs out from under him." I looked toward Lee to see if there were any perturbance, but there warn't any. "And when Shortie fell, he fell like Ajax on his own sword, but on his way down he landed on the little jockey and drove him into the grass like a nail into pine."

"So Shortie did it!" I says. "His luck turned."

"You think so, Joe?" says Zeb. "You think the rest of those jockeys would let any fool crawl off the beach and trample their own? No, bo. What followed was the tiniest riot you ever saw, with the smallest, proudest jockey in the lead, wearing a Frenchman's whiskers. That mini-mob picked up poor, disoriented Shortie Bigler like a sack of wet clothes and wrung him out good. Then they dumped him on a patch of prickly bushes on the Pennsylvania side!"

"That is a story," I had to admit. "But how'd you come

to know 'im?'"

"It was just a year ago that Shortie showed up here in Washoe County like tumbleweed in the desert, and that's where he finally settled. But the story don't end before one last gamble: he rode stagecoach just like we done, and that's how I come to meet him. He was so broke he couldn't buy shoe leather, so it was the charity of a lady that allowed him to ride as far as Washoe on her way out West. Her name was Sara and, get this, she was the daughter of a 49-er who'd staked a claim and found a vein of ore in the same county on the Pacific coast where Shortie's first gold-panning scheme had earned him only ridicule.

"The good lady's charity was the most luck Shortie ever had in all his years, and he fell for her even harder than he fell upon the poor rider of Mama's Pride—"

"—This don't end well," Lee put in.

"You're a quick study, Lee," Zeb says, "because on the way to Washoe, Shortie thought he'd try his luck one more time; he antes up and goes all-in, and in his foolhardiness confesses his love, and before they reach St. Louis, he's already asked Sara to marry him."

"What'd she say?" I says.

Zeb lifted the corner of his lip. "She says the worst thing a girl could ever say to a man in Shortie's position."

"'Let's not ruin the friendship'?" guessed Lee.

"'I wouldn't marry the likes of you if I was starving and you was made of taffy'?" I hazarded.

"Them's both good, but here's what she sure says: 'Shortie, *let's make a deal.*' Sara says that if this down-on-his-luck gambler can guess her one heart's desire, then she would marry him. Futhermore, since Sara was an only child, as her husband Shortie would receive a handsome dowry and be named sole beneficiary of her father's wealth. He spent the rest of their long journey pondering and pondering, and it warn't until they reached this very encampment where we now sit that Shortie spoke up. So ten miles outside of Silver City, without a wooden nickel in his pocket, his fate resided in a man's ability to guess what was in a woman's heart."

Lee whistled. "What did he guess?" I says.

"He dasn't," Zeb says. "Shortie, finally, had learned never to trust his instincts, and he resolved that ruther than toss out a bad guess and insult Sara with his poor insight into a woman's heart, he'd let the woman he loved go free and bear the familiar burden of poverty. He said goodbye at the Silver City station, and was never heard from ag'in, until I spotted a tombstone in the lonesomest corner of the Dakota territory.

"And *that*'s why there ain't ever been a worse gambler than Shortie Bigler, here or anywhere."

Zeb folded his hands in front of him like it settled the matter. The wind pushed gently at the tip of the fire, turning our faces orange, then black, then orange again.

"I reckon you got the score wrong, Zeb," I says.

"Why? D'you know of a worse gambler than Shortie Bigler?"

"I reckon Shortie came out further ahead in this game than any man I know."

"How d'you reckon?"

"He ventured acrost the country twice, saw more of this great land than a body can say, keered about his Mama, fought for the pride of his family, and fell in love with a good woman. It warn't a long life, but in the end his balance was zero the same as any bo that ever walked the wanderpath."

Zeb nodded at me slowly like it was precious wisdom, even though't was only so much rationalization and defensiveness. Here we was chasing after the scoundrels who kidnapped Ruth, and I was suffering for hope. I'd gone broke near as many times as Shortie, and I was looking for some assurance that by going West I was moving in the right direction. But the fire went cold, and the black wood smoked but gave no warmth, and all that was left to do was put the embers out in the Missouri way.

Chapter XXXII

To the immediate North of the last natural spring before the true desert begins, just East of Silver City, there is a big house called Grand Hotel, set up for visitors who've struck ore to enjoy the spoils of wealth in the company of fellow men and women of leisure. The pillars of Grand Hotel declared its importance from a distance, and as you approached it, the friezes and moldings, with its baroque detail, confirmed it. Within this oasis, there was every manner of distraction and every category of food. We reckoned, if anywhere, that this would be the ultimate destination of these deceivers who called themselves Pastors and robbed churches and kidnapped Amish girls and turned honest hoboes into dishonest churchmen. The only hazard was the local politicians and religious leaders who came there to hunt big-game contributors to their churches and campaigns. Seeing as we had no money to give, I reckoned it warn't much of a hazard at-all.

Soon as we learned of Grand Hotel, Zeb, Lee, and I designed to gain entry, infiltrate their rank, and reconnoiter the Ruth situation from a more comfortable spot. Whilst we did, it was only good disguise to enjoy the bounty within. Wearing Tomlin's fine clothes—though faintly worn down already—we'd begun to feel entitled to other fine things, and Lee's feasting at the Denver ballroom in partic'lar had accommodated him to the palate of the leisure class. It was only right, Lee says, that such things be enjoyed by all. So we started in the kitchen, and went about liberating the fresh fruit, then the French pastry with cream, then the pig roast, and finally the wine.

While the quality was all attending a speech on good colon health in the north wing of Grand Hotel—a big house has wings, Lee learned me—we lifted the lids off of pots and let the steam enter our noses. When I accidentally spilled a covered pan on the floor, I near fainted from the robust aroma of poultry and spice. Zeb played look-out in the hall until we was sure the cooks and maids was all gathered in the lecture hall.

In the kitchen, Lee assumed the posture of a connoisseur. He began stirring soups, sampling aperitifs, adding herbs to the sauce, and ladling it into our bowls until we was full. It was as though we stepped into a gymnasium and he turned into a gymnast. He was just a tramping fool like us, but in the kitchen, he reverted to a former, civilized self in a way that gainsaid the hobo life.

When our bellies were taut against our belts, Zeb struck on the idea to take in a sweat lodge, which was a quarter mile further West, over a path of cold rocks. This was an amenity for the idle rich, and our burden was to fit in. We carried our clothes in our arms, and sneaked through the chill air of December until we could shepherd ourselves in with the quality. When we got a mite closer, I seen a dozen or more russet triangles poking out from the ground on the horizon like pyramids, or spires, or spear-points. These hot-stone tipis was made by the Injuns, but had been taken over mostly by the richest and whitest Coloradans on holiday. Now that it was nearly Christmas, and our tan skin from life on the road had growed dim, I reckoned we'd fit in with the average. Fortunately for us boes, beards was still the fashion in the year of our Lord 1871.

In the steam lodge, it was a rum crowd, as jolly from wine as any hobo in a jungle. But instead of boes, these was bankers and astrologers, rich doctors and mental patients, the sons of industry and their "gurus" who'd taught them neat phrases like "find the god within yourself" that they may or may not have taken from shastas and vedas from the East. In their bare skins, you could scarcely tell the difference between them and regular folks.

As they talked stock-trading and villainthropy, I fought with myself on how to broach the subject of Ruth to these strangers. "Not to slander the present company," I says finally, "but I wish there was womenfolk somewhere in this lodge."

A couple of the corpulent rich nodded their assent. "I wish there were women in this *country*," says one with a confidence borne of his station. "But ladies are too delicate for the rugged landscape of the West."

"D'you know of any exceptions?" I says.

"Ho-ho!" says another one, just as privileged to assert his opinions. "This fellow is looking for a madam in the desert, and I reckon he'll find one."

That's twice, for the Lord's book, that I'd been mistaken for a man looking to pay for a woman's affection.

"I've seen a lady," says Lee, pretending for the moment that he warn't in my company, but just an unattached Chinee of independent means, "who come into Grand Hotel in the company of two gentlemen. She was fine and richly dressed, but her choice of traveling companions suggests she's... less than respectable."

"I seen her too," says one, the rare skinny feller with pop-out eyes who looked like a George but never said his name. "She was with them Wesleyans and such."

"They're *Wesleyans* now?" says Zeb, almost exposing our gambit, but since Zeb always spoke in such a manner that all present felt at liberty to ignore him, the only thing he exposed was his hairiness, compared to the sow-like skin of the rich folks, who was every one pink and hairless. Their backs flared as orange as fire.

"Grand Hotel has every kind of cult and false religion you can name," says the one skinny feller who looked like his name was George. "Those Wesleyans, they all go out to The Bulge and copulate with the Spiritualists and the Swedenborgians." For all his attempt at scorn, I never seen a judge so eager to detail the crimes he was presently condemning.

"That's what happens," he says, "when you remove God's judgment and try to decide right and wrong for yourself." Sussing out where his moral authority came from—to condemn the moral authority of so many sects who made it their business to challenge the moral authority of other religions—just made my head hurt.

"Well," I says, "they say it is easier for a camel to fit through the eye of a needle…"

No sooner had I begun to recite this scriptural wisdom, when these unclothed captains of industry turned on me with unfriendly eyes and stood up in the lodge naked and menacing, so we had to scramble away nude in the darkness or be revealed as impostors and assailed by the quality. We clumb over an outcropping of rocks—the same we'd traversed on the way in, luckily, since we'd left our clothes upon them—and as soon as we got beyond the range, we reckoned we was home free, since we was now past carriage-country and heading west through the rocky desert on foot.

West of Grand Hotel is a formation all the locals refer to as the Bulge, where all the land is made up of rust-colored stone, which is bordered by a ridge that forms a near-perfect circle. Within the circle there was a couple of bulbous stones out of which sprang an obelisk with a slight curve, making it look to all appearances like men's parts. So the local folks took to calling it the "Male Bulge" instead. And this bulge presided over a bacchanal.

It is here, at the hour of long shadows, that we encountered among the strangest scenes I ever had the misfortune to witness. We mounted a ridge, and below us in the recess of the Bulge was a tangle of human souls—or ruther, bodies— writhing in a cold imitation of pleasure, spread across the red sand like worms festering a crabapple. These men and women had an Oriental guide from California—same as I did!—by the name of Gary Ong, who led them through the naked motions they was expected to make, barking like a general to his army as they fondled each other anonymously. There was curious sorts and curious behavior amongst these sorts, such as men with faces planted flat against the ground and their rears up, men contorting their bodies and stretching their necks around so that their heads appeared to be turned the wrong way on their torsos, men walking on hot coals and lifting heavy rocks—even a woman or two laying prone exposed fully to the sun and covered in a dry layer of manure, expressing an apparently serious hope that this would draw "toxins" away from their skins.

Now and then a feller would object to the abject treatment he was due to receive, and Gary would oil things by saying, "Do it for *The Lord*. You will not please Him until you have tried *every experience* the world has to offer." Pleasing our Lord, from what I gethered by listening in, was a matter of becoming "actualized," which only come after experimenting with every kind of depravity. The less willing a body was to compromise itself to this guru's whim, the less "actual" he was said to be.

I've been a dozen different things in my life, but I'd never learned to be a moral man. Now, in a foreign land once again, suddenly I found myself counting heresies, listing and cataloguing every sin like a priest. Why should I care about a few dozen of the bored rich prodding themselves with hot pokers just to remind themselves they still had nerves? Yet in my judgmental heart I grimaced and deemed them most foul. But even as I wagged my finger, I dasn't look away from the object toward which I p'inted.

"Is that man your kin?" I asks Lee.

Lee squinched up his face and says, "Why don't you ask 'im?"

Taking his expression to mean "no," I says, "Well I reckon I will." Leaving Zeb and Lee hidden there on the crest, I skittered down the rocks to the makeshift courtyard where all the bodies was writhing. Having narrowly escaped that sweat lodge with only our skins—and not yet garbed with the glad rags bunched up in my arms—I reckoned I fit right in with this crowd.

"Anybody seen a girl by the name of Ruth?" I says, descending the sheer face of a yellow rock at the same time that the sun begun to creep below the horizon. To that crowd of bodies, I must have cut a strange figure, a shadow emerging from a beam of light. Yet this crew had long become accustomed to miracles, deadened to strange phenomena.

"We don't use our given names here," a "lady" says who'd got tired and set herself apart from the tangle. "We use our spirit-names."

"Well," I says, "spirit-Ruth was dressed like a society lady, or she may just have got on her old clothes, which was simple, Amish…" Seeing her blank and sympathetic look, I remembered that clothes, too, were unknown in this land.

"Now that I think about it," she says, bug-eyed, "there *was* a young lady with two gentlemen who sheltered themselves among our order." I wouldn't say she had a penetrating stare, but a stare that was trying its hardest to mesmerize, though all it did was cause her hair to stand out from her temples. "They acted awful suspicious, like they were uncomfortable with their beautiful human bodies."

"Did they use her in immoral ways?" I says, my voice peaking slightly, trying my best to disguise my fears.

"Not that I know of," she says, and winced when she heard the word "immoral" spoken aloud. "None of them were actualized, or even *focussed*."

This was a new one to me. In order to get actualized, she learned me, folks had to be focussed first. To be focussed meant to be so in-the-moment that you give your body over completely to Master Ong, who helped you to become actualized.

She led me to Master Ong, who she promised could answer *any* question I could ever devise, but would only answer three from a stranger unless he swore to join his movement. But, I wondered, which three questions should I ask him?

Talking to Master Ong, I learned, a body needn't worry about asking too many questions, as his preferred manner of speaking was the soliloquy. Master Ong, I learned, was the sorter man in possession of a great many fascinating facts, and if all those facts happened to concern his achievements and virtues, and if you happened to harbor a deeper respect for him as a result, he warn't accountable for the consequence. Did you know, fr'instance, that a bald man is more virile than a well-coiffed one? Or that men of median height are said to be the most intelligent? It was only coincidence that the feller who told me so was exactly five-foot-eight-inches and down to a couple a tufts behind his ears.

"Do you mean to say you could answer any question I throw your way?" I says, skeptical.

"Yes," Master Ong says.

"And I don't get but three?" I says.

"Yes," he says. "Well, you just asked two. So now you only have one left."

"Dang!" I says. There were loads of questions knocking around in my skull, and it would have been a rare peace to unburden them.

"Those men who came here from Grand Hotel with a lady, then moved on: where was they headed?"

Master Ong folded his thin arms. "They spoke about going West, to Injun country."

"That's the way we're a-goin'!" I says, and skated away before he could rope me in again. I rejoined Zeb and Lee by and by, and my legs rejoined their trousers. It was another hour down the road before I realized Master Ong had never answered the question proper and just told me where they *spoke of* going, ruther than where they sure went.

Chapter XXXIII

We was nearly out of Nevada before I ever seen a real Injun. For all the months I spent heading West on the hobo road, I never came across one until we went overland by carriage. I s'pose the Injuns warn't as fond of riding the rails, for reasons I reckon I can cipher out. But soon as we reached the border of California territory, dried out from so many desert miles, we come upon Injun land. It was a valley full of horses and Injuns—more of the former than the latter, I believe—and to my surprise there was as many children as full-grown men and women. I must have known that Injuns started out the same way as white men—starting out as babies and growing upward—but it was a shock to see the young ones parrot the behavior of their elders, and twice the shock to see the elders engage the young 'uns in their play and sport. They warn't so severe and somber as the pictures I'd seen.

Approaching the Sierra Nevada range now, looming so vast in front of us like there warn't any such thing as a horizon—like they was all tired giants, crouched and rain-drunk—my need for rest, before undertaking the overland haul, was absolute, and it wouldn't have mattered to me if we settled in a badger hole. Even if these Injuns *had been* the severe and somber sort, I still would have seen them as saviors from the empty desert.

In the foreground, a camp of pointed tipis emerged, looking at first like foothills to the mountain range. When we come near enough to see the spars crossed at the peaks where the hides didn't fully cover the wood, we was met by a welcoming party who greeted us as though we was expected guests.

I fancied an Injun guide, like ole Squinto had been for John Smith or Sack-o-Jawas become for Lewis and Clark, would be the right thing for this venture. Somehow I was led to expect that when I finally came across an Injun, he'd be an elf of a man, small but proud, always speaking in haltering half-sentences or not at all. But these men was loud and regular-sized; and one partic'lar Injun was a giant, clear over seven feet tall, and full of boisterous laughter and idle talk. His name was Honi, and his English was perfect because he had traveled around the country with the circus when at the age of fifteen he reached seven-foot. He'd met kings and queens, shook hands with Lincoln, and traveled in the company of artists and rich men. Once, the mayor of Providence presented him with a giant-sized bed, in case he should ever choose to set his head down there.

"Why'd you give up the sideshow life, Honi?" I says. "You could a' seen the whole world, made a fortune, and become a celebrated figure like Chang and Eng."

He sat down and held his knees. Even so posed, he was nearly my standing height. "Well, why do you think?"

Lee and I looked at each other. "You became disillusioned with the cosmopolitan life and decided it was a purer, simpler life at home amongst your people?" Lee ventures.

"They whipped you like an animal?" Zeb guessed.

"You didn't like folks staring at you all day and night?" I put in.

"No, boes," Honi says. "It's simpler than that. They found themselves another giant, from a bush tribe in central Africa, near a full inch taller than I am, so they sent me home."

"So you ain't the tallest man in the world after all?" Zeb says, reluctant to believe there was a man in the world as tall or taller than this giant.

"Nope," he says. "But I am glad of it."

I never asked Honi why he was glad to learn he warn't the tallest man in the world, but I wish I had. It left me unsettled. I'd have thought it would be a great comfort for a man to know he was the best, the most, or the onliest in something, anything, he does or is.

"Well, Honi, since you've got the highest perch, maybe you've spied what we're looking for from that height?" I says.

Honi gestures wide—wider than I knew was possible for a man—encompassing the big flat desert at the foot of the range, and says, "If it passed through this country, I saw it."

I exhale audibly, bracing myself for the prospect that we'd taken the wrong route, and would have to double-back the way we came before long. "We are looking for a white woman," I says, "by the name of Ruth."

"Well," says Honi, and he settled his chin on his wrist and creased up his brow. "I might be able to help you," here he looked up and cracked a smile, "but you might have to be less partic'lar about the name."

Zeb laughed a guffawing laugh, then catched himself, then found he cain't stop laughing even if he tried: holding it in just made a chuffing sound, until it come out in tears. Seeing me and Lee's expressions, Honi mimicked our air of solemnity and says, "There was a family of whites come through here and tried to take refuge amongst our people, for they were being pursued by a posse of miners who come all the way from Kansas. But our people weren't interested in a shoot-out with white strangers to protect a bunch of other strangers, so Chief Askum asked 'em to leave our land. Instead they give up the girl to the posse, who all high-tailed it into the range."

"Do you remember the feller's name who led that Kansas posse?" I says.

Honi struck a thinking pose, and in his stillness he looked even more made-of-stone than regular. "It was an English name, and it was a fine Palomino he rode," says Honi.

"That's Pendleton," I says, despairing at our ill luck, but feeling fortunate that we was on the right trail. Then, after I took up a think, I says, "What happened to the other strangers who brung her?"

"The fat one and the thin one?" says Honi.

"I would have gone with 'the short one and the tall one,'" I says, "but I reckon neither of them seems partic'larly tall from up there. They go by 'Fermat' and 'Desmond,' as I recall."

"Not anymore," says Honi. "Now they only answer to 'Uncas' and 'Chingachgook,' and occupy themselves these days with going amongst the people and propositioning 'Indian Princesses.'"

Eager to see the two swindlers thus engaged, I asked Honi where we might find the scoundrels Uncas and Chingachgook.

"Inola!" Honi calls out, and a large Injun woman—but hardly large enough to be Honi's equal—came our way and crouched beside us. I offered her my rock to sit on, but she declined, in English. Then Honi asked her a question in their vowelly talk—long and breathy, like Ruth's Pennsylvanian—which I later learned translated to "Where did the two crazy men go?"

Inola laughed heartily and responded—as Honi relayed to us—"We told them that we would all marry them if they built their own teepee, so they have been trying to figure out how to make a Numa home." *Numa* was the name by which "the people" knowed themselves.

I reckoned from their general mood of amusement that they never intended for Inola to marry poor Uncas or his companion Chingachgook. This seemed to me a reckless promise. "So what will you do if they actually succeed at building themselves a teepee?" I says.

Inola demonstrated her knowledge of our language by wiping tears of laughter from her eyes, and when she regained composure, says, "There's no risk of it. But it's good distraction to see them try."

"Is it too difficult?" says Zeb, who was as flummoxed as I was.

This one Honi had to explain to us, because Inola was lost to laughter again. "Well, Uncas and Chingachgook think it's easy, and they're not wrong, but there's a trick to it that they aren't accounting for. So I reckon there's no risk of success."

To appease our morbid curiosities, and thinking that the former Fermat and Desmond might be able to answer questions about Ruth's whereabouts, Honi and Inola brought us to the place where the men were trying to erect their teepee. They did an admirable job gathering materials, and they even went so far as to draft a construction plan, but for all their engineering, they warn't any farther along the job than laying it all out on the prairie grass. Uncas and Chingachgook was so absorbed in their colossal task, they scarcely noticed they was now in the company of other white men, including the one whom they duped into acting the part of a minister before an unsuspecting congregation, so they could kidnap an Amish girl.

Even when I hailed them, meaning to confront the rascals with their deception and criminality, they ignored me. 'T was almost as though they was truly changed, truly different—or *in*different—ruther than just adorned in the latest disguise. But Lee punctured through all the hey-theres and excuse-mes and grabbed Uncas by his bony shoulders, shaking him free of his contemplation of the wood, the hides, and the long grass in front of him. "Where's Ruth, you sons-a-devils, and what'd you do to her?" Then Lee threw Uncas to the ground, where he now lay amongst the flat idea of a teepee.

Chingachgook made a ca'ming motion with his hands, acting the peace-maker priest again after all the rottenness he'd done. "Your lady-friend ain't harmed. We never had to threaten her or tie her up; we only told her that the hobo and the chinaman was abducted at night, and we was goin' to go after 'em. So she come along without a fight, but when we arrived here last week and she seen how we intended to hide out, Ruth got wise to us and tried to light out. By then 't was too late, and she was abducted by another gang."

"Where'd they take her?" Lee says, raising his hand to a flinching Chingachgook.

"West, to the Sierras," he says. "There's but one path that heads that a-way, but they've got a day's head start."

Lee tightened his fists, and I was mighty impressed with his instinct for protecting a girl he hardly knew. But Honi reminded us that his people warn't inclined to allow white men to kill each other on their land. It'd invite more questions and controversy than they cared for. And besides, we was eager to catch up to Pendleton and rescue or ransom the girl from his gang. Though at the same time I reckon we was sick with the prospect of failing, and what would become of us if we caught up with the gang but never got Ruth back. We was now living in a story of the True West, I reckoned.

Then Lee he asks, "How did Pendleton get ahead of us?" to which I can give only a weak shrug.

"As much charm as Old Lady and Midnight have to you and me, Lee," says Zeb, "all their personality don't count for much when it comes to speed and endurance and good old-fashioned mettle. You get what you pay for, and our nags was free."

"*And*," says Lee, "somebody shot a bull that got stuck in our path."

"So, what now, boes?" says Zeb, eager to change the subject.

"Nothing's changed," I says, mustering the anger to overwhelm the fear a-stirring inside, "'cept that, ruther than hunting down a couple of lousy con men, now we are pursuing a whole posse of armed riders, hardened in the mines and motivated by a reward."

"Everywhere I go," Lee says, the scratch in his throat like the sound of a train docking at the station, "I become a hunted man."

Though before we went, we bade a fond farewell to Honi and Inola and all their hospitable siblings and cousins. Honi's hand swallowed mine when he shook it, and he patted us on the back in such a way that it propelled us onward.

"So, the teepee," I says to Honi. "What's the trick?"

"Since you're leaving, I suppose I'll tell you the great secret. The trick is this," Honi says, leaving all three of us in wide-eyed, gap-mouthed suspense. He counts out a single secret on his p'inter finger before we realize there's just the one step: "Ask for help." Seeing how our curiosities warn't fully appeased, Honi says, "It takes four to hoist the frame, and at least as many to tighten the buffalo skins. But if you ask for help, it ain't hard to accomplish. But so far, no white man who passed through has figured it out yet, though they drive themselves crazy making plans."

"Ain't it cheating?" I says. "To ask for help when they's the ones who are meant to build a teepee?"

"Says who?" says Honi, and afterwards, as the three of us ride West into the awesome ranges of the Sierra mountains, I wonder at the eternal spectacle of the natural world.

Chapter XXXIV

Some places I seen announce their beauty like a lady's laugh: it scarcely matters if it's meant as kind or scornful or indifferent, it's music. The products of nature might be there to serve our senses and affirm a Lord who could make such things as stars or oceans or egrets, or it might obey its own prerogatives, but either way you pluck it, what it amounts to is a world beautifully fatal or fatally beautiful. To straddle every gorge is to step lightly over death's maw; to cross over each narrow path lining each cliff is to dance on her collar. The gooseberries are all thorn and the corn lilies all p'ison, but the white and burgundy spots in the fertile green woods will garland our tombs nicely one day.

As I took the Sierra Nevada range one sun-speckled step at a time, I thunk on the Collinses of Denver, Colorado, and how they had bored us stiff with their prattle about how partial they was toward walking upwards. Now at last I seen what the dull Collinses was a-talking about and had a mind to go find some bystander and interrupt his bystanding by asking Had he ever considered the vertical?

There was still bramble and stuck tumbleweed low to the forest floor, but close up and at eye level it was all stalks of lily that circulated in the breeze and hanging willow aster that put out its honeyed-milk aroma; on every upward slope, sparrowhawks clumb the wind and osprey dove, leaving the river to spill sideways forever and rival the birdsong with its rambling.

Zeb, Lee, and I never says a word. There was nothing *to* say in such a place. Our input on the subject of this god-made world was super-fluidous.

Could you ever picture such a place as the showdown between a tribe of hungry hoboes and Pendleton's roughneck miners? I always believed that, once found, paradise would be a place for peace to reign; that the presence of Eden would suggest to every human heart heaven's grace and tend us toward mercy. But I've witnessed too many times beauty bring out man's worst, and the blood-hunger increased by the desire to lay claim to her spoils. What is mining about, I've had many an occasion to think since, but breaking the rock and anything else that stands between a man and his coveted shininess? How else is there to mine but to open the Earth's rich veins?

It was a lamentable error I made, to keep the fire lit through the night. These ranges were so vast, and we so small, and the night came so cold, and we had gotten so lucky so many times before, we figured we owed it to our bodies to bathe them in the light and the warmth the fire shed. Even Zeb was silent as we lay down our bedrolls, and we let the river lull us into a blessed sleep.

But when I woke, it was to the sound of horses clopping and stomping the earth, churning the loam and grass; we found ourselves suddenly surrounded by a half dozen old men of leather and a passel of red-cheeked young men. Old Lady ejected an unpleasant whinny, and Midnight looked bored in our general direction. "Lord protect us!" Zeb says, and shoots upright, a startlingly brave instinct for a man I'd come to think of as lacking in spirit.

Lee sat there with a patient expression. Only if you'd been traveling with him for months, as I had, could you detect the fear stirring just beneath the ca'm visage.

"What do we do with this bunch of dogs?" says a familiar no-necked feller who rested his beefy forearms on the pommel.

"I don't know, Cubie," Pendleton says. "What is to be done with a dog who bites his master?"

"Cut up his bitch?" says one fat whiskered feller.

"From the inside," says one man too young to be having such thoughts. The other men laughed to hear such wit from their junior.

"Well, I'd kill these men where they stand," says Pendleton, "except that they owe me their labor. A shoot-out, though it would be justice, would be the easy way out. I wouldn't want to honor them with such a noble death in such a paradise as this. If they die by my hand, I'll be holding their heads face-down in the gutter."

"Hands up where I can see 'em, boy!" Cubie says, when he sees me moving my hand down to my poke, where I'd gotten in the habit of putting it when backed into a corner. I lifted my hands, and so did Zeb, but Lee just sit there. "You too, coolie! Hands up where I can see 'em!"

Lee stuck where he was, and I wondered if he was stricken by rational fear or by his own stubborn nature.

"First you tell us where Ruth is at," he says.

"Don't talk tough unless you got lead enough to kill ten men and a draw so quick it's already over before you pull," says Cubie.

"Ruth is safe," Pendleton says, "and unharmed. See how gracious of a master I am? Instead of shooting you in the neck, as these men are eager to do, we are engaged in manly conversation. I am even answering your tedious questions, though nothing in our situation compels me to do so."

"Nothing but your pride," says Lee.

Pendleton shook his head. "Not pride," he says, "but fair play. You set this game in motion when you unchained those men and stole away in the dark. Now it's only sporting that we bring this match to fulfillment."

"You just cain't stand that I got the better of you. Twice," says Lee.

"You misunderstand me most grievously," says Pendleton. "I do not imagine myself to be in competition with a hobo chinaman on the run from the law and his own deviancy—" Here Lee finally stood up, and as he did, about ten loaded rifles and pistols were suddenly aimed his way.

"—That's right. I've looked into you. This is where greater resources mean the world, and all this scrambling around just makes you nothing but a caged rat." Pendleton's first-mate Cubie snorted a laugh and the chorus took up this theme. "It's not your fault. When you entered into this game with me, you had no way of knowing that I *write* the rules, and enforce the outcome, and judge the results."

The sun fully crowned now, we could see the men in all their sordidness and filth. I could also see that, among the unwashed rabble, there was a few men whose attention was unengaged from this menacing activity, who did not believe earnestly in the task to which their labor had been put. How to use this knowledge, however, eluded me, as it was clear that, for every man in which I could sense apprehension and doubt, there were two with a need for blood like a toothache needs tincture.

"You'll just have to put us down right here," says Lee. He never noticed Zeb shaking his head and his hands frantically, trying to express, I s'pose, his reasonable wish not to be put down by Pendleton and his men. "I wouldn't give you the satisfaction of parading me in front of your miners like a prize fish, to make an example of me."

Pendleton sighed. "I can parade you any way I like, dead or alive, *or* gutted like a fish. I just assumed you wanted to go back to Kansas without more holes in you than The Lord gave you when he made your mouth and your arse."

The men all chuckle like they'd never heard such a knee-slapper. Lee kep' silent as a whore in church.

"Well, I guess we can start with your friend here. As much as I can imagine ways to use your Amish runaway, I can't discover any reason why I should haul his bones around." At this, Pendleton turned his pistol upon me and fired, without a blink.

Lee's face registered a keen pain that made me think somehow it had missed me, hitting a rock, and Lee had been

204

caught by the ricochet. Then my bottom half feels warm, and like an image on a stereoscope coming into focus, my once-remote nerves report sharply the sensation of burning from within. I look down at my thigh and see a gush of surprising dark blood, then look up at Lee who, I realize, is feeling only the pain of sympathy. He jumps then and covers the wound with his hands, while Pendleton's posse looks on and laughs some more.

Poor Zeb cries out and runs off down the steeper side of the mountain, hoping, I reckon, that he can't be followed on horseback that a-way. But this doesn't skeer Cubie none. He even 'lows Zeb a head start, then pads after him at a trot. Pendleton only shakes his head as Cubie's shape disappears around the bend after the fleeing Zeb. Pretty soon a shot is heard throughout the canyon, and Lee is left tearing at his sleeves to make a bandage for his one remaining companion, which is me.

How quick it all happened, and how slowly too. Writhing in the grass, my vision blurred with wet, time passed far too lingeringly, as I awaited any sort of relief that could deliver me from this moment; yet there was a bustle all around and a commotion that I lost track of, and left my muddle of perception with only one fixity: that I had a body that I wished to depart and return to when it was less intensely absorbed with its own injury.

Chapter XXXV

The flurry of images that appeared before me next was the more startling for my conviction as to its reality: Ruth bound and strapped like cargo to the hind of a pony, Lee being roped like a steer and drug around the field in clothes that was shred up and falling off his torso like flat noodles, and Zeb dead and scalped like an Injun, face down in the torn grass. I lay face up, under the blinding noonday sun, which gave a touch of warmth to the cold altitude. Now suddenly Tom Sawyer's face was hovering above me, tapping my cheek. Was it really Tom Sawyer?

"Tom?" I says.

"What went on here, Joe?" the man says.

"Tom?" I says again.

He laughed then. "You was always delicate, Joe Harper, warn't you?"

I stir up quick when he answered me back a second time. "Is it really Tom Sawyer?"

"Deputy U.S. Marshall Thomas Sawyer," he says, like it was his habit. Out of the collar of his coat, I seen the flattened bullet he wore on a chain to commemorate the first time he'd been shot as a boy.

I give Tom a fierce hug, and clung to him like grapevine. For a figment he was ruther substantial, and I filled my arms with him.

"So what's going on here, Joe?" Tom finally says. "Why is there a dead man a-lying on the grass with his top off? And why're you full of buckshot? Was it men that got you, or was it Injuns?"

Now that I looked down at the rest of myself, I seen he was right. There was pellets that pocked my skin on an area covering an upper arm and a shoulder. Strange to say, but what I felt most keenly was the cold. My body had been trembling in that spot going on five hours, and my merciful memory erased the suffering of those eternal seconds in the aftermath, and brung back only the numbness and shock.

"Here's our situation, Tom," I says, as he huddled in. "There's a posse of ten armed men a-horseback; they've kidnapped a chinaman and an Amish girl, and are on their way to Kansas to turn them into slaves or worse."

"Well I don't know what the law has to say about a man's right to keep chinamen and Amish girls, but I know that this—" he gestured to encompass the scene that included, still, a dead Zeb— "runs afoul of the law, which it's my sworn duty to protect."

Now that he was a respectable Deputy Marshall, Tom had taken to shaving his chin, but kept his whiskers, which fanned out from under his nose wide but trim. His hair darkened with age, but never thinned. His complexion was the fairest I ever seen on a Western man. All those years sailing the open sea, the ocean air did for Tom what Doctors are always fond of saying it will do for the ailing—it brung him health and youth and vigor that defies time and nature.

As the older boy in our gang, Tom was the closest thing I ever had to a brother, and just like a little brother, I growed up with the expectation that one day I would fill out to become his equal, while secretly suspecting he was endowed by nature with a greatness neither I nor history had ever seen. But that couldn't be true, could it? What I didn't count on was that Tom Sawyer was always Tom Sawyer, and The Lord ain't ever seen fit to make another.

"You all right to ride?" Tom says, helping me to stand. Maybe if I was born Tom Sawyer, you could fill me with buckshot and I'd hop right back on a horse, but I warn't. After plucking out the shot that was buried skin-deep, I bandaged the wound with the torn up sleeve and drew it tight around my shoulder.

"I need a doctor, Tom," I says, "or a coroner."

"It ain't so bad!" Tom says. "How about we do it this way: go recover the captives, arrest the ringleader, and get you fixed up after."

"But…" I started.

"Remember that business in the Med'terranean? Off the coast of Morocco?" he says, as though what I *really* needed was just another story. "That was a miscalculation that left scars on all of us, and that was the day One-Eyed Billy became Blind Billy, and Mouthy Meg became Pegleg Meg. That was as bad as a bad day ever gets. But we didn't stop and see the doctor then, did we?"

"I s'pose not," I says.

"Don't bother s'posing, 'cause I can tell you we ain't!" Tom clapped my shoulder, which was friendly enough, 'cept he forgot that shoulder was full of buckshot. I nearly shrieked from pain, but swallowed it quick before I proved to Tom that even ten years a pirate never made a man of me.

I considered arguing more with him, but Tom had saved my life, and along with his immunity to the physical signs of age, he never acquired the habit of compromise. With Tom, it was always better to just go-along, even when it meant mounting a horse when your wounds are still open.

Now came the question, though, of whether I'd ride on Midnight or Old Lady. Old Lady was the steadier, which would have been a relief to my body, but it would have meant enduring the sound of his whinny. Midnight would have afforded the silence I yearned for, but I might've fallen off and paid for it with my leg. This led me to wonder, melancholily, whether I'd ever be right enough again to ride the rails.

If this were my last journey, I decided, I would spend it in silence, so we left Old Lady behind.

Chapter XXXVI

It was the first time in months I found myself riding East. To consider this sad fact lengthened every mile ahead. Even the presence of my oldest and best friend couldn't shake the sorrowful feeling of backsliding in the direction of my boyhood. I was too desperate to get my companions back, and suffering too much from the constant pinching everywhere, to think on how Tom once'd abandoned me on an island in the wide Atlantic.

"How much did you save, and how much did you squander?" Tom asks me after a long stretch of saying nothing, since we knowed each other well enough not to chatter.

I pull out my poke and toss it to Tom. If I'm to speak true, it was a relief to pass the burden of wealth upon another, and I was glad somehow to be in Tom's confident care. And it was my good luck that Pendleton and his men thought me so worthless that they never bothered to rob me, and Cubie's greed was such that he would never have searched me for a di'mond with his men in view, and likely aimed to come back later and pluck it from my corpse.

Tom emptied it into his palm, where a single di'mond dropped like a cow pie. "One di'mond?" he says.

"Least it's a di'mond," I says. "It's more'n I ever needed, or ever expect to."

"How d'you reckon?" says Tom.

"Well," I says, "once I recover Lee and Ruth, and lay Zeb in the ground, I aim to find a cave to die in."

Tom laughs his vigorous, manly laugh. "If you've a mind to die in a cave, Joe, then St. Petersburg would answer," he says.

"It's no joke, Tom," I says. "It's my plan. Mama Sereny is in heaven, and I never got to say goodbye because I was too busy robbing innocents of their money on the high seas. She only ever wanted goodness from me." On this last p'int, I showed my weakness by 'lowing my voice to crack like a boy's.

"You may be right on that score," says Tom. Was it Tom Sawyer telling me I was right to feel lowdown and mean? "But there warn't no innocents among the men we robbed, nor the poxy one you killed."

A cold cloud obscured the sun for a dark moment. I froze up, worried that my body was going rigid, but when it passed, my body slumped against Midnight as though hit by another bullet.

Measuring my reaction, Tom shook his head, upon which he wore a prospector's hat. "Joe," says Tom. "Is that what it's all about? You kill a man who was after death anyway, then suddenly you think you ain't worth living a life neither?"

It was such a mental shock to be reminded of my great sin on the same day I was shot so full of pellets that I could hardly muster a proper response.

"You done what you had to," says Tom sternly, almost meanly, "and there's nothing in the law that says you cain't." Though 't was Tom who was wearing the badge, I was righteous sure the law didn't leave room for doubt on the question of whether 't was right or wrong to rob a man, then shoot him dead when he resists, and leave his child for good as dead. "Once they make you a Deputy," says Tom, "you represent the law and the gov'ment, so it's your *job* to kill bad men. The only thing you did wrong was fail to wait until you had the authority."

"Tom," I says. "I'm thirty-five years old and got no home but the road. When do you reckon I'll have the authority?"

Tom tossed me back my di'mond. "This here is the kinder authority that'll earn you respect anywhere."

"So d'you have the authority to make me an authority?" I says. "Can a deputy marshall deputize a feller and make him a deputy-deputy?"

Tom took my inquiry as a challenge. "As sure as clouds make rain," he says, and reined in his horse, pulling her alongside us so that, when she flipped her tail, it brushed Midnight's rear. "I hereby deputize you in the name of the gov'ment of these United States, with all the rights, burdens, and such-and-such of this office. You will hereby and henceforward and forthwith assume the title of Deputy Deputy Marshall Joe Harper." Tom shot off his pistol in celebration, and I was grateful now that I didn't bring Old Lady, who would have made noise about this.

"But Tom," I says. "Even with all the privileges and authority of the law on our side, how're we goin' to get through more'n a dozen armed men, all a-horseback, to save Lee and Ruth?"

"Follow me," says Tom, with the long wink I'd come to fear.

Coming upon the encampment of Pendleton and his men that night, with Tom Sawyer beside me, it was easy and natural to become tender about our pirating days. I was never so fond of danger and excitement as Tom was, but in such a predicament I'm reminded of the way that fear fixes your attention, draws your focus upon a thing so exclusively that it amounts to an Eastern meditation, and the mystery of the universe seems knowable because it suddenly contains just one thing.

Atop the small, muscular frame of Midnight, I blended well into the wooden darkness. There was never another horse so quiet, and when he stood stock-still, 't was as though the dark took on a physical shape, without even displacing a leaf from a reaching branch. Keeping low to the ground and moving on his elbows so as to disturb not even the grass, dragging the rear half of his body behind him, Tom could have been a turtle making slow progress towards a cricket that, with a quickness you wouldn't have thought possible only a moment earlier, becomes his supper.

The men camped there warn't so cautious as we was. A pyramid of brush and dry twigs had been set up at the end of the encampment, awaiting a spark, as though it, like the pyramids of the ancients, was meant for the dead. Without a body sensible enough to bring along matches, they resorted to repeated attempts to light this would-be campfire with their pistols. Having sensibly arranged themselves in a circle around the wood pile, there was an occasional howl as a man found himself grazed by the ricochet.

"What's the plan?" I says, whispering extra-quiet just in case the men warn't sufficiently deafened by the sound of their own gunfire.

"Wait," says Tom.

Soon the men give up on the campfire and raised a shuper of beer to their victory, then raised another to their cleverness, and one more to their employer's money. Pretty soon the ale was a-flowing like a barrel without a stopper, and, giving up the fire, they warmed themselves instead on the spirits.

We stood by in the mountain dark for so long I wondered if we was waiting for morning to come, and kept looking in Tom's direction for a signal, as each man sunk into the depths of his own inner landscape, and I nearly sank so myself.

What was Tom's plan? Was I about to cause a distraction so that he could stroll into an empty encampment and free the prisoners? Was I a-goin' to fire off a volley in the air and he would holler out and pretend they was surrounded by marshalls? I was eager to know what clever strategy the old hero came up with this time.

Well, in a moment I found out. Tom reached in his pack and brandished a saber, same as we used to carry in our pirating days. Then I watched in horrified silence as the man

I call my brother went from one body to the next, holding one hand over a man's mouth to tamp the noise, and using his free hand to cut the throat of every sleeping soul one by one. Dark blood spilt from their necks onto the hard earth and made quick rivers in the grain of the earth. The leather of their tunics absorbed a portion of this elixir, and sent the rest with gravity to feed whatever stubborn plant-life imposed itself on this rough mountainside.

Despite Tom's silent maneuvers, we were eventually detected, and with only one tent left, these men were up in arms. There was three men left, already a-horseback, and only two of us, so, overcoming my shock, I shouted for Tom to scram, and I started to about-face, but then Tom called out, "Derrick Hivey!"

After a silence, he repeated, "Does one of you go by the name of Derrick Hivey?"

"Yes?" says a pug-nosed feller with a scrawny frame. Next to him was a man you might call barrel-chested and I might call neckless—ol' Quentin Blutes, or Cubie as I'd known him—and next to him was Carl Pendleton himself.

"Derrick Hivey! You are wanted dead or alive by the U.S. Gov'ment," says Tom, "but the price on your head ain't high enough to waste my time. So I want you to run along now and continue your unlawful ways until such time as you can fetch a price worth goin' after."

Derrick Hivey looked back and forth between Tom and Pendleton. "Did'ya come after me jus' to say your piece?"

"No, Derrick," says Tom. "Your hide ain't worth fifty dollars, but your pal Quentin Blutes here clears three hundred."

At this figure, Hivey looked over at Quentin with wolfish eyes. Quentin raised a bushy eyebrow and tucked his chin further into the folds of his "neck."

"If you shoot 'im on my authority, you and I will split the bounty, then go our separate ways," says Tom. "But if you try to fire on me, I might get there first, and even if your luck holds up today, you'll get nothing from it but more marshals on your tail."

Needing nowise to be asked twice, Derrick Hivey turned his pistol on Quentin Blutes and before he could say "Let's make a deal," his body fell from his horse and the blast echoed through the canyon. The scene around us was like the gore of the big one, from all the tales I'd heard told. I've seen nothing like it in my pirating days. 'T was odd that, for all this death, Derrick's pistol was the first one to really fire— the rest of this work had been done in silence, a monument to Tom's terrible skill.

Pendleton stood by and did nothing. He may have been the only sober man, but he never drew his pistol. Raising his arms slowly, with a flinch in his eyes that betrayed his fear, even as he forced an amused smile, he says, "I broke no law."

"You shot my friend," says Tom, his voice as flat as the dreary plains of Kansas.

I reckon Pendleton had dealt with zealous lawmen, revolting miners, bounty hunters, and meddlesome vigilantes out for blood, but he never faced off with Tom Sawyer.

"If you're a-goin' to end 'im," I says to Tom. "Let Lee fire the fatal shot. It's justice." It may have been my secret desire—to have plugged Cubie with my own hand—that spoke up at that moment.

"No, bo," says Lee, tied up with Ruth against a tree, like they was captives of savages. "I won't kill a man. It's against my principles."

"But you're not a *real* Christian," I reason. "You was born pagan. And where does it say 'thou shalt not kill' in the book of pagans?"

"There is no book of pagans," says Lee. "It's just right and wrong."

"Exactly," I says. "So there ain't no rules to say it's wrong to kill a scoundrel like Pendleton."

"Even so," says Lee. "I want no part of a man's murder."

"'Cept it ain't murder if it's a marshal that does it," I says, quoting the wisdom of Tom Sawyer.

Pendleton's forced look of amusement became an earnest one. "Could I interject something here?" he says.

"No, sir," says Tom. "I don't care to hear another man beg for his life. The man you wronged says you're not to be harmed, and I have no price on your hide, so I guess you're free to go."

Pendleton gave a nod, looked like he was about to say something, then thought better of it and turned his horse around, heading East.

Tom pulled his pistol out, mounting it on his steady left arm. With the first light of morning improving his aim, Tom squeezed the trigger and Pendleton fell from his horse the way a chess piece falls, with a wobble, then stillness.

Tom warn't looking in my direction, but if he saw me out of the corner of his eye, he would have seen a question in my eyes.

"He drawed on me," says Tom. And no man argued his assessment.

Derrick Hivey turned kindly all a sudden. "You don't need me in chains, d'ye?" he says, an exaggerated friendly grin on his face.

But Tom did not return the expression. He was grim with awful purpose. "No, I do not," says Tom.

Derrick flinched, and he was hardly turned around when Tom fired again, and another man fell from his horse like a stone into water.

Tom left the bloody scene with a smile, knowing the law was served that day, and telling us so afterward, and repeating it, in case there was any doubt.

Chapter XXXVII

The uphill path was warmed by the morning sun and charmed by the view of the gorges, yet marred by the stink of blood, which had long lifted from the air but lingered on in my nose like skunk. A single cloud in an otherwise clear sky moved in front of the sun and made a lone shadow over us.

The men had dragged and whipped and tormented Lee so cruelly that, despite the short duration of his captivity, he had the wild look of one who'd been trapped for weeks, starved and beaten like a dog. He hung back and clung to the reins of his horse like a drowning man to a buoy.

I warn't all right myself, but the cold, dry, clean air must have disinfected my wounds because the skin around each rupture never turned gray or black, just every other color in the rainbow. So we rode three abreast, Tom and I like sentinels on each side, and Ruth bewixt, with all stolen horses 'cept for Midnight, the mare I rode.

"I'm so glad you warn't harmed at-all," I says to her. "Those men never used you in any unchristian way, did they?"

Ruth was shy to speak around Tom for reasons I couldn't cipher out, and I felt a pang when I get the idea she might be fond of his heroics at the camp while I'd just stood by, paralyzed with shock. I expect I will never remember anything in such detail as I remember watching Tom cut each man's throat precisely, expertly, as though he worked a slaughterhouse and they were no more than hogs.

"As is often the case with a rapscallion," Tom says with authority, "his need to abuse and humiliate a chinaman is greater than his need to satisfy his sinful nature, even if it be with a woman of surpassing beauty."

For some reason I was moved to assert some authority of my own. "But, Tom, you've got to figure in the fact that these men had never seen a woman with as much grace and innocence and loveliness as Ruth."

"I agree," says Tom. "Yet thankfully they didn't have enough time to slake their animal natures upon the lady. Their leader fancied himself a gentleman, and would have kept them off of her as long as he was able, if only to prove himself a hypocrite by forcing himself upon her when it suited him."

"Well, that's one theory," I says.

"Theory nothing," says Tom, bristling at my attempt at claiming the privilege of knowing. "It's the way it went. As a lawman, my instincts for the criminal mind are sharp, and my conclusions are unassailable."

Tom must've forgot who he was a-talkin' to. I seen him living the life of a pirate all the years of his youth, and I seen him oaring away whilst I was stranded on an island in the great gray Atlantic. And I seen him, in the deep of night, slit the throats of a half dozen men, shoot two in the back, and neglect to bury any of 'em.

Ruth 'lowed her horse to draw back a few paces, so that Tom and I were now side by side, without her presence to buffer the off-kilter feeling between us. She and Lee kept up a quiet conversation a ways behind whilst Tom and I was blustering and palavering at the head of our caravan.

"It ain't wrong to ask whether she was harmed any while in captivity," I says.

"If she was," says Tom, "then it's too terrible for the lady to talk about. And if she warn't, then I reckon she don't care to dwell on the possibility."

"So you mean to defend her honor against me?" I says. "Deputy Marshall Tom Sawyer, who just met Ruth and who ain't even addressed her yet by her name?"

Tom looked at me like he'd never seen me before. "Who ever said such nonsense as that?" he says.

"Look, Tom," I says. "I appreciate you riding in like the cavalry and saving my hide. But here you are stepping into a situation you can scarcely appreciate. There's history between me and Ruth."

"Is this Joe Harper, *terror of the high seas*?" says Tom. "I wouldn't recognize him for all his prattling on about a churchlady."

"She ain't a churchlady," I says. "She's my intended."

Tom gave a laugh that was half mean and half genuine. "Was you born a fool, Joe?" he says. "Or did your mama just raise you that a-way?"

It was a suspenseful minute in which I could hardly muster the will to say anything in a human tongue. I expected Tom to combust, raising a cloud of ash, and to burn down to cinders on the very spot; but I never so much as heard Mama Sereny's voice. Rows of leaves, riffling in the wind, sounded like chattering teeth. The clacking of insects like an impatient woman tapping her shoes. And there was no birdsong. We were riding down from paradise into the grim valley, about to hit a stretch of road that bore us west with no gaps, bumps, or detours.

"Mama Sereny died, Tom," I says. "She died *dead*."

There was another quiet span, and for a moment the wind and insects hushed, joining in on our silence, during which I wondered whether Tom might have taken to heart my plea for compassion—or whether I'd even spoken those words aloud.

"Joe Harper," says Tom. "You had so many Mamas growing up I could never tell which one was the flagship. What kind of a yokel calls his sisters 'Mama' anyhow?" This last one he said loud enough for Ruth to overhear. There was gamesmanship in this. Tom meant to p'ison her against me, and in this way to take what I had come to think of as my own. And I could scarcely raise my arm in objection without bringing fresh pain all over my healing shoulder. I could only hope that, like Mala, Ruth had a heart that leaned toward the protection of a wounded bird ruther than one that yielded to the hunter.

Next week we blazed through California like a wick on dynamite. I heard music in the stomp of hoofs. We was almost to the goal, where Lee would at last be home in San Francisco and I would finally reach a cave worthy of dying in. But I started to think about Tom's a-laughing at me and calling me a yokel, and then I thunk about Tom's trying to protect Ruth from my questions about her captivity, and then I thunk about Tom's abandoning me on an island with no food or water, and finally I struck on the moment when Tom slit the throats of the rapscallions, and my mind stayed there because it couldn't get away from it.

"Ruth," I says, as we slowed up on the approach to the city. "I have an earnest proposition—" then I remembered the sad story of Shortie Bigler that poor Zeb tole me, "—well not a *proposition*, but a serious question I'd like to ask."

"Joe," she says, and wears the first smile I seen since we recovered her. "Are you asking vether you can ask a question?"

"I s'pose I am," I says, grinning back a bit too wide and cheerful, so that her own smile shrunk away like a burrowing worm. "Could I?"

"Of course," she says.

Now I was reminded of Gary Ong, who according to his followers knew 't-all, and his one rule that a body could only ask three questions before joining his tribe.

"D'you miss home?"

"Never," she says, then adds, as though any more emphasis was needed, "Never ever." "We come all this way to bring Lee home, and it occurred to me that all this time we been taking you further and further away from yours," I says.

"The more I am avay, the more I believe my fader was being cruel ven he forced me to marry Abram," she says. "The God who made me cannot vant me to be unhappy."

She never knowed how this news lit up my heart. But

then it just as quickly sank back into the darkness it rose out of. "Don't you mean when he *tried to* force you to marry?" I says, to which she clammed up like I'd lain an unwelcome hand upon her.

"No, Joe," she says, finally. "I vas given in marriage to Abram Hershberger, but our life vas miserable, and by running avay I have surely added to the sum of happiness in this vorld."

"But, Ruth," I says, unable to say clearly what I meant. "You told me that marriage is 'a holy thing, ordained by God'."

She nodded a tearful nod. "I shtill believe this to be true, of a true marriage."

Our steeds had slowed even more now, having already fallen several paces behind Tom and Lee, and I brought Midnight to a full stop. "What d'you mean, 'a true marriage'?" I says. "You says the words 'I do,' that's as true as it gets. In the eyes of God and the laws of man, you are wedded and that's the way of 't, unless Abram gives his consent otherwise."

Ruth's tearful nodding turned instead to a tearful face cast down into its collar. I was ashamed to draw from her well of sorrow, sure, but I was even more ashamed that here Mama Sereny had been watching us and I'd proven her right yet again.

When Ruth judged that no comfort was forthcoming, she instantly recovered, dried her unpainted face with a dark handkerchief, and started off at a trot, leaving me at the tail of the party, a sullen fool alone.

Chapter XXXVIII

We come to the border of the city now, where instead of patches of dry grass separating each, the buildings was crushed together, sometimes one on top of another, or so it appeared upon the steep hills that ranged the city line.

Sure enough, we were half a block into the city proper when we saw another Chinaman. He looked near enough like Lee to be his brother. "Lee. Is he a relation?" I says.

"No, bo," he says. "But maybe he can give us directions."

I looked oddly in his direction, since for uncountable days Lee'd been telling me that San Francisco was his home, but he neverminded my look since he was already engaged in conversation with his countryman. The man was followed by another Chinaman, who happily discoursed with both of 'em. He too looked like he could be Lee's brother.

"Is *he* kin to you?" I says.

"No, bo," he says. "And our time in San Francisco will pass painful slow if you ask me that question every time we see a Chinese."

"Well," I says. "Would you ask 'im what month it is?" Lee grimaced, but he done it. An answer came back quick, for these were more Christian Chinese, like Lee, and they was sorely offended that we failed to observe Holy Week, from which fact I judged it was nearly Easter, and already halfway to Summer, though you wouldn't know it from the chill wind blowing over San Francisco. 'T was cold as January in the Midwest—or worse, because the sun always reminded you of the warmth you warn't feeling.

From an elderly Chinawoman, Lee learned where the best and cheapest place in San Francisco to stay was—in Chinatown, at her own establishment, as it happened. Her name was Soon, and she had vivid facial expressions that spread outward to surround the general company, leaving only Tom Sawyer unmoved by an upturn of the lip or a sinking of an eyebrow; and as she set the pace leading Ruth's pony, her langorous walk was not like the curious shuffle of the Chinee that Tom and I used to imitate in our pirating days, but more like a barefoot maiden stepping over rocks on her way to the beach.

There was a hanging mist, with no threat of rain in it but just a dampening of the hair and clothes. Ruth and Soon talked the whole way through town, under the curved balconies of a city both ghostly and lively. It struck me strange that here Tom and I followed two ladies at an ambling pace, and gave no hint of protest.

"Ve have two men who are injured," Ruth says, nodding at me and Lee. "Do you have a room on de virst vloor vor dem?"

"Hurt man should not share room with hurt man," Soon says. "Each one need healthy body to watch them."

"I suppose Tom and Joe vill room toogether," says Ruth, with what I chose to interpret as a faint melancholy, "and I must bunk vith Lee."

"Always this way," Soon says. "Opposite make balance."

"Is dat your guiding philosophy?" says Ruth. "Dat everything needs its opposite?"

"Best way," Soon says. "Otherwise too much of one thing. I give example. You and friends bring too much strong body smell. Tonight, you will meet strong soap, and together will make balance."

The thought of a bath and a bed, the chance of lying down on one, all a sudden made me wearier than ever before. As we ascended a partic'larly steep hill, a downwind draft caused me to hug myself, and I felt the bumpy flesh of my own arms, wondering if I ever remembered being so cold, whether it was sleeping with no blanket in the Kansas winter or clinging to the deck of a freight car.

Upon the threshold to Chinatown from the downtown, a red-and-gold gate loomed above us, engraved with whole passels of figures including a dragon in flight, which spanned the arch. Soon says that, far from the fearsome attitude it presents a stranger with, the visage of the dragon is peaceable and divine.

In fact, there's lots of ugliness in Chinatown that Soon says ain't ugliness at-all. Dead animals hang in the open-air markets, some shorn, some still dressed in feathers, or scales, or skin. Strong-smelling roots and fruits draw flies even in the cold, and the proprietors of these tiny, raw establishments have ceased to bother waving them away. But all the complaints among Chinatown's neighbors, Soon explained, concern its love of fire. The streets are aglow with puffy red lanterns hanging from ropes between the buildings, and firelight turns the windows of houses into lively screens through which one can see old men dealing cards, and ladies shifting tiles around checkered boards. The air is thick with smoke in the market, turning it into a hot core in an otherwise cold-swept city.

"Dead animals, strong-smelling spices, and fire?" says Lee. "That just means we love food. America is young yet. She'll learn to eat proper by and by."

At Soon's establishment, the Lucky Good Fortune Happy Time Hotel and Hungry Friends Palace, she took us immediately to the baths and handed us towels. Ruth got a different treatment. I reckon she was pampered like a queen as soon as Soon sensed that she'd been treated roughly on the road, whether it were or it warn't on our account. Sounds of merry-making came from the ladies' salon while Tom, Lee, and I bathed in aching silence. There was a row of descending rocks that made a waterfall, and the gentle sound soothed Lee near to sleep, while it made me restless in my bladder. Tom all a sudden stood and dressed himself, declaring that it was his duty as a U.S. Marshall to check in for an interview at the local precinct.

In the dining hall, Lee proceeded to show me how a Chinaman eats, using two hands—one to hold the bowl, the other to shovel food in with sticks. The supper table ain't the place to be shy, says Lee.

"Tell that to Mama Sereny," I says.

"What's to be shy about?" says Lee. "If I'm proper hungry, I don't aim to hide it. You ought to be proud of working your body hard enough to need a meal the way grass needs sunlight."

The food was spread out on the table in covered pots, and I had to lift them one by one to survey what I might put in my mouth first.

"It ain't what civilized folks do," I says.

"Says you," says Lee, filling his plate by dumping the contents of several pots onto it. Halfway into his feeding, he looked up at me with a look of perplexity.

"You look like you're about to ask that bowl of rice to get married," he says. "And that pork? It ain't a virgin bride."

We'd feasted on mulligan and dried meat and bread loaves many a day together, but other than the Denver ballroom and Grand Hotel, this was the only time I'd seen Lee eat as much with his eyes as his mouth. So I took a serving spoon to use as a fork, and scooped it straight from the pot.

The first bite I took confused my tongue, sending it in and out a couple times like a panting dog, before I discovered the red-flecked rice and pork warn't hot, as I'd thought, but full of contradictory flavors so I needed to take another bite right away to figure out what I'd just et. Eventually I'd done more'n my share to finish off this spread, but my mind still spun from the confusion.

Sitting across from Lee at a lacquered wood table, my

blood rushing and my body fidgeting from unexpected doses of salt and sugar and crazy flavors I don't know what, I wondered when Tom planned to return from his interview with the local authorities.

As soon as Ruth appeared in this establishment, with her heavy cotton blouse worn to the threads and her cheeks roughened with dust, Soon and the ladies in her employ undertook to give her the completest comfort, and would take no pay for their service. There was as much insinuation of guilt as there was kindness in this gesture, I reckoned, but the result was the same: a Ruth at rest. Considering how poorly she'd been used by every man on the road to California, I was glad for that.

At night Tom and I found ourselves in a mostly empty common room slurping up Chinese noodles with sticks—having taken my first Chinese meal, I was now the authority on the subject, and aimed to illustrate that authority to Tom Sawyer—waited upon by Soon's sister, a squat lady with streaks of silver in her hair, tied up into a bun, and a tall feller I guessed was her son, who never spoke but only nodded. There was the most ornate claw chandeliers and leaded stained-glass windows, that I wondered at the patience required for its assembly. There was a feller in the corner playing a stringed instrument, and it was unclear to me whether he was paid for this occupation or deriving only intangible benefits from it.

I never could get used to seeing so many Lee-looking folks all in one room. For every soul that entered, I had an instinct to greet them with a "Hey, bo!" and a clap on the shoulder, but checked myself from doing so lest I frighten a stranger.

But as it turned out none of it was strange or new to Tom Sawyer, who had spent the last year and more in California as a Deputy Marshall. He seemed to have scarcely any reaction to Chinese at-all.

Once I had confided in him the extent of my plans, though reluctant at first to take up this mission, Tom had opinions on how a cave ought to be acquired. Most importantly, the cave should be undiscovered. That way you warn't just an old hermit, but an intrepid explorer to boot.

"How's a body s'posed to discover an undiscovered cave, when nobody ever discovered it before?" I asked him.

"That," says Tom, "is the reason folks come to California."

I took him to mean that California is a good place to look for caves, but I reckoned that, if everybody came here to find one, then wouldn't the chances of being the first one to find it decline considerably? And more to the p'int, once I find a cave, should I expect waves of would-be hermits to "discover" my home by walking in through the mouth?

"No, Joe," says Tom. "California cave-finders don't just crawl into holes the way we done it in Missouri. They look for a vein, then use dynermite to blow it open."

I begun to understand the kind of "discovering" he meant, and I amused myself with the thought that Tom must have had me confused with Pendleton, who "discovered" so many mines for his indentured men to fall into.

"So the only hazard is that the cave could be blowed up while I'm in it?" I says.

"But the use to which you aim to put the cave is to die in, ain't it?" he says.

I warn't up to the task of explaining to Tom how I preferred to die slowly of hunger and cold, so I told him that first of all we had to deliver Lee home—one mission at a time—but Tom was bored by a homecoming.

"If you're hunting up a cave, and Lee is bound for home, then what's Ruth a-looking for? Is she fixing to marry?"

"No, Tom," I says with a disgust in my voice that was

only scarcely hidden. "That's what she's a-runnin' from!"

Tom leaned forward. He took an interest in what I accidentally let drop about Ruth's past. "She was nearly forced to marry a man, and then she run away with you on the hobo road?" he says, giddy from the improbability of it all. I bristled at the word "nearly." "And now she's been saved by a Deputy U.S. Marshall!"

"Well," I says. "I reckon you saved *me*, anyway, and *together* we saved Ruth."

Tom remained quiet, and at first I wondered if I'd stumped him for once, until more than a moment passed and I reckoned his silence meant he was busy plotting his next adventure.

—

Dreams cain't kill a man. I repeat that to myself, since I knowed I was in the shadder-world now. But the man kept cutting me anyway. I sat on a barrel on a rocking boat, and though there warn't any ropes, he had me tied down with his eyes. There was two cuts now on each thigh, and punctures on my chest and shoulder and gut, plus a gash where the man had pulled the knife upward from my armpit. It ain't hurt quite as much as a real blade in the waking world, but it kept stinging like bees, so I was stricken with fear since it warn't s'posed to hurt at-all, and I cain't wake myself up.

"Ain't I familiar?" he says, but I am mute.

The man wore an evening-coat and a stetson, and seemed to rock the boat with his feet, so that on top of it all my head spun and my stomache roiled. The sky behind him was full gray, without any variation in tone, so that we may as well have been drifting in a vast cloud. His large, dark Mediterranean features made him look sad at the same time he was cutting at me. Here he was advancing on me ag'in! I was stung between the ribs now, and it felt like jelly sliding out of me sticky and warm and churning. He pulled back his hand then, seeming for all his scrunching eyebrows and tilted chin like a painter disapp'inted in his creation.

"Ain't I familiar?" he says ag'in, and I can only cry in answer. So he gets me with the knife, uncomfortable close to where the pelvis joined with the leg, jiggling a bit to spread the sting around.

"I have my mother's dark complexion," he says, "and her mouth." I sat there open-jawed but dumb. The man's upper lip was straight-across and prim, while his lower lip jutted out like a precipice.

"I have her wide nose, too," he says, "and her small chin; her neck, her ears." He smiled, thinking on the memory of his mother.

"But I have my father's eyes." Here he covered the lower half of his face with a palm, leaving only his sad and severe eyes, bushy brows, and premature forehead wrinkles. That was the clincher. I reckoned I knowed who his daddy was, and who he was.

"Ain't I familiar?" he says, holding the jagged-edged knife vertical in his fist, with bits of gut attached, even a belly-hair or two pinched in the handle. He stabs upward in the air, and at the gesture alone there's a tightening in my groin.

I nod my head, and look down at my feet, which blended right into the planks of the floor and the gray mist of the sky, to avoid his awful eyes. I shouldn't have, since it brought a fresh wave of nausea, and it was the emptying of my bile upon the ground that inspired him to go for my throat, a move which shook me up in bed with a cry that sounded like a yipping fox.

—

Lee got away early, and Tom slept, so I walked crazy-haired down to the common room to find Ruth in a patterned pink-silk dress dandelioned with blue and silver rosettes, the fabric folding in at the neckline, showing the depression of her delicate throat. She had finally emerged from the comfort and care of the Chinese ladies to stride out like an empress. It was a vision to make me forget many another vision I'd seen—almost enough to erase the memory of Tom sawing men's throats with his saber like a woodsman with his logs, soaked in red spots like sawdust.

Soon's sister served us a breakfast meal despite the late hour—rice porridge with pork, which I judged was the same ingredients we et for dinner, but differently arranged. I was glad to take a meal with each of my road-kin, feeling privileged to have leisure at last to focus on something other than saving my own skin, and I was partic'larly keen to spend time with Ruth, since I'd been on the road with Lee so long already, and spent most of my life in the cursed company of the man who called himself Deputy Marshall Thomas Sawyer.

"Ruth," I says, in a panic all a sudden for how little I had to say that warn't in praise of her beauty. "You ain't touched your food at-all."

"If I stay here very long, I vill grow fat," she says, patting her middle as though it held a baby, though 't was as flat as Kansas.

I would feed you every day till you grew fat on my generosity, I wish'd to say. *I would learn your desires and go on quests to accomplish them—even if 't was for a spoonful of honey straight from the hive.*

Then to my poorly concealed displeasure, Tom meandered down the stairs and into the common room. He sat at the end of the table, in the man-of-the-house position. "I think we can finally put the Pendleton affair behind us," he says, with a look of knowing that suggested something exclusive.

There was a halo of sun on the shiny wood table between us. The rice porridge still sat there uneaten, since I learned growing up that a man waits for a woman to eat before he begins to take his meal.

"The sheriff here has been apprised of the unfortunate circumstances of the shoot-out and massacre up there in the Rockies," Tom says. *Massacre*. Didn't it take a special sort of devil to own up to his own acts of murder and still sit conscience-free at the breakfast table? "It's a shame Pendleton ever employed such men as Quentin Blutes and Derrick Hivey, since they turned against him in the end."

It just then occurred to me what Tom was doing by narrating things that a-way. I had the curious thought that maybe *this* was how history was written.

"Ain't it, Joe?" he says.

"Ain't it what?" I says.

"Ain't it a shame?" Tom spoke slowly and purposefully, a pace that asked *repeat after me*.

I dared myself to look him in the eye, and then surprised myself by doing so. "A *damned* shame," I says. How much time elapsed in our fix-eyed stare I cain't properly judge. Here was a man no different from Quentin Blutes or Big Belly Rob or any number of jack-rollers I come across in my endless travels. *But*, I thunk, turning away my eyes, finally, *this one was also a man of the law.*

"The only inquiry the sheriff made was after the Chinaman," says Tom. "What's a body doing so far away from Chinatown anyway, that he could get in trouble with a mining posse from all the way on the other side of the Nevada territory?"

"I'd say it ain't our business what Lee was doing, time of his unlawful capture," I says.

"Don't misunderstand, Joe," says Tom, with what could have been another long wink but could have also been an eye going lazy with too much drink. "This is a high-stakes game."

"When it comes to my road-kin," I says, "it ain't a game at-all."

"The sheriff's concern here," says Tom, finding it easy to ignore me entirely, "was that more than a dozen white men was killed, and the Chinaman he lived. How d'you reckon?"

"Tom," I says, a-standing. "Ruth and I are a-goin' to see this mission to the end, and we've almost got Lee home now."

"Why ain't he home already?" says Tom. "Why would a Chinaman return to Chinatown and choose to stay in a hotel where nobody knowed him?"

Ruth stood up and left our company, her breakfast and mine still untouched. Once she had gained the top of the stairs, and Tom and I were good and alone, I leaned in to him and says, "Soon as this is over, you make yourself scarce and never bother me or Lee, or Ruth."

Tom reached across the table, gathering in the bowls of porridge that once'd belonged to me and Ruth, and starts eating of the gruel without any pretense of asking.

"What's a cave-man like you got to do with my business?" says Tom with a growl I never heard in his voice before. A bite of wind blowing in from the window turned San Francisco a few degrees colder'n it already was. I hoped to God that he'd been drinking all night long, and that this warn't a sober Tom Sawyer a-threatening me by the cold, clear light of day.

Chapter XXXIX

Four blocks into the Chinesiest part of Chinatown, the colorful paint and stable structures end, and a row of decrepit half-houses begin, one of 'em with its front walls fallen in, appearing as a dollhouse with its contents exposed, but with none of the latter's tidiness. All the gloss and shine in the rest of the neighborhood had the effect of imbuing these ruins with an odd beauty. The peeled paint married intention and accident in ways its applicant never knowed it would.

Amidst this chaos and rubble was the remnants of its former owners. For these are some of the oldest structures in this shining new city—older than Chinatown itself. It's original settlers was Dutch by the looks of it, the sturdy blue-gray curtains flapping in the wind, enduring time and salt and weather. Broken beds with tall-headboards had lost their down, and an indoor tub was caked with mold of every color except for white. A Swiss cuckoo clock stood perfectly straight and unmolested near a hearth with gaps in the stone face, like missing teeth.

There was a curious bo below it, gray of hair but still upright in posture, flanked by a pair of dogs standing unnaturally still like sentinels guarding a castle. He wore gold epaulettes on his blue uniform, and a beaver hat with a peacock feather tucked in the ribbon. A rusty saber hung at his side, and in his hands he cupped the head of a walking-stick.

As we approached, his posture and expression never changed. Upon our arrival at this squalid scene, he measured us with black eyes buried deep in his worry-lined face like coals bedding in a cold furnace. What a sight we must have cut! A hobo dressed as a torn-up gentleman, a Chinaman dressed like a Christian, and a Dutch girl dressed like a Chinese doll.

Then, an event short of miraculous but far from predictable occurred. Lee bowed and folded at the middle and kowtowed his head, with a kind of sacred purpose that was at odds with the broken-up sidewalk beneath him and leaky awning above. I never seen Lee so much as nod and smile; now here he was prostrate upon the ground in front of a man I never seen before. This uniformed fellow looked at us like it warn't the strangest thing that ever happened. Who was this bo, the Airedale?

"It is my honor to greet Your Majesty, the Emperor of the United States and Protector of Mexico," says Lee, who I'd always suspected of being a bit funny in the head, but never so far gone that he'd mistake a bum for an emperor. Perhaps, I thunk to myself, Lee had suffered one too many blows to the head from Pendleton's men, and his brain warn't working properly.

Well, that old raccoon just played along, and why wouldn't a body consent to being called the Emperor of these United States? History records that there have been less charitable cases of mistaken identity.

"From whom do I receive the dignity of being so addressed?" says the strange bo in the limeyest way you could imagine, maybe moreso. For some men, like Lee, being away so long from their home country separates them from their past, speech and habit alike. But to others, such as our newly dubbed emperor, great distances exaggerate the effect of their foreignness.

Then, despite my gesturing him to hush up and step away from this unfortunate entanglement, Lee spoke again. "My name is Lee Bao, and I was born in Chico, California to Chinese parents. I am a poet by profession, and a man of learning. Five years ago, while hosting a guest from my parents' home country, I became part of a roundup of Chinese by a mob of white men disposed to violence, exiled from my home, and subsequently survived a massacre that claimed the life of my guest. That guest was Win Chu, a newly arrived messenger from China. As he lay with his wounded head resting upon my lap, I swore to the dying man that I would fulfill his duty and deliver his message to Emperor Norton. I have been living in exile in Missouri for the past five years, but now I return to fulfill this mission."

Lee received no reaction so far from the bo, so he spoke more loudly. "So it is that I bring a letter from the Tongzhi of China, Tenth Emperor of the Qing Dynasty, to be delivered to Norton I, First Emperor of the United States and Protector of Mexico."

This hobo emperor nodded ceremoniously and invited his subject to continue. All this time I thought Lee was a plain bo, or the Airedale, or some other such thing, but all the while he was a chinaman poet working as a stand-in messenger on behalf of the king of Qing?

Ruther than produce a letter, Lee begun to recite this message from memory. I thunk back to Lee's stack of papers, all the time he spent studying them and re-writing them on the road, and how when he finally give up his luggage he insisted he ain't have a need for it no more. It was on the carriage-ride through Nevada, I judged, that Lee finished filing the entirety of this dispatch to the cabinet of his memory.

"It is with gravity and sympathy that we mourn the passing of Lazarus, your great and loyal companion, who has inspired generosity and good will among the people of the United States and who keeps San Francisco free of vermin. Your goodness extends to all creatures, and the dog Lazarus endures as a testament to that goodness."

The uniformed bo nodded slightly in response.

"The Tongzhi is not naive. Among your subjects, your sage proclamations fall upon deaf ears. They regard you and your Imperial decrees as jokes and whimsy—parodies of the old monarchies of an old world and its false claim of authority over the rightful will of the people. But you

234

are currently the only voice calling for kindness and respect toward the Chinese people in a region void of compassion, and so it is that I regard you as the true and rightful authority in the United States, and the only man worthy of my Imperial communication. In my country, any man who looks upon the emperor is promptly sentenced to death. Yet I send my most trusted personal advisor Win Chu to deliver this message, recorded by my own hand, knowing, upon his return, that he must suffer this selfsame fate."

Emperor Norton, who had been standing the while with whiskered chin poked in the air and eyes closed, says, "The Tongzhi is wise and munificent. I am grateful for his words, and for his expression of sympathy upon the death of Lazarus." The emperor gestured to his dogs, and it was only then that I judged his two canine companions to be stuffed and taxidermied.

Lee continued. "It is with solemn and clear-sighted resolve, then, that I hereby propose that a bridge be built between our peoples. A bridge that, spanning the Pacific Ocean, will put to shame every other product of man, including our illustrious Great Wall. The Yi Wan Li Bridge, or 'the Bridge of Ten Thousand Miles,' will not—as the Great Wall was intended—serve to keep barbarians out, but to welcome friends from your nation to our side of the world, and ours to yours. It shall consist of one million bents and trestles, eight million spars and beams, uncountable rail ties, and a marker for each mile extending from the great city of San Francisco to Shanghai. It shall make provision for persons traveling by foot, by horse or carriage, and by train.

"If Norton I, Emperor of America and Protector of Mexico, is disposed to make a commitment in kind, then I hereby declare this to be the sacred obligation of the United States and China, sealed on this the sixth day of the month of Sanyue in the Chinese year 4563, to be shared in equal portion and fulfilled within a period lasting no more than thirty years." Lee paused here, and stood erect, with breath to spare.

"I am so inclined," says Emperor Norton, with great pride. Here was a man I just met, yet I instantly gleaned from his strange comportment that he was a man who had been powerfully moved by this gesture, who was otherwise not easily moved.

"Therefore," continued Lee, "Let the moon and stars stand witness to this union of purpose. As long as we two draw breath and command loyalty from our subjects, a bond stronger than a paper treaty has been formed on this day—" at this p'int Lee puts in, "there was a paper treaty too, but it was lost in the journey—" then clears his throat before finishing his recitation. "As witness I offer my steadfast subject Win Chu to your mercy, whose office demands he bring me news of your reply. Sincerely Yours, the Tongzhi of China, Tenth Emperor of the Qing Dynasty."

At this p'int my shock was no longer for Lee's power of memory—that he spent a year or more entrusting this duty to perfect recollection—but for his voice. Having settled just South of the region, Lee nearly spoke like a born-and-bred Pike County boy, but now I reckoned he spoke the King's English as good as he spoke Missourian.

As it turned out, the Tongzhi Emperor had no power to make good on decrees, being himself governed by his mother, the Dowager Empress, whose habit was to treat him like a child, which he nearly was. So the Tongzhi understood well Emperor Norton's circumstance, which he shared: he was a figurehead who was beneath even a figurehead and could just as well have been the dead wood that a figure-head is carved out of. P'raps that explains why these two men of vision was so quick to make proclamations. They knowed it was just a doll's house.

Many a time since, I have been asked what I made of the only monarch of America when I met him. The truth is that I reckoned Emperor Joshua Norton was a kindly and well-meaning man of former wealth, in the mold of our old friend Tomlin, whose only form of purification was to play at scarcity. The shame of it is that such a man can never ride the line for long without reminding his road-kin, by his very presence, of the stark reality of their own honest lack.

Chapter XL

I had more questions for Lee than we had miles of travel behind us. Walking in the direction of "The Lucky"—the name for our hotel I'd settled on, having failed to commit it to memory—we was now completely surrounded by chinamen a-carrying steaming pots and laundry-bags and timbers, engaged in the various occupations of the Chinatown chinee. But his kind warn't the talking kind, and after clearing out his file-drawer of memory, Lee was so drained of speech even his monotone response was scratchy and dry-mouthed. But I never give up on him. I couldn't let go of it.

If he come back to California and was this close to his home, why ain't he on his way to Chico now? Was that where he was headed? "No, Joe," he says. "They rounded us up and hounded us and harmed us until we was either too scared to stay or too dead to say no. I wouldn't go home now if I lived at the bottom of the sea and had an anchor tied to me."

Warn't he a railroad worker at-all? "Sure I was," he says. "But it warn't a day after the last track was laid that the white workers come together and threaten us to leave town or else. They'd rather kill than compete for labor. So I rode me a train all the way to Missouri—on the same tracks I once'd built—and nursed my wounds in a forgotten place, and took up the path of independence."

So why, God Almighty, had he kept his story—and his mission—a secret from me this whole time? Lee threw this one back at me. "Why'd you keep that di'mond of yours a secret?" he says. "You told Ruth and every stranger on the road about it, but only got around to showing your road-pal Lee when you promised it to Quentin Blutes." Now warn't the time, I reckoned, to confess that I carried *two* di'monds most of the way acrost the country, and the one he seen had a cousin.

"I cain't account for it," I says. "I never suspected you would hive it, but you might have had notions about how it'd be best used, and I never wanted luxuries to tempt you when we was still throwing our feet at strangers' doors and sleeping in bedrolls in trainyards. By and by, it was too late to say anything without revealing the prior deception, and it was easier to go 'long that a-way without saying boo."

"I'll accept that," he says, more settled with my answer than I was with any of his'n. "We was both hobby hoboes from the start, and it's no use pretending otherwise. Unless... Did you show *Tom Sawyer* that di'mond you stole?"

I stopped now at a high crossroads that afforded a view of the bay that morning in all its sparkling indifference. "It was Tom who was with me when I pirated it!"

Lee shook his head and looked away in the opposite direction, toward the hills. "That Tom Sawyer is canny as a fox, and twice as dangerous," he says.

Even though I know he spoke true, it was my instinct to defend the man I spent most of my life following. "Careful who you talk rot about. I've knowed Tom Sawyer since I was smaller'n a fox myself, and he warn't much bigger."

"If you can stand up for a man like Tom Sawyer, Joe, then I guess I ain't know *you* at-all," he says.

Come my reply, "If you can stand up *to* a man like Tom Sawyer, Lee, then I guess I ain't know you at-all."

There was a silence that prevailed briefly before the dinging of a carriage-bell interrupted the nothing. "I reckon I'm simple," he says, "since I ain't take your meaning. D'you mean I'm yaller?"

"You're yaller," I says. "Sure as clouds make rain."

"Okay, I'll bite," says Lee. "What's your quarrel?"

I was committed to the row now. We was standing on a corner in chinatown and though we warn't the only folks on that part'cular street in contention that morning, I was the only white man around and I warn't about to concede. "You ain't want to open the door to Big Belly Rob's den, thinking it was haints that dwelt there; you ain't want to throw your feet at The Summit on account of the bulls; you ain't want to come with us to the dance in Denver, afeared you'd be caught; you ain't want to perform the part of preacher to the horstile congregation of Salt Lake City; once more, whether it was Injuns, or Morons, or occultists, or men of business, every time you step back and nudge me forward." I says, near out of breath from the effort, before adding: "And you warn't the one who Pendleton shot!"

Lee looked down at the toes of his boots. "I am sorely ashamed that you got shot on my account, Joe," he says, "and if that's what it's all about I can't be sorry enough. But if you think that list of yourn adds up to less than a man, I disagree. Let me ask you, which of those adventures of yourn come to a satisfactory result?"

I tried to marshal my righteous anger in defense of my cause, but it come to naught and instead I stood there growing warm in the cheeks and my mouth agape.

"At Big Belly Rob's, you was drugged and left nearly for dead, and 't was me and Ruth who saved you," says Lee. "Then, when you was arrested and stuck on a chain gang, it was me and Ruth who saved you ag'in; at The Summit, the bulls nearly nabbed you for being accomplice to a robbery, and I rescued you ag'in; Pendleton learned to recognize your face from the debacle in Denver; and your 'preaching' in Salt Lake was just the distraction those rapscallions needed to git away with Ruth." Even if he settled it there, I would have adopted the shame and raised it on my own, but he a-carried on. "As for Pendleton, I'd rather have died than have been party to such a massacre as that. Black, white, or yaller, there's not a cause in the world noble enough to justify forfeiting so many human souls like they was a pack of poaching hounds."

By gum Lee was right. This was the man who carried me on his back acrost half the country and here I was calling him a yaller-dog. "Don't listen to me, Lee. I'm just a-biling on account of being told a lie by my brother on the wanderpath," I says. "And I'm struggling to make sense of it-all. You run away from a round-up in Chico, spend five year in Missouri, then come to San Francisco to make good on an old promise. That your whole story?" I says.

"No," he says. "There's always more to a man than what you know."

"So why'd you stay in Missouri five year?"

"That part of my tale was true," he says. "There was a young lady who charmed me and kept me there, and we met in that cabin every chance we get, to talk and laugh and keep each other company the night-long. We was deep in love like storybook love; moreso, in fact, since we was skin-pinching real and reminded every day of how real we was."

"So what happened?"

"In the end her father made her to marry a man—she never tole him about her chinaman—and I was so sore about this arrangement that I left town and promised never to return. So you see I warn't a free spirit or a phi-landerer like I made out, but just a sucker whom the Lord made a cuckold."

"D'you mean you took up home with a Christian woman and expected to marry her? She warn't Chinese at-all?"

"Not even a little bit," he says.

"And she warn't from a house of ill repute?" I says.

"No, Joe," he says, curling his lip and letting his eyes strain angrily. "She's a good, devout woman who was forced to marry against her will."

This one flummoxed me. Lee always showed himself to be a moral man. But now he'd let spill that he had been living in sin with a white woman for years. I couldn't conscience it. So I about-face and walk that a-way, with Lee calling after me, "Wait, Joe!"

At the arched entrance of The Lucky I met Tom Sawyer and without a how-d'ye-do he pulls me aside and says, "I found the perfect cave, Joe. Let's have a look and you can thank me later." And I was deep into the thickest woods I ever seen before I realized that I was a-following Tom Sawyer once ag'in.

It was still daylight when we reached the entrance, but I judged we'd have to wait another day to explore on account of the descending sun. This warn't a hill cave, like all the ones I'd known back home—cracks underground that widen for thousands of years until a man can fit through; 't was more like a hollered-out mountain. Burrows blanketed a whole wall of rock and moss on the side of this sheer cliff, but none of 'em punctured it but one. The rest was full of birds' nests and still water. I could see immediately why Tom Sawyer called it "perfect," since it only had one way in, and 't was large enough inside to accommodate a dance hall. It made an ideal home for a live hermit and a perfect tomb for a dead one.

"Nevermind waiting for tomorrow," says Tom. "Let's lay our claim." This "we" was troubling, but I managed to ignore it.

"How'd you ever find this place?" I says.

"Just the way we do in Missouri," he says. "I brought a hound out to the woods and let him run loose, and followed 'im."

So we crawled through a hole as wide around as a dog, and just as wet as a dog's nose. When I emerged on the other side, I was birthed into a windless, airless, motionless cavern—a cold cloud that seemed to hold the two of us suspended like berries in gelatin. Once inside, Tom lit his lantern. I seen his face, and it was grinning wide. I couldn't stop the flood of memories that come back to me—Tom and I as boys, all the time we spent in the damp cold of a cave, imagining in the darkness; the times we used to hunt up foxes in the forest, get lost, and go to sleep in the dead leaves and wake up in the rain; the thrill of the approach when we overtook a ship laden with tin, or coffee, or ore.

I found a tick affixed to my ankle and plucked it off, watching it wriggle helplessly in the lamplight. The hours Tom and I spent making these critters suffer in turn! P'raps it was this boyhood memory that led me to ask whether Tom ain't have a ken to poke the tick a little before I crushed it.

"Shore!" he says, just like he always done.

Smiling so hard my cheeks hurt and my ears popped, I placed the tick on a stone and pull out my Jim Bowie knife. Then I took off that mite's legs one by one until Tom called out, "Don't hog it all, Joe," and took him a turn. It warn't the occupation of a gentleman by a long sight, but it was pure joy to a couple of St. Petersburg boys who lived to thirty-six years but harbored dreams of remaining boys forever.

Before leaving, we posted a sign that staked our claim to this cave. Tom had checked with the county, and it warn't owned by a soul 'cept the public trust. So now it was my own, and someday soon I'd be a happy dead hermit at the bottom of a cave.

Chapter XLI

That night in The Lucky, I was a-setting down on a real bed for the last time before my forever-descent into the darkness and cold of a great cave, adjacent to a snoring Tom Sawyer. Having fulfilled Lee's strange mission, I reckoned there was no more excuses to keep me from my own ambition, and it was time to make good on the promise I once'd made to die a hermit. But I kept stirring in my sheets, troubled by my own mind. Half of me had grown sorely dependent on the company of Ruth, so that it was painful to imagine going anywhere without her forever. There she was in my thoughts, setting in the straw of a barn in her humble dark clothes; there she was ag'in in the tattered bo-clothes of a deafie; there she was got up in the costume of a rich lady at the ball; and again, adorned with china silk. As she rode, Ruth often kept her head p'inted down to evade the attention of strangers, but I knew it was a ruse, since her nature was proud. I resolved then and there that I would invite Ruth to spend eternity in a cave with me, and even though it warn't a common proposal, she warn't a common woman; she was as comfortable on the road as if she had been a-traveling with a family. In fact, as I thunk on 't, the notion occurred to me that she acted so ca'm and comfortable sometimes 't was like we was already married in every way 'cept for sharing a room—hold on now, reader, and hold your tongue, for if you've arrove at the truth already then you are way ahead of Joe Harper, blinded by his affection and deafened by the nattering of his road-kin— but warn't it Ruth and Lee sharing a room together, while Tom and I plotted? Come to think on't, warn't it Ruth and Lee who always rode together, and whispered together, and pestered each other like an old married couple?

There on my dreamless pillow, I arrayed the evidence: First, Ruth confessed that she was forced to marry Abram

Hershberger 'gainst her will, and now Lee says he'd been a-carrying on an affair with a girl who was forced to marry 'gainst her will. Lee says he was sore at that girl for a- marrying another man, and he'd acted sore towards Ruth from the first hour they met on the road. And didn't she live awfully close to Lee's cabin, and didn't Lee know the way to the rail, and from the rail to the goods station where she was a-hidin', awful easy?

My blood pumped in my extremities like my heart split up into little hearts and a-wandered out to my fingers, my toes, my groin. If this was true, it was most awful truth, and a worse betrayal even than Tom Sawyer leaving me oarless in an uninhabited island in the great Atlantic.

One thing I couldn't cipher out: Why'd they want old Joe Harper along, and never tell 'im the whole time that they was carnal with each other? Warn't it cruel, to let me harbor feelings for a woman who was not only married but promised to another man? When I imagined what those two might look like, a-riding the road without me, I struck upon the truth: they needed Joe Harper to pretend he was husband to Ruth, in case she was ever discovered. A chinaman and a white woman going alone on the wanderpath would never have made it to California.

I stirred and rumpled the surface of the bed, my comforter twisting into a rope strand, and humid with sweat like newly wrung clothes. The bile rose up in me as I thunk how, the one time I was laid out by the po-bro, we was pinched by bulls who, like me, couldn't abide the thought of a chinaman corrupting a woman like Ruth with a foreigner's perversity. Sure, Lee come back to rescue me, I thunk, but only so he could a-carry on this disguise, using Joe Harper as his mustache.

Poor Zeb, too, had been employed in the unwitting service of this foul design. That man—a simple carriage-driver and story-teller—helped us recover Ruth from her captors out of a sense of goodness toward his fellow-man, and was now dead and in the ground because of the shifty deceit of a sinful and unrepentant chinaman.

And to think, the depth of degradation to which Tom was forced by the circumstances of our rescue!

"Tom!" I says, a-shaking him awake. "You were right about Lee—it's his fault that Pendleton and his men are dead, and once more, he has been miscegenating with poor misguided Ruth!"

"Ruth?" he says, then just as soon remembering. "Oh, you mean that sour Dutch girl who's dressed up like a china doll?"

"The very one," I says.

Tom frowned, and his mustache frowned on top of his frown. "Why, the underhanded, soulless deviant!"

Tom crept out to the hallway and crouched in front of Ruth and Lee's room, where I joined 'im; the night was soundless 'cept for the occasional ding of a carriage-bell or the clop of horses' hooves. He turned the handle and the door creaked open, shedding a warm lamplight into the room, which revealed two empty beds, pushed together to make one.

"I'll inform the sheriff," Tom says, standing up to his height and bearing the posture of his rank.

I misread all the signs. Ever since her rescue from Pendleton, Ruth warn't sorrowful because of any harm or indignity she'd suffered at the hands of her captors. She was dreary because she'd watched Lee—with whom she'd been carnal—whipped and abused in heinous ways, with no power to intervene. On that account, there was more dreary days ahead for Ruth, I reckoned.

Chapter XLII

Sheriff Curly Cobble and Deputy Marshall Thomas Sawyer sat athwart their horses like army generals. Around them, a crowd of authorities was gethering in the twilight. I never seen so many authorities in one place, every one with a star on his chest, badge in his pocket, and letter of title in his satchel attesting to his worth as a man of rank. It was a comfort to see the situation was being handled so squarely and solemnly. If Ruth was kidnapped a *second* time now, at least I could guarantee that she'd never be used for the pleasure of her captor.

"California is a large place. She's harsh, and pock-marked, and full of hiders-outers," says Cobble. "Squatters, Injuns, horse thieves, cattle rustlers, and chinamen. This Lee feller will try and stash his plunder in some hole and wait us out." I startled at Ruth being called *plunder* by this man of the law, but then I reckoned this warn't the first time the sheriff had to recover a captive woman from a treacherous foreigner. "But just like an Injun he underestimates the white man's resolve. So go and look under every rock and inside every mountain and down every mine shaft, for that chinaman is as good as a worm… and, men, we are huntin' up fishbait." At this I become worried that, if they look up in the hills, these men might trample upon and ruin my tomb.

But before the posse could disperse and blanket the hills, one authority raised his arm and says, "'Scuse me, Sheriff, but why do we have so many Deputy-Deputies here, some of whom I seen on the other side of the prison bars more than once?"

"Now, now, Jim Paddock, these boys have been tested and proven," says Sheriff Curly. "They're *all* good boys. If by 'Deputies who was once on the other side of prison bars' you mean Tom Sawyer, well he's the one who brought this rascal chinaman to our attention in the first place."

"I'm talking about honest-to-goodness outlaws," says Jim Paddock. "There's enough arrests 'mongst this crew to qualify as an insurrection 'gainst the gov'ment. Hell, there's enough arrests with that rogue Pat Chester by hisself!"

As their palaver continued, one feller in a scoop-brim slunk lower on his saddle and hid under his hat. I reckoned this was Pat Chester. Pat Chester, it turned out, was a horse-thief and swindler who achieved the status of local legend. For every time he committed a crime, he made sure that he committed a dozen at once. He'd live a peaceable and trouble-free life for a spell, then turn himself loose on the Bay. For all the trouble he made, the courts always took it easy on this feller who had the courtesy to confine his bad behavior to a spree, so that it only took one trial to send him off to jail for more crimes than you can count on both hands. He economized his wickedness, and the public expressed its appreciation by housing him for a month in county prison then sending him home every time.

The mob arrayed there agreed that such good will on his part redeemed him, and Pat Chester was again in the good graces of the law. It warn't long before Cobble had persuaded this rabble that his troubled past in fact made of Pat Chester a better sort of man—it was his redemption after the fall from grace, they agreed, that constituted proof of his goodness. You couldn't trust a man who'd never done wrong, because you never knowed how they'd handle a transgression. On t' other hand, a Pat Chester could be trusted to follow a pattern, from sin to grace to sin and back ag'in.

The matter settled now, the crowd whooped, scattered, and pressed on into the enormous woods. Before I mounted up, I reached down into my trouser inseam, as was my habit, and found no poke, I felt no shock but a clarity and understanding that molded my resolve. Though how Lee managed to sneak into my room and pluck my poke from my trousers, I cain't guess. He must have been a more experienced lousy yegg than he ever let on, I reckoned. *Airedale*, stuff and nonsense!

I rode alongside Sheriff "Curly" Cobble, Deputy Marshall Tom Sawyer, and Deputy-Deputy Marshall Pat Chester, the four of us astride a quartet of lawfully acquired horses—mounts worthy of Pendleton himself. Lee had made off with the horse we called Midnight, along with poor Ruth and, I now discovered, my last di'mond too—just like a horse-thieving, miscegenating, jewel-nabber.

We covered the same thick woods to the North where Tom and I'd found our cave, sending other authorities off to less likely destinations for fear that they would discover my home-to-be. This warn't a moist, dark, and viney jungle like the Osage plains, nor a leafy paradise like the Rocky range, but ruther 't was a landscape of vertical shafts that bisected your vision on every dip, turn, and rise, and which on the approach grew to fill your sight entirely before it dwarfed you and everything else with its godly proportion.

If'n Lee chose to hide behind one of these trees, I judged, we'd hardly know it, since by the time it took us to get to t' other side, he'd be gone. So we exhausted our labors peeking underneath roots large as houses and inside shallow caves that were hardly blemishes in this ancient forest. The sun was past its peak when finally I struck upon a thought. Lee and I had ridden together two thousand miles, and here I was expecting he'd hide out in a hole, when the only thing I ever seen him do was run. The truth is that *I* was always the one hunting up a dark hole, but Lee was always on the move, always restless for traveling on. The only place I'd known Lee to duck out was in a jungle of another sort, and I reckoned it was a waste of manpower to exhaust the woods where I knowed he warn't hiding. I conveyed this intelligence to my company, who all agreed it was a welcome mercy on their necks to keep them out of holes in the ground. So we come

249

back to the outpost where Sheriff Curly Cobble wired all the train stations around and warned them to be on the lookout for a chinaman and a white woman.

Then we waited. These authorities picked their teeth with Jim Bowie knives and talked 'bout what they'd do to Lee when they found 'im—and where they'd stick those knives. All this talk of revenge left me in the throes of pleasure and torment; I twisted between wanting to cry out for Lee to run and wanting to turn the knife in him myself. I remembered Lee's tenderer moments, like the bo stories he always told about the Airedale, and the god Zoos, and his haints; but then I'd always strike upon the time he played me a fool, and how he was revealed to be a shameful deceiver all along, which put me much at ease with this talk of revenge, and pretty soon I warn't shy to join it.

It warn't long before the wire come back to us that these runaways was caught like rats in a trap. After using Joe Harper as a vehicle to make it clean across the country, Ruth and Lee ain't lasted a day on their own without 'im. Ruther than hiding in a hole somers, as the Sheriff had anticipated, they found Lee and his captive in a dank, abandoned Southern Pacific freight car in Daly City Station.

Standing arm to arm with the authorities in the light of a train yard was a strange and unfamiliar perch for a man who once traveled the hobo road. It warn't as though this route was original. I knowed boes who turned shacks then lost their jobs and went to hunt up work of another kind—some of 'em end up yeggs, and some of 'em end up bulls. But everything looked different, clearer and less complicated, from this side. Actions had predictable outcomes, and that gave me some comfort that they were the right ones.

As soon as the shack at Daly had spied Lee and Ruth in the abandoned blue boxcar, he'd shut the door on them and locked the latch, where they'd been held until sunset, when we finally arrived with the sheriff and his men.

"Lee Bo of Chico," says Curly. "You are wanted by the law of California and the United States, and are charged on one count of horse-thieving, one count of larceny, one count of miscegenation, one count of fornication, fifteen counts of murder, and twenty five counts of nigger-stealing. As a man, you are entitled to the due process of law…" here he seemed to bow for a moment under the glare of an invisible eye, but he just as soon lifted his gaze and glared back. "But as a foreigner and a chinaman, you are entitled to only scorn for the perverse uses to which you put these men, and that poor woman. I hereby condemn you to death by the whip, which is the only death you deserve since your life ain't worth a bullet."

What fresh happened next took us by such a surprise, it warn't until long afterward I could even make sense of it. I reckon Lee had clumb up to the top of the boxcar, broke the lock, then stood astride it like a ranch hand about to rope his tenth steer of the day. There was seventeen rifles and at least thirty pistols p'inting in his direction, but Lee stood with a wide and comfortable stance as though a hail of gunfire would have fallen on him like a light rain.

Then he comes out reciting lines of poetry, like he was an old biddy learning her boys and girls in a one-room all-grader. The thing of it is that his words was all in Chinese. I never heard Lee speak Chinee before, and when I finally did, the voice was so foreign to my ear that the only emotion I experienced from his recitation was a tickle, which grew into a laugh, which spread to the whole posse and poured out in guffaws that drown out his queer scritching and whiny peals.

"Creepin' Jesus!" says Curly, amused by the unexpected show they was putting on, "that yaller dog has some grit, I tell you."

"Should we cut 'im down?" Pat Chester asks, a loyal dog

himself.

"Send him a warning," says Curly. Pat Chester eagerly complied, but his aim warn't true and the blow sent Lee reeling, then falling, from the top of the car straight to the road bed. I felt afresh the shot in my arm I once'd received from Pendleton's pistol—the sound, the posse of men surrounding a helpless captive, the sudden memory of Lee covering my wound to stanch the blood—it all come back with a flood of feeling. Then there was a scream, and Ruth appeared at the top of the car, where she ran from one side to t' other, unable to find a ladder or low place from which she might descend, and so she resigned to kneel down and pray for her fallen paramour from all the way up on deck.

I tried to drown all the sympathy within me, as the laughter of the men persisted, but the pitiful sight of Ruth shifting around tearful and desperate calculated to undo my resolve. Lee may have been rotten, but he was rotten human. He writhed in the dirt and gasped not from the bullet-wound or the shock of the fall, but from the winding he received from the landing. And he never took his eyes off the praying girl high above him like she was an angel hovering up in the sky.

"Well, we done wasted a bullet after all," says Curly, then he invites Tom Sawyer to stand beside 'im. "Marshall, you took the lead on this here venture and gave good information that led to the villain's capture. D'you want the honor of finishing it?"

Tom lifted the fold of his coat and reached for his saber. Down at his hip, dangling near its sheath, was my poke—the same poke that held the last, and the largest, di'mond—which I'd come to believe that Lee stole. I hollered, "What's goin' on, Tom?" All the men there arrayed turned in my direction all at once, as though attached to the same spindle, and I was faced with the choice of accusing the formidable Marshall in front of his posse or pardoning myself for the intrusion.

Then, somehow, I struck on a plan. I drew upon my experience as a biblical preacher in the Evaginical church, and called forth a sermon worthy of the grand-deceivers who installed me in that church. "How're you goin' to cut down a wounded man in front of a lady kneeling in prayer? This pair may be sinful, but they're to be pitied more than punished. No matter where they go, they'll meet with scorn and violence." I stopped my speech to spit on the fallen Lee, for dramatic effect. "Gentlemen, that might be the first time this chinaman was spat on for his wicked ways, but it shore won't be the last. Folks will spit on him until the day he dies. And when he does, it will be on his own, since the Lord is bound to turn her heart and allow the good woman to see the folly of her ways.

"Scripture says, 'Give unto Caesar what is Caesar's.' Let the villain take his prize, even if he ain't fairly earned it. Because your rewards are higher rewards, and will be granted you in heaven." I take a solemn pause as I let the warmth of this sentiment insinuate itself in their hearts. "But if you abide the killing of a man whilst a lady is praying over him, you cain't be sure."

The gates of dawn begun to open just then, and a tall light populated the horizon for which the low clouds served not to dull but to scatter its rays more fully upon the new day. "I was a sinner who came to the lord for redemption, and he sent me this chinaman instead. He was my guide through hell, and saved my hide many a time, and shared me his meals," I had to stop, for as I strung together this testimony, its truth begun to insinuate itself. "Though in the end he was revealed to be a betrayer and worse, an unrepentant miscegenator, Lee is born of Christian parents, and must live to see the error of his ways. The Lord does not ask forgiveness, He commands it."

To my infinite surprise and relief, the momentum toward violence that had been building since morning dissipated with the sun. In the gloaming light, this crowd appeared to me in the exact way that Lee addressed them—as children eager for direction and anxious to please. I heard grumblings of "C'mon, Sam, let's get a pinch," and "I ain't come all this way for a sermon," but their gruff and snarling voices were at odds with their actions, as each man slouched away, conscience-stricken, from the ugly scene they nearly made.

I discovered that, during my speech, I had taken Tom Sawyer's hand in mine, preacher-like, and held it tightly. He locked eyes with me, and I looked down—not to suggest defeat, but to direct his own gaze to the belt at his waist, from where my poke dangled, worn to the threads, seam-lined and testicular.

Ruth had come down from the deck of the boxcar by hanging off the side and dropping. Though she fell on her hind, she never bothered to brush herself off and went straight to Lee's side, ministering to his wound and elevating his back, stroking his cheek until his breathing came regular again.

Lee did me a bad turn and betrayed me. But when I pled his case in front of that crowd of authorities, I reckon I was speaking to myself. I reckon an act of mercy made me square in the eyes of the Lord for all my wretchedness, and now I could go on the rest of my days believing I was a good man.

Lee hobbled away, never turning back to me or the crowd, leaning upon the rough-and-rouge-cheeked Ruth. I've never had a moment of peace since from this memory: the pair of 'em dwindled East away from my watchfulness.

Chapter the Last

In the end I agreed to let Tom keep the di'mond, as long as he relinquished his claim on the cave, which he done—as soon as he bored of being called a Deputy Marshall and found his true calling as a campaigner for President Grant's reelection. Discovering there was considerable advantages to being a Republican, U.S. Deputy Marshall Thomas Sawyer became machine-politician Thomas Sawyer. But before he left for Sacramento, there was a signing, and a handshake, and he left on a train, and I never seen Tom again but in the papers.

I was clear out of di'monds now, but I was blessed free from the yoke of Tom Sawyer. Though he always brung a drop of excitement to the proceedings of a day, I never wanted to share my last years being interrupted with his holts and schemes. He offered to take me east all the way to Washington, and set me up with a clerkship and be his second-in-command, which he insisted would have been a finer way to decline than rotting in a cave. But I reckoned it was well enough the way it was.

When I finally returned to the cave-mouth to confront the fact of my death, there was already a crew of men working the mountain! I'd sat on it two months, and already it was too late. Good luck, Joe Harper, becoming a hermit in an already-discovered cave. Not only was it discovered, it held ore—ore so precious that superstition prevents me from saying it aloud, or writing it down, suffice it to say that 't was the mineral for which this part of the country was made famous—which meant that this was to be a more enduring distraction.

Since the claim officially belonged to me, these men were considered squatters by the law, and ruther than boot them, I soon made them my paid-men, extracting and weighing and building and channeling the earth until the cave turned to a bustling mine, and the bustling mine turned to a dead mine; I had to hire men to secure the site, and other men to haul the goods, and still more men to handle my economic affairs; since the cave was the vessel of my escape from poverty and the reservoir of all my dreams, once the mountain was empty of its glittering contents, I built my own home there—a high ceilinged palace that surpassed any construction, public or private, that the region had ever seen.

Locals called it Xanadu, but I never fit the part of Kubla Khan, with all his armies and harems, though 't was well within my power. I preferred, at last, to be alone, now that I knowed how to be. I reckon it warn't Lee that learned it to me, either. I figured it out on my own.

I think about Emperor Norton and the time Lee bowed down to him. The Emperor once'd been a rich man too, they say, but he lost it all speculating on rice and spent the rest of his life treading the sidewalks of San Francisco and making proclamations. I reckon I can appreciate why Lee fulfilled his promise to deliver the message on behalf of that dying chinaman. But Lee was smart enough to know it warn't a real emperor in front of him. So why'd he bow? That cigar-store-Injun emperor died last year in the streets, a charming bum, maybe, but a bum nonetheless, leaving nothing behind but his walking sticks and pockets full of play-money.

The story of that man's once-great wealth is a sober reminder to me to hold on to my fortune and guard it jealously from the takers of the world. My education in scarcity, furthermore, has taught me a habit of thrift exceeding the rational. I make certain investments, and reap certain profits; the only gambles I make are in the art market. Long as I hold steady, I'm 'most guaranteed to go out of the world a rich man.

So it is I am standing on the top rung of a ladder in my study, where I keep my Turners and Whistlers to remind myself how far I've come since the day I met Bring'Em Young and he asked which of the two painters I preferred, in order to adjust the Turner painting which he named "Rain, Steam, and Speed—The Great Western Railway," which had gone crooked with gravity. The painting is mostly a big blur, but now it's *my* blur and worth more'n most men make in a lifetime. Once I have it straight, I start down the ladder one rung at a time, feeling strangely disoriented like the floor is the ceiling and the ceiling the floor, and this topsy-turviness persists long enough that on the cave ceiling, my body p'inting down like a dripping stalactite.

Acknowledgments

I begin, as always, with a heartfelt appreciation for the love and support of my parents Hien and Emily Nguyen, and to James and Dorothy Hershman, without whom I never could have written this book. And to my wife Sarah Nguyen, my best critic and most enduring source of inspiration.

I had many early readers for this book, and each one provided specific feedback that changed the manuscript in significant ways: thanks to Jake Sentgeorge, who assisted with pinning down Ruth's Pennsylvania Dutch; to Ben Johnson, without whom my Missouri geography might have been all wrong; to Steve Nelson, who wisely suggested the addition of an "exhibition meal" in Chapter XIII; to Tom Dillingham for his astute critical comments; to Carolyn McCarthy, without whom I might not have added the character Soon in Chapter XXXVIII; to Joey Franklin for helping me navigate the Utah chapters; to Gail Crump, who gave detailed feedback on every aspect of the novel; to Art Ozias, proprietor of Java Junction, where the book was written from 2012-2015.

The episode in chapters IX through XI appeared in very different form as "The Pendergast Musket" in the anthology *Kansas City Noir* (Akashic, 2012).

Brian Blair came up with the "head-in-a-bag hobo" from chapter XIX.

Thanks to Evelyn Somers, Michael Pritchett, Trudy Lewis, Michael Nye, Rose Marie Kinder, Debra Brenegan, Michael Czyzniejewski, Michael Kardos, Zachary Mason, Rebecca Makkai, Kiik Araki-Kawaguchi, Alexander Weinstein, Seth Brady Tucker, and all the other friends of *Pleiades*

Thank you to scholars Kevin Michael Scott, Shelley Fisher Fishkin, Justin Kaplan, Ron Powers, and Ben Tarnoff for providing me, through your critical and biographical writings, with a solid foundation of understanding Twain and his work.

Thank you to my colleagues in the Department of English & Philosophy and the College of Arts, Humanities, and Social Sciences at the University of Central Missouri for supporting my writing habit.

Finally, thank you to the doula, midwife, and doctor who helped deliver this book into the world: my agent, Leslie York, of Fredrica Friedman Literary Management; my publicist, Gretchen Crary, of February Media; and my editor, Jon Roemer, of Outpost19.

About the author

Phong Nguyen is the author of two short fiction collections, *Pages from the Textbook of Alternate History* and *Memory Sickness*. His stories have been published in more than 40 national literary magazines, including *Agni, Iowa Review, Kenyon Review Online, Boulevard, Massachusetts Review, Chattahoochee Review, Florida Review, Mississippi Review,* and *North American Review.* Nguyen's stories have been given special mention in the Pushcart Prize anthology, and have won the Mary Wollstonecraft Shelley Award. He is Editor of *Pleiades: Literature in Context* and serves as an Associate Professor of English at the University of Central Missouri. He studied writing and publishing at Emerson College (MA) and creative writing at the University of Wisconsin–Milwaukee (PhD).

CPSIA information can be obtained
at www.ICGtesting.com
Printed in the USA
LVHW091917250419
615549LV00003B/523/P